WOOING
THE
DEVIL

VIRGINIE
MARCONATO

OLIVERHEBERBOOKS

PROLOGUE

"Well," the woman mumbled, stretching lazily by Rune's side. "I think I know now why they call you Devil."

He smiled. A fellow Dane, who had been coming to this country for years and knew the Saxons' language and culture better than most, had explained to him that they believed in an evil creature living in the middle of a fiery pit populated by the mangled bodies of people atoning for their sins. It seemed a rather fanciful notion, but there was no going around it. As soon as they saw him, the Saxons took fright, gave him the creature's name and mumbled what sounded like protection charms.

The men, at least. The women's gazes seemed to linger a while longer.

"Yes. My hair," he drawled, running a hand through his shoulder-length fiery red hair.

"I think it's more than that," the woman said, placing a hand on his naked chest to circle his nipple in a sensual caress. "I think it has more to do with the way you behave in bed. I've never seen the like and I should know. I've had my share of men, amongst which some have been your countrymen, but I must say, none of the other Norsemen were half as wild as you. Not that I'm complaining."

"Mm," he answered noncommittally.

What was she blabbering on about, Rune wondered? Having not learned more than the basics of her language on the way here, he could only understand a few words. 'Norsemen,' 'bed,' 'wild.' She must be praising his performance, he decided. Male pride surged inside him. He would rather have her remember him as an insatiable, skilled lover than a ninny who could barely string two words together. Conversation had best be avoided. Because he didn't want to admit to his lack of knowledge, he decided to silence her before she could ask him anything else.

Besides, if she could still talk, he hadn't done his job properly. He would not be satisfied until she passed out under him.

Without a word, he slid down the pallet and placed his hands on her slender thighs. Growling in anticipation, he pushed them open to expose her swollen folds. She had been thoroughly loved tonight, he could see, but dawn was not here yet. By the time he was finished, she wouldn't have the strength to call him after a ridiculous Saxon deity made of flames, she wouldn't even remember what her own name was.

His tongue darted straight to the center of her, so sweet, so alluring.

The woman bucked. "Yes! Ah, please!"

Rune smiled to himself.

This, he understood.

CHAPTER ONE

EAST ANGLIA, SUMMER 1039, A YEAR LATER.

Another weed, and then another. And another.

Eowyn sighed. This really was a relentless, thankless task. Why was it that weeds always took root much more easily and quickly than useful herbs and vegetables, she wondered for the hundredth time? It seemed to her she had been toiling all day and despite her efforts she still had to clear the corner where the onions grew. As if that was not enough, the day was scorching hot and the whole of the vegetable patch was in the sun. Sweat was trickling down her spine. In a moment she would have to go get a drink.

She wiped her brow with the back of her hand and went down on her knees. Forget dignity, being on all fours might spare her back somewhat. Besides, she wanted to be finished before—

"I have fond memories of you in that position, you know."

Eowyn froze, her hand clutched around dandelion leaves. That voice. That accent!

They could only belong to one man.

Slowly she sat back on her haunches and placed the handful of weeds in her basket, giving herself time to recover from the shock. Rune. It had to be him. But what was he doing here? She had never thought to set eyes on him again. Last year he'd told her he was only staying for a few days.

"I thought you'd gone back to Denmark," she said, keeping her back to him.

"I did. And then I came back with some traders. Good afternoon to you, too."

She made to stand up but after so long spent weeding, her legs felt both stiff and weak. She stumbled. Immediately, Rune was at her side, holding out his hand to her. There was no choice but to accept it, for fear of falling flat on her face.

Once she was back on her feet, Rune drew her to him as naturally as if they were lovers being reunited after a long absence. His hand slid down from her waist to her buttocks in a sensual caress. Though she wanted to rant at the liberty he was taking and push him away, she could not. With fiery long hair braided even more intricately than it had been the year before, pale cream skin that begged to be licked, ice-blue eyes and iron strength coursing through every inch of his chiseled body, Rune was one compelling man. Even his scent, his clothes, his voice, his silences were enticing.

No, the appeal he exerted over her, unfortunately, had not diminished.

It had not taken her long to fall into his arms last year, when he had come to her hut one balmy evening and asked if she could offer him something to drink. She had watched, fascinated, as he drank the ale she had given him with long pulls that caused his throat to ripple. By the time he'd finished his cup, she'd known they would sleep together. As soon as he'd touched her, she'd melted, and understood she would spend the wildest night of her life with this man. And when he'd left at dawn, leaving her sated and limp on the pallet, she had feared that one night with him would not be enough.

But he had left without making any promises, like a thief in the night. There had been no choice but to accept he would only become a distant memory.

And now he was back.

Why? She had never thought to see him again. Had he changed his mind? The questions must have shown in her eyes because he tilted his head, as if to invite her to speak out.

"You came back to East Anglia with Danish traders. That's all very well. But my village is nowhere near the coast. So why are you here?"

He answered with his mouth at her ear. "We don't know each other very well but I think it won't take you too much time to guess why I'm here."

She stiffened when he ground his hardness against her hips none too subtly. "I dare not think," she said icily. How had she thought he would be any different from other men? Why couldn't they see past what was hidden between her legs?

"Come. You were not so shy last year."

No, she hadn't been shy. But he hadn't been so crude either. He hadn't acted as if her agreeing to a wild night with him was a foregone conclusion. But here he was, holding her against his hard body, rubbing himself against her, looking at her like a wolf about to pounce would look at his prey. She knew that look all too well. He was about to tumble her into bed.

"Let's go inside." He nudged at her stomach again. "I've got an itch to scratch."

The crudeness of the statement made her bristle. For a moment she had feared she might not be able to resist his allure. Thankfully, his attitude was making it easy for her to behave as she should. "Is that supposed to entice me?"

The wretched man did not even blink. "I don't know, you tell me. Does it?"

"No." How could he even think it would? Or... Could it be

that he didn't know what he was saying? He spoke her language better than he had a year ago, with a less pronounced accent and complete sentences, but that didn't mean he couldn't make mistakes. Hope surged through her. "I think you meant to say something else."

"Perhaps I should stop talking then," he purred. "Perhaps I should use my mouth in a different way."

Her whole body went liquid at the suggestion and her answer almost escaped her lips.

Yes!

Yes, she wanted him to use his mouth on her. An image of a fiery red head cradled between her thighs burst through her mind. Rune had been a relentless lover, skilled and shockingly wicked. Never had a man made her feel as if she was granting him a favor by letting him pleasure her so intimately. But Rune had relished every moment, groaning as he licked her to mind-numbing pleasure. Their night together had been truly wild. In fact, she had relived those moments so often since then, she was starting to wonder if she had not dreamed them up. Surely no man could be that enticing? Now that he was in front of her, all brooding intensity, she knew she remembered him all too well.

Strong, confident, handsome, he really was the most decadent lover imaginable.

"Yes, you should definitely stop talking," she snapped to hide the turmoil the memory created inside her. For she remembered all too well what his sinful mouth could do. And she could not allow it to sway her and make her do something stupid, like allow him to get inside the hut and see—

"Ah, Angel," he said, cutting through her thoughts. "You wound me. I will admit I was hoping for a warmer welcome."

Angel.

Absurdly, the name sent a shard of pleasure shooting up her spine. No one had given her any nickname before, and certainly not one as lovely. She squashed the blooming sensation spreading through her chest before it could reach her heart. "What did you call me?" Was he trying to woo her, after having talked to her so crudely? Well, she was determined it wouldn't work.

"Angel." One side of his perfect mouth curled up. "My friend Magnar told me about the beautiful creatures you Saxons call angels. It seemed appropriate, what with me being called Devil. As I don't know your name, I had to—"

"Wait, what do you mean? I told you what my name was last year, right before we... Before we went to bed."

Eowyn was outraged. Did he remember her as a woman with no real identity, nothing more than a warm body to rut on? He had not meant to woo her by choosing a nickname he thought fitted her, he had simply tried to establish her as his by choosing a name that echoed his own.

If he'd been called Hammer he would have called her Anvil.

He shrugged, not in the least put out by her fury. "You might have told me your name but I didn't catch it. I barely understood a word of what you said that night. I could not speak your language very well then, as you might have noticed."

Yes, she had noticed, but she had not thought he had wilfully ignored the fact that theirs had been a one-sided conversation... Rune was making her feel worse and worse by the moment. The rush of happiness she had felt upon first seeing him was well and truly dissipating.

"My God, is that why you were only interested in getting into bed?" Not that she had put up much resistance, she had to admit. After months without a man, she had been too desperate and he too beguiling. But still, she had thought the attraction was mutual, and bedding her more than a way of shutting her up.

"I'm sure I would have enjoyed teasing you beforehand if I

had been able to converse. But I wasn't." His blue eyes seemed to catch on fire. "I will admit I was relieved when you knelt in front of me and finally stopped talking, because there was no mistaking your intent then."

"Oh!" Eowyn was incensed, embarrassed and aroused all at once. "I thought you liked what I did, and now I'm being told you only let me do it to silence me?"

The hold around her tightened possessively. "I did like it. Loved it. Nothing had ever felt so good," he growled, leaning in. "Why do you think I flooded your mouth so quickly? I dream of it when I pleasure myself, if you must know, I imagine your pretty lips wrapped around me and your tongue licking me clean afterward."

She couldn't answer, couldn't think, couldn't move, could hardly breathe. How could he say such scandalous things? Though not a shy maiden, Eowyn wasn't used to men talking to her in such a way. They behaved wickedly once they had her in their bed, true enough, but outside of it they usually held on to some semblance of propriety. The most they did was allude to what they could do together. Rune talked about dreaming of filling her mouth while he stroked himself and his scandalous words had made her weak at the knee.

"Let me go, Rune," she croaked.

"Mm. I will if you give me a good reason to. Good luck. I don't think you really want me to release you." His smile was arrogance personified.

That did it. She was not going to be made a fool by a cocky stranger. He thought he only had to take her into his arms to make her melt, grind his hardness against her to make her open her legs, talk to her crudely to make her fall at his feet?

She refused to give him the satisfaction.

He wanted her to give him a good reason to release her?

Well, she would give him one. She needed to make sure he left and never came back.

"You stink. And I don't bed men who smell like goats."

WHERE COULD HE GO? There was a village of Norsemen on the other side of the lake, he seemed to remember from what he'd heard the previous year. Perhaps someone there would offer him shelter for a few nights, while the Dane merchants completed their business in town.

Rune grunted in annoyance. What a comedown! He had imagined, or rather hoped, that he would spend the night in the arms of his fiery Saxon lover, instead he was going to ask strangers for hospitality.

Why had she pushed him away, pretending he stank of all things? He knew he didn't, as he had bathed just before going to her, and besides, he had not missed the light in her eyes when he had held her in his arms, or the limpness in her body when he had reminded her of their night together. She had wanted him, say what she might, and his scandalous talk had not shocked her. It had aroused her. As for him... He had been almost demented with need.

She had been so beautiful, even more than in his memory. Her long black hair, fanned over her shoulders in a sheet of silk, had made his fingers tingle, her skin, the shade of his favorite wood, and just as smooth, had made his mouth water, her cheeks, flushed by her exertions in the garden—or perhaps his proximity—had caused his blood to roar.

As if all that hadn't been enough to make him wild, she had been wearing a dress whose bodice could be unlaced from the front and barely contained her generous breasts. Had he tugged at one of the laces, she would have been bared to his gaze and mouth in an instant. He had almost reached out to it. The idea of falling to his knees to suckle her perfect breasts out there in the sunshine had been irresistible. For a moment he had been certain she would agree to it.

But then she had pushed him away, invoking the paltry excuse of his smell.

Why?

Perhaps she had a good reason for it. Perhaps she had gotten married in the interval, and been afraid her husband would walk in on them locked in a passionate embrace. But then, why not just tell him as much instead of pretending he stank? He would have understood. He would not have liked it, but he would have understood.

Let me go, Rune, she'd begged.

It was only when he exited the forest that he realized she had called him by his name. How did she even know it? He had not introduced himself last year and, like all the other Saxons he'd met then, she had called him 'Devil.' That was why he'd started calling her 'Angel' in his mind. His friend Magnar, who'd been coming to this country for two decades and knew Saxons customs, had told him more about the people's beliefs on the boat on the way home. In the last year, he had even taught him the language.

Rune had not thought he would ever want to return to East Anglia, but when the opportunity had presented itself to sail with local merchants, he had accepted. He was not quite sure what had motivated his decision but he suspected the beautiful angel with whom he'd spent the most satisfying night of his life had something to do with it. He'd wanted to see her again. Why else would he have learned her language?

Well, he might have spared him himself the bother of a long, perilous journey.

She, evidently, had decided to write him out of her life.

He set off at a run only to come to a halt a moment later. In front of him was the village he'd been looking for. The first person Rune saw at the edge of the forest, a Norseman, looked oddly familiar. Tall, lithe, with a striking angular jaw, he was talking to a petite woman who, by contrast, appeared to be Saxon. Her hair was not the right shade of blonde to be Norse, and her skin was too dark. He definitely didn't know her but he was certain he had seen the man before. Where?

Back home, he suddenly realized. The man was none other than Sigurd, the orphan who'd lived in the woods behind his village. What was he doing here, so far from home? There had been rumors saying he had gone to live elsewhere, but Rune had not imagined the man would have gone as far as leaving Denmark altogether and settle in such a remote place. He walked forward, causing the Norseman to turn his attention to him. His eyebrows shot to the top of his forehead, proving he had recognized him as well.

"Rune?" he asked in disbelief. "Is that you?"

Obviously he'd spent too much time away from home for he'd not even spoken in Norse. So he was Saxon now, was he? Very well. Rune would play along.

"It is me, Beast," he answered, causing the man to roll his eyes at the use of the nickname. Then before Rune could ask anything else a sharp slap landed on his shoulder. He cried out and whipped round. "Ow! What the—"

The blond Saxon was standing behind him, a look of outrage on her face.

"Meet Frigyth, my wife." Sigurd chuckled. "I'm afraid she won't take it too kindly to you calling me 'beast.'"

"So I see." The woman was scowling at him as fiercely as if he hadn't stood two hands taller than her. She put him in mind of his Angel, who'd glowered at him in a similar fashion earlier. Were all the women as spirited in this country?

"Sigurd's no more a beast than you are a..." She gestured wildly at him.

"Devil?" he suggested, crossing his arms over his chest.

She nodded. "Exactly."

"Yet that's what your people call me."

The tiny Saxon only shrugged. "It only shows how imaginative they are. They chose the name on account of your red hair, no doubt."

"That, and the way I behave in bed, of course." He wiggled his eyebrows suggestively. "Positively wicked, or so I've been told. Would you like to—"

A heavy hand landed on his shoulder, cutting the sentence short. "Careful," a voice growled in Norse in his ear. "This is my wife you're talking to. If you even hint that she might like to see for herself what it is you do to women in bed, I will rip your filthy tongue out."

"Ah, please, not the tongue." Rune gave a mock shiver. "It is the part that earned me the nickname, if you must know."

Sigurd was not impressed by the jest. "If you want to keep it then you will stay away from my wife. Is that understood?"

"Loud and clear, *Beast*." This time, as he had spoken in Norse, Frigyth did not hit him for using the reviled nickname.

"Watch your mouth, Devil. You're not a helpless pup anymore, so I have no reason to hold back. This time I *will* kick your ass." The Dane glared at him. How he had managed to ensnare the beautiful little Saxon with such rough manners, Rune could not begin to understand, but his wife seemed utterly devoted to him.

As if to prove it, she placed an arm about her husband's waist and gazed at him in adoration. "Shall we? We were on our way to the lake for a swim," she added for Rune's benefit.

He raised his hands in surrender. "Don't let me stop you. But I was wondering if I could stay in the village for a few days."

Sigurd stayed silent, clearly not thrilled at the prospect, so Frigyth answered in his place. "Go and find the Icelander called Wolf. He will help you."

"Thank you." He smiled his most wicked smile and laughed when she dragged a scowling Sigurd away before he could make him regret the provocation.

In the village, the man called Wolf was easy to find. Everyone seemed to know him. The Icelander informed him of the fact that one of the huts was empty for a few weeks, its owner having decided to make the most of the warm weather to visit his children, who lived further south.

"You can stay in his house if you promise to replenish the stock of wood before you leave."

"Naturally."

That night, as he stared at the dried herbs tied up to the ceiling, Rune wondered what had possessed him to come here. He should have gone back to the harbor and boarded the first boat bound for Denmark.

CHAPTER TWO

"Rune's father is back."

Eowyn could tell the announcement had taken her friend by surprise, which she had fully expected. She had meant to shock her. Just then, as if he'd guessed they were talking about him, the baby stopped suckling. A drop of milk still lingered at the corner of his rosebud mouth and his eyes were closed. Eowyn's heart contracted with love. How had she created such a perfect little boy? It never ceased to amaze her.

Frigyth held out her hands to take the child from her. "Give him to me while you put yourself to rights."

"Thank you."

As soon as he was upright, the baby let out a loud burp, causing the two women to laugh.

"Someone's drunk more than his share as usual, it would seem!" Frigyth settled Rune on her shoulder and turned to face her. "You were saying? His father is here?"

Eowyn sighed. There would be no avoiding this conversation now. Why had she blurted out the shocking truth? Because she had been bursting to tell someone since yesterday, that was why. She'd known as soon as she'd left the hut that morning that she was only pretending to go hunting for food. What she really meant to do was go see her best friend and tell her about Rune's reappearance.

"I was weeding my garden yesterday when he appeared out of nowhere."

Demanding to be bedded—or rather to have his 'itch scratched.'

She didn't mention that part. No need to share her humiliation. Her friend knew about her active love life and never judged her, but she didn't need to be told how men treated her as a consequence.

"My... I can imagine your shock—and his." Frigyth's eyes almost popped out of her head. "How did he react when you told him about the babe?"

"I didn't tell him." Eowyn lowered her eyes to the floor. This hadn't been her proudest moment but she could not lie. She hadn't found the courage to tell him about his son. There was a silence, during which she sensed her friend was doing her best not to remonstrate with her.

"You have to tell him," she said eventually. "It's only fair."

"I know. But I was taken by surprise. I never thought I would one day be in a position to introduce him to his son. And as he only appeared interested in bedding me, I didn't think it a very—" She stopped as a terrible thought crossed her mind. "What if he wants to take the baby back to Denmark with him when he finds out?" That was what she would want to do in his place, a natural reaction she could not even blame him for. After all, as the father, he had half the claim over the little boy.

Frigyth looked at the baby sprawled over her shoulder as if he would provide her with an answer. "I don't think that's a possibility," she said slowly.

"But you don't know for sure, and neither do I."

"No. I suppose not."

Eowyn wrung her hands on her lap. She didn't know anything about the man, except that he was incredibly skilled in bed and had a penchant for crude talk. Oh, and lived at the other end of the world. What if he decided to take his son with him, if only to spite her and make her pay for refusing his advances yesterday, for hiding his child from him? Everything was possible.

"I can't take the risk of telling him until I know what his intentions are. I will never surrender my son. In any case, I doubt I will see him again. After the way I sent him away, he will probably find himself another woman to 'scratch his itch.'" This time she spat the words. "He might even be on a boat back home right now."

"Wait." Frigyth gave the baby's downy hair a stroke. "Is his hair the same color as Rune's by any chance?"

As always when she looked at her son, Eowyn smiled. "Yes. He certainly didn't get that from me. Why?"

"As it happens, Sigurd and I met a red-haired man called Rune yesterday. He wanted a place to—"

Just then the door of the hut opened on Sigurd. Eowyn's greeting died on her lips when she recognized the man coming in after him.

Rune, come bursting into her life. Again.

ANGEL WAS HERE.

Rune blinked. What was she doing in Sigurd's hut? And why did she appear panicked at the sight of him? Surely she wasn't afraid he would hurt her? Had he mistaken her reaction the day before? Had she sent him away because she was actually scared of him? It didn't make sense. She hadn't appear worried in the least the previous year.

What had changed?

Unaware they already knew each other, Sigurd began to introduce her. "Rune, this is my wife's friend and her—"

Frigyth cut in to beam at her husband. "Ah, finally, you're back!"

"Back?" the Dane repeated, frowning. "I only went to see Wolf at the other side of the village, Birdie."

"Yes, well. I've missed you terribly."

She planted a passionate kiss on his lips, even though she was holding their newborn son in her arms. Rune arched a brow. The baby's hair looked different today. It had been blond last night, he was sure of it. Now it was red. So red it was impossible not to notice.

Frigyth saw his surprise when she drew back from the kiss. "I guess Sigurd didn't tell you we'd had twins," she said, wrapping her free arm around her husband's waist.

"I—"

"Otherwise you wouldn't appear so shocked to see me holding our other son," she carried on, cutting her husband off by pressing herself tighter against him.

My, these two were sickeningly in love. The Saxon couldn't keep her hands off him, even though he'd only been away for a moment.

"How many sons do you have?" Rune asked, crossing his arms over his chest. He'd already seen at least two other boys, all under the age of six.

"Four. Elwyn, Eirik and the twins."

"Well, you've been busy, Beast. Sorry," he added when Frigyth glared at him. "Force of habit."

"A habit you had better get out of, and fast."

When an uncomfortable silence stretched in the hut, Rune

realized he had been glad to talk about Sigurd's children to avoid having to look at Angel. She seemed equally reluctant to tell her friends they knew each other, which did not surprise him.

"I suppose I will get going," she said, her voice barely above a whisper.

"Wait," he could not help but say, taking a step forward. But once again, Frigyth spoke up before he could say anything. He barely refrained from snarling at her. Did the woman ever shut up?

"I will accompany you to the edge of the forest," the Saxon was saying, oblivious to his scowling. "Sigurd, why don't you take Rune to meet Magnus? He said he would like to meet him."

The Dane nodded slowly, as if not sure he understood what she was referring to. Certainly Rune had no desire to see this Magnus, whoever he was. He would rather speak to the woman who had not once met his eye since he'd entered the hut.

But she'd already gone, taking advantage of Frigyth's distraction.

Eowyn rushed past Rune, and out of the hut. She couldn't deal with the idea that he could demand to be handed their son so he could take him home with him, all the way to Denmark.

Thank God for her friend's presence of mind. Now Rune would be unaware she had given birth to a child in the spring, in other words, nine months after their night together.

"I don't think he suspected anything," she told Frigyth, who joined her a moment later.

"No. And by the time I'm back without the babe, he will have left the hut, Sigurd will see to it. Fret not, he will be none the wiser."

"Your husband is going to ask you why you pretended the babe was yours, you know."

Frigyth giggled. "I'm sure he will, but don't worry. He's used to me making odd demands of him. You saw how he didn't give me away."

Indeed. Eowyn remembered her friend telling her that she had once asked Sigurd to pose as her husband and how he had slipped into the role without so much as a blink. He would not give her secret away.

Once they were out of sight, she took the baby back from her friend's arms, relishing the warmth of his perfect little body against her.

"Thank you. And I'll think of a way to tell Rune about his son, I promise. I just need some time to prepare myself."

———

RUNE WATCHED the two women disappear through the trees together and turned to face Sigurd.

"So you have twins, hey?"

The Dane's mouth quivered. "Apparently. No wonder you're surprised. Last night you only met Moon and for some reason I completely forgot to mention his brother."

"Moon. You called your son *Moon*?"

Rune was incredulous but Sigurd merely smiled. "It's a jest between Frigyth and me. His real name is Halfdan, but he has a mark on the inside of his wrist shaped like a moon crescent, just like his mother and I do."

"Ah yes, the mark of the beast." He remembered how the village boys had mocked him for it, and given him the nickname because of it. He'd never seen it himself, but it had been all the others could talk about.

"You had better not mention this in front of my wife."

Rune grunted. "No." The woman was formidable. So formidable she had allowed his Angel to slip away before he'd had time to talk to her. Nevertheless, he would have insisted had she not appeared so panicked, so afraid of being on her own with him.

Why? What had happened? Last year she had been anything but afraid, initiating their lovemaking even before he could make his move, a rare enough occurrence to be noted.

"What happened to you after I left?" Sigurd's question cut through his musings.

"What do you mean?"

"Come. Back in Denmark you were the youngest in that pack of boys, and somehow frail looking." The Dane eyed him up with an arched brow, as if to indicate things had changed since then. Yes, they certainly had. Now Rune towered above most men. "You never dared go against what they did or draw attention to yourself, but I always sensed you would not remain the victim for long."

How had he guessed? Indeed, for years Rune had had to earn his place. And then almost overnight, or so it seemed, he had started to grow. Finally he'd been able to lead the scoundrels rather than suffer their jibes.

"When the oldest boy left, I took his place."

Sigurd laughed and gestured toward the forge, indicating they should start walking. "Just like that? Yet you weren't the oldest in the group, not by a long shot, if I remember."

"Yes, just like that. As you say, I was not cut out to be a victim. And I was stronger, taller, more intelligent than all of them put together."

"More arrogant as well, I bet."

"I know what I want and I make sure I get it." Rune shrugged. "If that makes me arrogant then I guess I'm arrogant."

By the time they had reached the blacksmith's workshop, his decision was made. He always made sure to get what he wanted, didn't he?

Well, then, he was going to see Eowyn again.

CHAPTER THREE

I f ever Rune had needed confirmation that Angel was the perfect nickname for the woman, there it was. Magnar had told him the creatures looked like humans, only they had wings like birds and were supposedly gifted with non-human abilities. Well, the dark-haired Saxon didn't have any wings but her singing was... unnatural.

That voice! It sent shivers all the way down to his toes.

He stopped in his tracks before she could spot him. From what he could gather, she was at the back of the hut. Closing his eyes, he let her voice wash over him. Never had he heard anything so beautiful.

Suddenly she stopped singing and gave a laugh.

"Oh, look at your face! Didn't you like the song then?" She giggled again, a sound so full of joy it tore at his heart. Why couldn't he make her laugh like that? He'd not realized she was not alone. But she clearly wasn't, and the person with her had not like her singing. The fool. "Rune, I love you, you know. With all my heart."

He froze.

She was talking to him. But how she had seen him, hidden

where he was, he could not fathom. And why was she saying... saying that she *loved* him? It made no sense. The last time he had seen her she had seemed petrified, and the time before that she had sent him away, telling him that he stank.

He stepped forward, careful to remain hidden. She was sitting on a bench, with her back propped against the hut, her face lifted up to the sun, a smile on her face and a... a baby in her arms. Not just in her arms, but suckling at her breast, thereby proving beyond doubt it was not just a young nephew or a neighbor's child she was looking after. No. It had to be her own child. It was testimony to his shock that he did not even register the fact that her breast was exposed.

The baby looked young, no more than a few months old. He looked familiar, as well. At least, his hair did. Flaming red, like the hair of the baby Frigyth had held in her arms the previous day.

Like his own. Devil red.

Did it... Could it mean what he thought it meant?

Closing her eyes, she started singing again. Rune took advantage of it to creep forward. Nothing could have made him leave now. Lost to the song, a lovely ballad about a little girl walking through the forest, she didn't hear him coming. Once he was in front of her he stopped, making sure not to cast his shadow over her and alert her to his presence. The baby suckled on, his own eyes closed. It was a perfect image of happiness.

Heart thumping hard in his chest, Rune waited.

At some point she would open her eyes again and see him. And then he would unleash the dozens of questions jostling in his mind.

"Ah. You've had enough then, sweetheart."

Eowyn felt her son release her nipple and smiled. He always drank greedily, before letting go with a contented little sigh when he was done. More often than not, exhausted by the frantic pace, he then fell asleep in her arms. She opened her eyes—and almost dropped the baby when she saw the man towering over her.

"What are you doing here? You scared me half to death!" she whimpered.

"Mm. I seem to do that, don't I?" He didn't seem overly concerned by the notion. "But I could tell you the same." He nodded toward the baby nestled in her arms. "Care to explain why you're feeding Sigurd and Frigyth's 'son'?"

There was no point even trying to come up with an explanation other than the truth. She might have been able to get away with pretending she was looking after the baby, unlikely as it was, if Rune had not seen her feeding him. But he had and he was not stupid. Only women who had recently given birth had milk.

"He's mine," she said, glancing at the little boy asleep against her. Only then did she realize that her breast was still exposed. Slowly, so as not to wake Rune up, she covered herself. Not that Rune—the other Rune, the one scowling at her— appeared to have noticed her state of disarray.

He was too busy glowering at her.

"Is that why you didn't want me to stay the other day? Because you'd just had a baby?"

She could not help a snort. Trust him not to consider his crude manners could be responsible for her decision.

"Yes. But I think I would have sent you on your way anyway. I didn't like being told you had a itch to scratch, if you must know. I'm not sure many women would. It's not a very flattering image."

He narrowed his eyes. Apparently, he didn't like being reminded of his vulgarity. Well, too bad. She hadn't forced him to speak so crudely.

"Why didn't you tell me I had made a mistake in your

language instead of supposing I was just being impolite?" he accused. "I didn't know that expression would offend you. You know I don't speak your language as good as a Saxon."

She let out a sigh. Had she been too hasty in her reaction? She had thought it reasonable at the time, but she now felt like a petulant child. Perhaps she should have guessed he wasn't as proficient as she'd thought and hadn't meant to offend her. "Perhaps I should have given you the benefit of the doubt."

"And the baby?" Rune's eyes glittered. "Why didn't you tell me about him instead of lying about my smell? What is a 'goat' anyway? Some sort of excrement?"

Eowyn shook her head, feeling ridiculous again. "I panicked. I told you, I never thought to see you again and I didn't know how you would react when you were told you had a son. I'll admit I—"

"I have a son?"

The words were little more than a whisper. Eowyn realized only then that she had not explicitly told him the baby was his, once again assuming he would reach the right conclusion himself. But it seemed that all along, Rune had tried to hold on to the possibility that he might not be the father, even though the dates clearly coincided. His hopes had just been dashed and he looked horrified.

Eowyn didn't know what to do. She had expected many reactions when the Dane found out the truth. He would rant, he would not believe her, he would storm away in anger, he would demand to be given his son so he could take him back home with him. She had not imagined this reaction.

Rune, the mighty Norseman, the tower of strength, the indomitable warrior, looked about to faint. No, not faint, she amended quickly. Rather... retch. His face had gone a sickly green color. Oh dear, this wasn't good. She'd been bracing herself for his remonstrance and felt ready to stand her ground.

Faced with such a reaction she didn't know what to do, or even if there was something she could do. He needed time to absorb the shock, and that was not something she could do in his place.

He staggered and fell on the bench next to her.

"I have a son."

Not knowing what to say, Eowyn stood up, deciding it was best to give him time alone.

"I will go put him to bed."

In the hut she tried to calm the wild beating of her heart. It seemed the discussion she had dreaded would not quite go as anticipated. She had no idea what she was to do.

Rune hadn't moved a muscle by the time she joined him back outside.

"I have a son," he repeated, dazed.

"Yes, you do," she said gently, handing him the cup of ale she had prepared. He looked truly stunned. She had not been half as shocked when she had found out she had fallen with child from the encounter with the red-haired Norseman last autumn. Perhaps she should have, but, oddly, she had welcomed the news with joy.

Rune emptied the ale in one gulp. "Thanks. Did I hear you call him... Rune?"

She nodded. "It seemed the only option. When I discovered I was pregnant I knew if it was a girl I would give her my grandmother's name and if it was a boy I would call him after his father, so I—"

"Don't call me his father!" The words exploded out of his mouth.

Eowyn recoiled. Because he had been so dazed just moments before, the outburst was all the more shocking. He hadn't seemed to doubt her word, but evidently, he did not believe the baby to be his. As much as she had not wanted him to take him away, it was unbearable to have him refusing to acknowledge the little boy.

"Why should I not call you his father?" she said, getting angry herself. Did he think this was easy for her? "That's what you are!"

He only glared at her. "Is it? I fathered a child here, miles away from home, in a country I don't live in with a woman I do not know, that's not quite the same, as I'm sure you'll agree. I have a son I almost never knew about, who I will never see grow into a man." He let out a bitter laugh. "Yes, I do have a baby, apparently. That doesn't mean I can be a father to him, though, can it, not with you living here and me being all the way in Demark!"

Lord. She had not thought about it like that. But how heart-wrenching for him to be told about a boy he had fathered and understand at the same time that he could never be a part of his life? How would she feel knowing she could never be a mother to her son? It would be devastating.

She swallowed, utterly at a loss.

"I'm sorry," she murmured. "I understand your shock. But I cannot pretend you didn't father him. You must know I'm telling the truth. We did sleep together when you came last summer."

"Oh, yes, we definitely did."

There was no missing his meaning. *We slept together, repeatedly, thoroughly, and I did not even try to withdraw. I filled you with my seed time and time again. And look at the result.*

Look at the result indeed. A little boy she loved more than life itself and a father who could not bear the thought that he had created him.

By the gods!

Rune didn't know what to think, let alone say. His mind was

numb. Angel was looking at him with glittering black eyes, eyes that had haunted him for a year.

"Are you sure—"

"Please." She raised a hand as if making the effort to try to understand he had to ask the question, but was still hurt by it. "Yes, I'm sure he's yours. There can be no doubt about it. That's why I went into town last winter and asked everyone if they knew the real name of the man named Devil, because I wanted to give my child your name if it was a boy. One of the Danes who'd traveled with you told me you were called Rune."

There it was, his last hope to have been mistaken gone up in smoke. Now he knew why she had pushed him away the other day, why she wore this maddening dress with the laces at the front. Because she needed to feed a newborn baby ten times a day. A baby he had fathered on her.

Bile churned in his guts.

"I need time alone."

She nodded and made to leave. At the last moment, she hesitated. "My name is Eowyn by the way."

"Thank you." How had she guessed he couldn't bear the thought of having a child with a woman whose name he didn't even know? Perhaps it was insignificant in the grand scheme of things, but he felt better for knowing it.

Once Eowyn had disappeared inside the hut, he took the road to the forest at a run. Perhaps if he exhausted his body, his mind would stop whirring for a moment.

CHAPTER FOUR

"Where did you sleep in the end?"

"In a ditch."

Rune's blunt statement made Eowyn wince, as did the idea of him being holed up in a ditch like an animal, hiding from the world. She had the uncomfortable impression she had destroyed his life when she had announced he had a son, quite the opposite of what she had felt when she had met her child. It had been love at first sight.

"Do you want something to eat?"

"Yes please. I'm starving."

Well, he would be if, as she could imagine, he had not eaten anything last night. But he made no move to follow her inside the hut when she went to get food ready. Instead he glanced toward it as warily as if it had housed a three-headed monster. Her heart sank further in her chest. She had not wanted Rune to take her son away from her but it hurt to think he didn't want anything to do with him, or even be in the same room.

Of course, if it was his way to spare himself from the pain of a pending separation, then she could not blame him.

"I can bring the food out here if you prefer."

He nodded his agreement, looking relieved, and made his way to the bench at the back of the hut to wait for her.

Eowyn placed a chunk of cheese, a piece of bread and an apple on a wooden plate and poured a huge tankard of ale. Then she paused. A man like Rune likely needed twice as much food as she did. Twisting her lips in consideration, she added an onion and a handful of nuts to the plate. If he was to stay more than a day or two, she would have to ask him to go hunting. Her provisions would not last long at this rate.

"Thank you." Rune accepted the plate with a quick smile. "Don't worry. I will go hunt for meat as soon as I have eaten."

She was surprised to see he had anticipated the problems his presence would bring and wanted to solve them before she even raised them. She forced herself not to betray how that made her feel. After all, he had done nothing extraordinary.

"Thank you," she said curtly. "That would be most welcome."

"Oompf!"

Eowyn walked into a wall that shouldn't be here and almost fell flat on her face.

"Eowyn?" Rune's voice reached her at the same time as two strong hands gripped her shoulders. "Be careful."

"What are you doing outside? You almost scared me to death again," she hissed, her heart thudding hard in her chest. She hadn't expected him to be standing right in front of her door. He should have been asleep. Only new mothers who had to feed their babies were awake at this time of night.

"I couldn't sleep," he answered, his hands still on her shoulders. Through her thin chemise she could feel the heat of his touch burning her skin. "I thought I'd come to see the stars.

Then I heard you get up for the babe, so I waited out here to give you privacy."

"Oh." She hadn't thought to look to the corner of the hut to check if he was still there before walking through the door. She had assumed he would be fast asleep. And if he hadn't stirred while she had fed Little Rune, it was because he was a man and men just slept through the commotion, no matter what. Her friend Cwenhild had complained about it many times.

"With both our babes, Wulfric was able to sleep the night undisturbed, even while they screamed and I fumbled around the hut to get to them," she'd sighed. "I have no idea how men do it. And the worst of it is, when I took him to task over it, he only asked why he should wake up with me when he cannot feed the babe anyway. I swear I could have killed him that day."

Eowyn bit her lower lip. Rune, who felt no special draw to his son, would have even less reason to help her. True, men could not feed a babe, but they could rock it back to sleep, clean its dirty clout and just... do whatever else needed doing.

"Sometimes, depending on the time, after feeding Rune, I find it hard to go back to sleep," she explained, lifting her face up to the skies. "I like to come out here and look at the stars. For that reason, I am glad he was born in the warmer months."

"Well, there isn't much to see tonight, I'm afraid. It's very cloudy."

"No."

But there was plenty to feel. Rune had come to stand behind her and wrapped his arms around her, drawing her against his chest. "Come here. It's not winter, but you're not wearing much," he purred in her ear.

"You're not wearing much either," she replied, her voice hoarse.

In the faint light of the moon she had seen he was not wearing his tunic, only his undershirt. He gave a soft snort. "I'm a Dane, remember? This is not cold for us. But I don't want you to catch a sickness."

"An illness, or a cold, we would say," she corrected automatically.

"Ah. Thank you."

She should perhaps have moved away from him, or at the very least protested that she wasn't cold. But the truth was that she relished the feel of his embrace. Her feminine urges had always been her downfall, but even if they hadn't been, she would have found it hard to resist this particular man. He felt delicious around her, and smelled even better, of spice and wood. To think she had accused him of stinking the other day. It was incredible he hadn't called her on the lie.

There was a chuckle as Rune placed his chin over the top of her head, mercifully breaking through the tension.

"You're quite short, aren't you, Angel? I hadn't noticed before."

Of course he hadn't. The differences in height between two people were negligible when they were both lying in bed or when one of them was on her knees in front of the other. She reddened.

"I'm not short!" she huffed, trying to fight the heat spreading through her body at the proximity of a strong, virile male and the memory of what they had done together. "Rather, you are taller than most. But I am not smaller than my friends."

"Mm." He didn't sound convinced. "You are a lot darker, though."

Rune felt Eowyn stiffen in his arms. His comment, innocent though it was, seemed to have displeased her. Had he made a mistake again? Did the word mean something he was not aware of?

"What do you mean?"

There was diffidence in her voice. But he had not meant to

offend or embarrass her. Her exotic, dark looks were certainly no cause for shame. If the truth be told, they aroused him like nothing else. The silence stretched between them and he realized he had to say something, for fear of having her think the worse of him.

"People here seem to be different from Danes, less pale and fair but still not very dark. Frigyth, for example, with her blonde hair, could almost pass as one of us. But not you."

Not her, with her hair as black as the blackest night and skin as golden as well-baked bread.

"No." There was a pause. Would she shrug it all off and disentangle herself from his arms or on the contrary tell him what he wanted to know? There was no telling. "I was raised by my grandmother," she said eventually.

Rune frowned. What did that have to do with anything?

"Your grandmother?" he repeated when she stayed silent.

"Yes. When my mother fell pregnant with me, she was still very young and unmarried. She was living with her mother, from what I heard."

From what I heard.

That sounded ominous.

"You mean you never knew your mother?" he murmured, lowering his head to speak in her ear. Against his chest, he felt her shake her head. It seemed to him only the fact they were not looking at each other and talking in the dark allowed her to persist with this conversation.

"I was raised by my grandmother. At least... I was until she died."

Rune's arms automatically tightened around Eowyn. He could sense this story would not be a happy one. "How old were you then?"

"About ten."

"I'm sorry." His heart twisted at the thought of her as a

lonely child and he fought the urge to tighten his arms further around her. He didn't want to smother the woman, merely comfort her.

"Anyway, what I meant to say is that I owe my coloring to my father, a merchant come from distant lands," she carried on, her voice a bare whisper in the night. "From what I can gather, my mother found it hard to accept. When they saw my dark looks, people mocked her for lying with a heathen, taunted her for choosing a lover who was not a Saxon."

"Oh, Eowyn." This sounded too familiar for comfort. He could easily guess that people now mocked *her* for having a child with red hair, and bedding a man who was not a Saxon either.

"She disappeared when I was about a year old. No one knows what became of her." He heard her swallow. "I often wonder if she didn't take her own life, too burdened by the shame of it all."

There was nothing Rune could say to that, so he waited to see if she would carry on with her story. She did not. Just then the clouds parted and he saw the Northern Star appear in his line of vision, unassuming amidst brighter, bigger stars and yet... Yet of vital importance.

"You know," he told Eowyn pensively, "the men who sailed the boat here used the stars to guide us. Out there, in the open seas, everything looks the same. With no landmark, so to speak, to help you, you could be going anywhere without even noticing. But the men set us on the right course using the night sky."

The stars up above seemed to wink at him. *We've led you here*, they seemed to say. *Right where you should be. No need to thank us.*

He tightened his arms around Eowyn. Suddenly it did feel as if he was exactly where he should be. Overhead the sky was now clear and a wide, powdery bow arched over them, blazing a trail amongst the thousand pinpricks of light. It was a breath-taking sight.

"Mm, I think... I think I'm ready to go back to sleep now," Eowyn mumbled, her words sounding somewhat slurred.

Before she had finished the sentence he had swept her off her feet and into his arms. He fully expected her to protest at this treatment but she didn't say a word, instead placing her head against his chest. He smiled to himself. She must be tired indeed for her not to balk.

"Let's get you back to bed, Angel."

She allowed him to lay her on the pallet without comment and mumbled her thanks when he covered her with the thin blanket. For a long moment he just watched her, asleep in the moonlight, admiring her midnight hair fanned around her as if it had a life of its own. Then he went back to his fur by the far wall and fell into deep musings.

What had he got himself into?

His life had been turned upside down and he wasn't sure everything he had fought to build would not come crumbling down as a result.

In the morning things seemed to have changed between him and Eowyn. Perhaps it was because of the unexpected intimacy they had shared under the stars, perhaps it was the result of his internal debate from last night. Rune wasn't sure, but for the first time in two days, since he had found out about the baby, he felt at peace.

Eowyn woke up to a table laden with food and a smiling Rune. Relief flooded her. Stupidly, she had feared he would flee during the night, scared by what had blossomed between them under the cover of darkness. She wasn't sure quite what had transpired during their conversation, but she knew things would be different from now on. There had seemed to be a new connection between them.

"Where did you find all this?" she asked, taking a loaf of bread in her hand. It was still warm and smelled delicious. Her stomach rumbled in anticipation.

"Yesterday I went round the village and saw a bench in need of repair outside a hut not too far from yours. I went to see the old couple living there while you slept and asked them for some food in exchange for my help putting it to rights." He spoke as if there was nothing extraordinary in that fact. "I thought you'd want something to eat when you woke up. Feeding a child must be hungry work."

Well. Eowyn was speechless.

Cwenhild's words came back to her. It seemed that some men were ready to compensate for not being able to feed their child, even men whose feelings toward said child were of an ambivalent nature... If Rune was prepared to see to her needs while he didn't consider himself Little Rune's father, she could not imagine how he would behave if they were a real family.

Thinking it best not to dwell on that thought, she sat down at the table and began to eat.

"So you repaired Gedla and Athelred's bench in exchange for a loaf of bread?" She had noticed herself a few times the state of disrepair it was in and wished she could help the old couple. But she had neither the time nor the skill for such an enterprise.

"I don't know what their names are," Rune answered, before tearing off an enormous chunk of bread with his perfect white teeth. For a reason she could not explain, the sight of those teeth caused her to shiver. Or perhaps she could explain it all too well. Because she remembered the delicious way they had nipped at her flesh.

"Let me guess," she said, steering her thoughts away from their wild night together and back to the conversation. "In your mind you call them Apple and Pear."

"Mm, no. I think Cat and Dog would suit better." He winked. "They appeared as if they like a good..."

"Bicker," Eowyn supplied when he waved his hand in search of the word, a giggle building in her throat. "Yes, they do."

"I thought so. And with those nails, the woman is clearly the cat."

So... There was more to the Norseman than arrogance and sexual prowess. He also had a generous nature, ready wit and a surprising sense of humor... Now that they could communicate better, she could appreciate all facets of his personality.

She chewed on her cheese pensively. What else would she discover about him? Would he even stay long enough for her to get to know him better? Did she want him to? Wouldn't it be easier if he did as she had imagined he would, and left?

"I think I will go to the Norsemen village today," Rune announced abruptly, as if he'd heard the questions whirring in her mind and thought he had better leave before she asked them out loud. "I want to see Sigurd. I need a word with him."

When he disappeared through the trees, Eowyn couldn't rid herself of the impression that she had just seen the last of the dashing devil.

CHAPTER FIVE

"**W**here is your son today, Beast?"

Rune planted himself in front of Sigurd, all menacing intent. He was itching for a fight and the tall Dane was the perfect man to indulge him. He would be both strong and skilled, ensuring Rune could exhaust his anger and frustration but he would be controlled enough so as not to seriously injure him.

More to the point, he deserved a good thrashing for his deception. What had possessed him to go along with his wife's outrageous lie and pretend to be Eowyn's baby's father? Didn't he think a man deserved to know he had fathered a child?

"You know the one I mean, Moon's elusive twin brother, the one with fiery red hair," he jeered, inching even closer. "Sun, is it, by any chance? Does he have a sun shape stamped on his ass?"

Though they were now within touching distance, Sigurd did not move a muscle. "He's with his mother, I should imagine."

"Mm. Yes, his rightful mother you mean. Not your wife because, of course, he was never yours."

"No."

Silence stretched between the two men. Rune brought his face a bare inch to Sigurd's, desperate to goad him into throwing the first punch. The Beast's temper had been notorious back in their village in Denmark. There was no reason this would have changed. Seeing that the wretched man did not seem to want to take the bait, however, he reluctantly took a step back.

Apparently, there would be no fighting today. But that didn't mean they couldn't quarrel.

"You never thought to tell me I had a son?" he erupted, finally breaking through the pretense.

"It was not my place to say anything." Sigurd's reasonable answer only incensed him further.

"You didn't think I had the right to know, seeing that the mother didn't find it necessary to inform me?"

That was another thing. Why had Eowyn kept the secret from him? All the frustration, pain, and fear of the last few days poured out of him. What would have happened if he had not gone back to see Eowyn? He would have returned to Denmark, not knowing he had a child. The mere idea sent chills down his spine.

"Are you saying you intend to raise this child as your own?" Sigurd crossed his arms over his chest.

Was that what he was saying? Rune hesitated, then decided to be honest. "I don't know if I want to have anything to do with him."

I don't know if I can.

"You don't *know* if you want to be a part of your son's life?" Sigurd's calm finally shattered. "Bloody hell, Rune, I don't blame you for leaving to get back home when you had no idea Eowyn was with child, you couldn't have known. But I will blame you if you leave now, when she's introduced you to your son!"

"What I do is none of your concern," he growled.

"It is my concern. Eowyn is my wife's friend. I've watched her waste away as she took care of your baby day and night all on her own and protected him against the malice of the people in her village. Now that you're back you will help her and take care of your son or so help me, I will shred you to pieces!"

Rune glared at him. "Who are you to order me about? You and I were never friends."

A few years older than him, Sigurd had always the been the village outcast, living in the woods all by himself. Rune had been secretly intimidated by the forbidding 'beast' and only too happy to join in the mocking. It had seemed the safest way to behave, as the last thing he had wanted was the boys' cruelty to turn on him. He regretted it now, but that was easy to say for a man who towered over everyone. As an eleven-year-old child, he had not dared draw unwanted attention to himself.

One winter, though, while out looking for wood, he had come across the infamous beast's hut. The miserable lodging was crumbling away, making it painfully clear no one living in there would manage to keep warm in such cold weather. Compassion had twisted his guts. Making sure no one saw him, including the inhabitant of the hut, Rune had left the contents of the leather bag his mother had given him for his mid-day meal in front of the door. It was not much but he just couldn't ignore the youth's plight.

"No, we weren't friends," Sigurd said, piercing him with a keen stare. Had he guessed what Rune was thinking about? Did he know he was regretting having joined in the boys' ribbing? Had he seen him deposit the food that day? It was not impossible. At the time, Rune had thought himself the epitome of stealth, but eleven-year-old boys rarely are. "That doesn't mean a thing anyway. We are not talking about me, but about Eowyn. You will do what's right by the woman."

Do the right thing? Surely he didn't mean...

"Are you mad?" Rune recoiled. "I didn't come here to stay! I have my life in Denmark."

"I know, I'm not asking you to marry her or anything. But you will stay until the end of the summer, give her the relief she needs for a couple of months, some time for her to recover and get the rest she deserves. Then in the autumn you will leave with the last boat departing for Denmark, if you wish."

If he wished?

What was the man talking about? Did he imagine Rune would drop everything he'd built to stay in a county where people viewed him with suspicion and called him after some sort of ludicrous demon, with a woman he barely knew and a babe he could not afford to see as his?

"Marriage has changed you. You weren't always such a romantic, Beast," he mocked.

"No. But people change. You were once afraid of doing what you knew in your heart was right. I don't blame you for it, as children will do whatever they need to survive." Sigurd shrugged and Rune swallowed. By the gods, somehow the Dane knew about the guilt he'd felt back then, in the pack of boys! "Well you are a man now, not a frail youth, so you are going to get back to Eowyn and you are going to do whatever she asks you to do, do you hear me?"

Rune could not resist. He cocked a suggestive eyebrow. "She might ask me to make love to her, you know. If we live together, it is inevitable she'd be tempted. She might even beg me to take her to bed."

Sigurd didn't even blink. "If she does ask, then you make sure you don't leave her bed until she's passed out from pleasure and while she sleeps, you go and change your son's dirty clout. Is that clear? Now enough stalling, go!"

THE MAN in front of the chicken coop was one Eowyn had not thought to see again. She stilled. Could she pretend not to have seen him? Probably not. It would not serve anyway. He had obviously come to see her. Even if she could slip back inside the hut unnoticed, he would only come knocking on the door a moment later.

At least she was not holding Little Rune in her arms right now. Without knowing quite why, she didn't want to share the news of her son's birth with her former lover. Ecberg had left the village a few years ago, after a glorious summer spent together. It had been the closest she had been to falling in love since Freodheric. Now, she could barely muster the energy to speak to him.

Taking in a deep breath, she walked up to him. "Good afternoon."

"Eowyn. Good afternoon. You look... incredible." His eyes were fastened on her bodice, which didn't surprise her. All the men she'd met of late seemed to share this fascination for her new, generous breasts. But at least Rune always made the effort to drag his gaze back to her face after the initial admiring glance to her bosom. Ecberg was all but drooling.

"Thank you," she said, wishing he would look her in the eye. "How have you been?"

"Not well, if you must know." Ecberg threw her a wicked smile and came a step closer. Finally he was looking at her. "I've missed our nights together."

"Have you?"

"Of course. How could I not? There is little time or opportunity for bed sport when one is surrounded by men all the time. Maybe I should have found myself another occupation. One doesn't meet many women while out in the forest cutting wood, you know."

Eowyn gritted her teeth. He hadn't missed *her*, only having a woman in his bed, which was not the same at all. And apparently he was now back for more.

"I think you must be hot for me me as well," he purred in her ear before drawing her into his arms. "Don't think I missed the fact that I was the man who gave you the most pleasure."

Up until then, maybe. She toyed with the idea of telling him that she had since been bedded by an insatiable Norseman before thinking the better of it. Ecberg would not take this humiliation too well and he was already holding her too tightly. She should focus on making him understand their time together was over. He was still as handsome as ever but today his beauty left her strangely cold.

"Ecberg, I—"

"Shall we go inside so I can give you what you need?"

As he approached the hut, Rune saw the tall Saxon draw Eowyn into his arms. His fingers bunched into fists. This was going too far. He had not objected while they had talked, even if he'd disliked the glint in the man's eyes. Even from a distance, he reeked of lust.

But now he most definitely objected, because it was clear Eowyn didn't want to be pawed at and yet the wretched man was pretending not to see it.

Before he knew what he was doing he strode over to them, intent etched all over his face. It seemed he had timed his return from the Norsemen village well, in time to dispose of the man.

"Do you need help getting rid of this stinking goat, Angel?"

"*Angel?* Who the hell are you to call her that? Or me a goat?" The man blinked at him. "I don't remember requesting your—"

"You didn't. Now let Eowyn go before I make you."

"I see. You want her for yourself, Norseman." The man finally released Eowyn and came to face him. He could almost look him in the eye and didn't appear worried. More the fool he. Rune was not above breaking arms and gouging eyes out when necessary. With a broken wrist and bleeding sockets, the wretched Saxon would not be able to grope or leer at anyone, much less his Angel.

"What if I wanted her for myself?" he growled. If that was what it took to get rid of the man, then he would gladly go along with the pretense. Besides, it was not a lie. He did want Eowyn, in spite of everything that had transpired between them.

"I wouldn't be surprised if you did. That woman is one hell of a fuck. Well, I got here first, my friend, so you'll have to wait your turn."

Wait his turn. One hell of a fuck.

Rune stared at the man in disbelief. How dare he talk about Eowyn thus or assume she would take one man after the other without a word of protest? Who did the Saxon think he was? At first, he'd taken him for a harmless idiot who had got carried away by desire in front of a beautiful woman, but the fool was actually treating her like a whore.

It was unacceptable.

He saw Eowyn bite her bottom lip. She didn't look outraged, rather worried about the issue of the confrontation between the two men. But who was she worried for? That was the question.

"You might have to wait a while, though," the Saxon taunted, taking his silence for surrender. "My balls are full to the brim and aching for release."

That did it.

Rune struck before the last word was uttered.

It happened so fast Eowyn didn't have time to open her mouth in warning. Quick as a snake, Rune raised a hand and hit Ecberg square under the chin. The Saxon fell backward without a sound, felled as neatly and as noiselessly as if he'd been a rag-stuffed doll. She stared at him, flat on his back, unconscious, eyes closed, then turned to look at Rune in horror.

"You—"

"He's not dead, no," Rune grumbled. "But he might think twice about trying to steal kisses from unwilling women and calling them whores when he wakes up."

Warmth spread through her. He had done that for her, to make Ecberg swallow back his awful words, not because he'd wanted to indulge in a male display of strength. Never had anyone taken her defense as unequivocally or as efficiently.

"How did you know I was unwilling?" she whispered. After all, from a distance, she and Ecberg might have looked like a pair of lovers. Which they had been, in a way.

Rune stared at her as if she'd asked him how he knew she was a woman. "It was quite obvious, I would say."

"Was it? Not to Ecberg."

"The fact that he did his best to ignore it doesn't mean it was not clear. A willing woman doesn't push at a man's chest when he leans over her, she doesn't laugh away his attempt at a kiss but instead lifts her mouth to him, and she doesn't have a look of panic in her eyes when he tells her he wants her."

Eowyn was stunned. She hadn't really pushed at Ecberg, even if she had wanted to, merely placed her hands over his chest, which he had interpreted as a sign of passion. She had laughed and he had thought her aroused. And he had failed to understand it was panic, not desire, flaring in her eyes.

Rune, who'd been yards away, had seen it all and had come to her aid unprompted. And then he had taken exception to the way Ecberg had talked about her and what he wanted to do. She could not deny being touched.

"Thank you."

"No need to thank me. Is that a usual happenstance?"

This time she did not bother to rectify the mistake. It was

clear what he meant. "Not exactly."

It hadn't been, but it was quickly becoming one. She had once been able to lead the life she wanted without being accountable to anyone but of course the more men she bedded, the more word spread about her supposed willingness. What some people failed to see was that it wasn't because she had bedded lovers of her choosing in the past that she would welcome just about anyone who asked for her favors. The men saw it as tacit agreement to tumble her into bed and the women as an excuse to despise her.

Eowyn wasn't fooled. The men knew full well they were pushing their luck, and the women were in fact jealous of the liberty she was taking. But it was making her life difficult and was quickly becoming problematic. Even if she had not bedded anyone for a year, her reputation as a wanton woman was now established.

It could not have come at a worse time, when she had decided to put an end to it all.

After her wild night with Rune no one had been able to tempt her. And once she had found out she was with child, she had wanted to focus on her role as a mother. All in all, she had not been with a lover for well over a year.

But apparently it was not enough to deter some men. She glanced at Ecberg still lying on the ground. He had been bursting with need and only thought of getting relief in her arms, not stopped to wonder what she wanted. What if Rune had delayed his return from the Norsemen village even by a moment? Would she have been able to make Ecberg heed her refusal? She was not certain.

"Will he be all right, do you think?"

"He will be well enough." Rune sounded as if he regretted it. "Don't worry about him. He has only himself to blame for what happened. Let's go inside."

Rune was seething with rage at the man's presumption. How dare he treat Eowyn thus? But as irate as he was, something was niggling at the back of his mind. This Ecberg had seemed pretty confident his offer would be accepted. Besides, he had behaved with the ease of an old acquaintance. Why was that?

He would just have to ask.

"Why would the man assume you were willing to be bedded? Why would he think I was 'waiting for my turn' as he said?"

Eowyn sighed and sat on a stool. "We slept together a few times about two years ago, before he left the village."

Of course, he should have known the man had already bedded her. He had called her 'a hell of a fuck' after all. He clearly spoke from experience.

"Is he your only lover?" She hesitated, too long to leave any doubt in his mind. He was not.

"No," she confirmed. "But he was one of my most regular ones."

"I see." He bunched his fists. The idea of other men bedding her bothered him, there was no denying it. Perhaps that was why his next words were more scathing than he had intended. "You seem to have earned yourself a reputation."

Far from shying away, Eowyn raised her chin defiantly. "Don't pretend to be surprised. How did you know who I was last year? Why did you come to me, confident in the fact that I would be willing to bed you? Didn't you hear about me from your countrymen on the way over here?"

Well... Rune ran a hand through his hair, feeling caught out. It was true he had been told about a beautiful black-haired temptress living in the village beyond the harbor and his curiosity had been piqued. As soon as he'd seen her, he'd known who she was. Raven hair falling in a sleek sheet over her shoulders, liquid dark eyes, sensual body, incredible skill at pleasing a man. Yes. Eowyn had lived up to his friend Leif's description and more.

And he had made the most of it.

"Are you saying that you sleep with a man just for the asking?"

"No!" She shot back to her feet, outrage painted on every inch of her beautiful face. "Of course not! I only mean that you would never have met me, or rather slept with me, if you had not heard about me. And you wouldn't have heard about me if I didn't welcome men to my bed. You knew what kind of woman I was at the time, even if you chose not to dwell on it. So don't pretend to be shocked now."

He blinked. She was right. He'd been told about her because she took her pleasure with men when she wanted. And not just Saxons, Norsemen as well. During the trip from Denmark, Leif had boasted about the exotic Saxon lover he'd bedded the year before, saying that she seemed to have a penchant for men from their country.

Rune remembered his friend's words all too well...

"She lives in the village just yonder. You're here for a few days, go and see for yourself, my friend. You'd be a fool not to. If I weren't newly-married, believe me, I would go with you. But unfortunately, I know that my wife would smell it from a mile out if I slept with another woman now."

Rune looked at Eowyn, who was still staring at him, as if debating whether to speak or not. Perhaps she feared she had said enough already.

"When my grandmother sensed she was dying, she arranged for me to be taken care of," she said eventually. "She had no family who might have taken me in."

By now Rune was used to Eowyn's habit of blurting out odd

things when you least expected it. He waited, knowing there would be a point to the story.

"There was a woman owning a farm in the next village. She was known for welcoming orphaned and destitute children. My grandmother asked if she could have me when the time came. The woman agreed."

Why did Rune have the impression this wouldn't have a happy ending? He lifted his chin. "What happened?"

"The woman was in fact little more than a slave owner. The majority of the children, some as young as four or five, had been recruited to work on the farm with no pay. They had been sold to her by their poor parents, or even stolen. Of course, I only found that out afterward, when it was too late. My grandmother thought she was safeguarding me by entrusting me to her care. She thought she was ensuring that I would not be left to my own devices, to beg on the streets."

"What did they do to you at this farm?" Rune asked, his jaw clenched. The thought of Eowyn as a child, all alone in a place where no one would know or care what happened to her was enough to make his blood race through his veins.

She shook her head like someone who did not wish to remember difficult times. "Nothing, except work me every hour of every day. There was no time to rest, barely time to eat. Until I found a way of escaping, it was hell."

"Hell?" He'd heard that word before, but he didn't remember what it meant.

Eowyn looked at him straight in the eye. "The place where the Devil lives. You might be familiar with the place."

"Mm, yes, I see. In other words, it was bad."

Her lips quivered, drawing his attention to her mouth. Not that he wasn't already very aware of how perfect and plump and red her lips were. It was all he could think about most of the time. "Very bad. No one wants to be too close to the Devil."

"No. I can imagine." For a moment the air between them seemed to sizzle, exactly as if it had caught fire. Maybe he did share more than a name with the fiery demon if he had the power to create such sparks.

"You said you had escaped?" he prompted. If she didn't carry on with her explanation, he might well kiss her and taste the juicy lips on offer.

"I didn't escape for real. I mean I found a way of making my life more bearable."

Ah. So now he had a feeling he knew where she was going with this. She had started to bed men as a way of bringing some much needed spice to her dull, hard life, to try and make herself feel as if she were more than just a slave.

"I see," he murmured. Even if he understood the thinking, the idea of a young Eowyn bedding men, perhaps older than her, was twisting his gut.

"One day my friend and I stumbled upon two of the farm hands hired for the season making love in the hay. It was... well, it was a revelation. They seemed lost in their own little paradise. The place where angels live and everyone wants to go when they die," she added for his benefit, which was just as well because he'd never heard the word before. Magnar had not been that thorough in his explanations of Saxon beliefs.

He managed a smile. If the place was populated by angels like her, it was no surprise people—especially men—wanted to go there. He might swap it for Valhalla himself.

"How old were you then?"

"Sixteen. We watched, transfixed, and while we watched, the oddest thing happened. My body started to tingle and heat all over. I know now that I was aroused, of course, but at the time I didn't know what was happening, only that it was delicious."

Yes. Delicious. His little Angel was brazen indeed. She was

discussing with him, a man in his prime, what most women would never even dare acknowledge to themselves.

"And your friend?" Rune cleared his throat. He would *not* be more embarrassed than her. "What did she feel?"

"*He,*" Eowyn answered pointedly, looking at him from under her lashes, "was aroused as well."

He tensed, guessing what she might tell him now. A green, excitable lad of sixteen next to an aroused young woman as enticing and open-minded as Eowyn wouldn't have been able to contain himself.

"That day we started experimenting with what we'd seen," she confirmed. Jealousy was like a knife to the heart but Rune stayed still. He would not ridicule himself by showing it. "It became our way of pretending we could have some freedom, of making sure our life was about more than backbreaking work."

"Mm." Deciding he had heard enough on the subject of Eowyn bedding a friend to make herself feel alive, he steered the discussion in a different direction. He didn't need to hear what Eowyn and the boy had done that summer, he could guess all too well. "Was this Ecberg?" Was that why the man had been so familiar with her? Because he'd been her first lover and considered he had every right to come back to her whenever he wanted?

"No." A shadow passed over her eyes. He could tell she didn't want to talk more about her former lover. As it suited him fine, Rune didn't insist. "I've always been more attracted to your people." She reddened at the admission but did not lower her gaze. He was impressed by her honesty.

"Why?" He could not think of anything less arousing than a Norseman.

"They tend to be taller and stronger than my countrymen, and as a rule they are also cleaner." The blush on her cheeks increased, as if she remembered how she had accused him of stinking the other day. Good. He really had not liked that. "Most conveniently of all, they do not live here."

He arched a brow. "How is that better? They would never be able to offer you anything long term."

"That is not a problem, as I'm not looking for anything long term."

"What then?"

She stared at him as she would at a simpleton. "The same thing you are looking for when you go to a woman, I imagine. Pleasure."

Rune wasn't sure what to say to that. He had never met a woman like Eowyn, comfortable with her needs and desires, not looking for marriage or commitment from the men she bedded, only pleasure, and happy to admit it out loud. He didn't know how to deal with it.

"And have you been successful in your quest? In my experience, women are less easily satisfied than men in bed."

She blushed, clearly remembering their night together. She had been satisfied then. Never had he heard a woman moan so much or be so clear with what she wanted. The mere memory caused him to harden.

"Some lovers are more talented than others, and I have been disappointed on occasion," she agreed. "But all in all I was quite satisfied."

At least she had been at first, Eowyn reflected.

She had hoped that having lovers who disappeared after she had taken her pleasure with them would ensure she didn't get a reputation as a promiscuous woman amongst the villagers. It had worked for a while but somehow, word of her willingness had started to spread. Either men had been seen leaving her hut too often or the few Saxons she'd bedded had boasted to their friends about their trysts, she didn't know. In any case, it seemed she was now considered fair game for the local male population and she didn't feel in control anymore.

The incident with Ecberg was telling.

He'd come back for her at the earliest opportunity, because he'd needed his balls emptying, to use his shocking words, and he had not thought for a moment that she would not be willing, had not even bothered to ask if she was still available. She could have gotten herself a husband or another lover in the interim but he had not seemed to consider that possibility. What if Rune hadn't been here? Could she have gotten rid of Ecberg on her own? She couldn't be sure. A few men had been rather forceful of late, and reluctant to accept her refusal. The fact that she had just given birth didn't seem to deter them, nor did they seem to accept it as reason to leave her be. On occasion, things had come too close for comfort, and she feared it would only get worse.

"So now you know why Ecberg thought I would be willing," she murmured. "Because usually, I am."

Rune stayed silent for a moment, as if lost in thought. He was trying to absorb what he'd been told. Eowyn waited, her heart in her throat, for the inevitable comments that would follow her declaration. As a woman she wasn't supposed to live her life as freely as if she were a man, to pursue pleasure for pleasure's sake. As an unmarried woman, she wasn't even supposed to know about such matters. It would not be long before he reminded her of the fact and concluded that, in the circumstances, Ecberg was not to be blamed for assuming she would offer him the relief he needed.

"Well, the next time one of your former lovers comes back for more and you don't want him, make sure to tell him as much before he gets ideas into his head, like you did with me," Rune said at long last. "Don't wait until he takes you into his arms, send him on his way with a curse, or a kick to the bollocks if needed. It could help avoid an unpleasant scene, although I fear not every man will be as compliant as I was when rejected."

She stared at him in disbelief. "Is that all you have to say?"

He stared back at her, jaw set in granite, as if he didn't understand what she meant. "What would you like me to say?"

"I-I don't know." Certainly she didn't want him to look at her in disgust, but this reaction was not the one she had expected. He was supposed to be horrified, or at least disapproving, wasn't he? Why was he so understanding? "I thought you would, well... judge me or belittle me," she mumbled.

"You wouldn't think of judging me or 'belittling me,' whatever that means, for bedding women, would you?" Rune asked, crossing his arms over his chest. Oh. It seemed she had angered him.

"No, of course not," she agreed hurriedly. "But you are a young, unmarried man, it is expected you would indulge your senses and—"

"I am also not a deluded hypocrite. I understand that men like me need women like you if they want to be able to 'indulge their senses' as you say. If the female population consisted only of virgins waiting for marriage and faithful wives, then we would only be able to bed old widows and disease-ridden whores. Not a particularly appealing prospect, you will admit."

"No, I suppose not." She had never thought about it like that.

"Sex is one of the greatest pleasures of life, not one I see any reason to deny myself if I find willing partners. Why should you feel any different because you don't have a snake between your legs?" She arched a brow at the unusual word but did not comment. There was no need, she knew what he meant. "At least you have the courage of your opinions."

Well. That was clear enough. He wasn't horrified. He thought her behavior perfectly reasonable.

She cleared her throat. "Thank you. And..." She hesitated but it was only fair she helped him improve his vocabulary after what he'd done for her. "We don't say 'snake' for that part of the body."

"Ah. Apologies. Snake made sense, I thought. What do you say then? My friend Magnar told me, but I've forgotten. I know it is the name of an animal though."

Eowyn groaned. Trust his friend to have taught him that particular word to name the male member! Now she would have to say it out loud. She raised herself onto her tiptoes so she could whisper it into his ear. It was one thing saying it, quite another to shout it out loud. "It's a male chicken. Cock."

"Mm. Yes, cock. I remember now." The growl he gave was pure lust. "Cock."

"Stop saying it," she begged. Hearing the crude word in his mouth was arousing beyond belief, as was the fact that she could feel the heat of his chest against her own. Why had she not taken a step back? She should do so, right now.

"Why should I stop saying it?"

"Because it's rude."

And it's making me want to touch yours.

"Magnar didn't tell me that."

"Well, maybe Magnar didn't know," she snapped, annoyed at her weakness. "But I'm telling you."

She should definitely move and she should stop talking about Rune's cock, stop imagining it, stop remembering the pleasure it had given her.

As if he could sense she was on the verge of an outburst neither of them would be able to contain, Rune did what she seemed incapable of doing. He took a step back.

"Let me go and see if the Saxon has come to yet."

With those words he left the hut and Eowyn knew she had seen the last of Ecberg.

_____

CHAPTER SIX

The next few days were spent in a peaceful atmosphere. Rune went hunting to keep them fed, he took care of the fire, and gave her a sense of security. No longer worried of seeing a man come to the hut in search of bedsport at any time of day, Eowyn finally allowed herself to relax. She had started to lose sleep she could ill-afford to lose over that eventuality. What if she got hurt in a confrontation with a man more forceful than the others? What would become of her son then? But now she knew if someone like Ecberg came sniffing, Rune would send them on their way before they could even open their mouth.

Even better, little by little, Rune seemed to come to accept the idea that he now had a son. He had been cautious around the babe at first, refusing to have anything to do with him but gradually, he seemed to have warmed up to the boy. How could he not? Little Rune was the most endearing child.

One morning, as he was looking for a ladle to stir the stew, Rune found her wooden doll.

"Did you make that?" he asked, examining the little figurine.

"No. If I had to sculpt anything, I wouldn't know where to

start. If I wanted to make a woman, I'd probably end up making a pig."

"This I would like to see, as women and pigs have very little in common in my experience." Rune laughed. "But you should try. Carving wood is not that difficult."

"For you maybe not, but you're very talented with your fingers."

He shot her a purely wicked look. "Ah. So you remember. I'm flattered."

Eowyn blushed all the way to her navel. Why had she said that? "I meant..."

"I know what you meant. And yes, I am more talented than most at carving. There is nothing extraordinary in it, though. I'm a boat builder, so working with wood is what I do best. Well, maybe not best..."

The heat descended further down, invading the place between her legs. Yes... He definitely had other talents. Now she understood how he had been so skilled with his caresses. He worked with his fingers, he was used to smoothing his hands lovingly over wood. He needed to be gentle enough to be able to detect faults in the planks he used by touch only. Those skills he'd honed in his trade, combined with his strength, pure wickedness and stamina, could not fail to make him an exceptional lover.

That and the fact that he had probably bedded his fair share of women, of course.

Her gaze fell to his fingers and her core started to tingle with need. Oh, she needed to distract herself from thoughts of those long, elegant fingers teasing indescribable pleasure out of her. She took the little doll from him and cleared her throat.

"My grandmother had her, and she gave her to me when she died. She was originally part of a set, there was once a man to go with her. I never saw him, but the woman doll has always fascinated me. I used to play with her as a child, I made her do all the things I wished I could do myself. Once I made her ride one of the chickens all afternoon."

Eowyn giggled at the memory. It had not been easy to tie the doll to the animal's back but she had not given up. Her doggedness had earned her more than a few pecks from the disgruntled hens.

"Did you now?" Rune smiled as if he was imagining her running after the clucking, ruffled animals. "Did the woman end up covered in chicken shit that day?"

"Of course not! And you're a horrid man for even thinking such a thing." His blue eyes gleamed at the scolding. "Anyway, that's why she's all chipped now."

She showed him a series of small indentations by the left arm.

He took the doll and nodded. "What happened to her that time, I wonder? Did you decide she would explore the inside of a dog's mouth in your stead?"

"No. I don't remember. This is all the result of a series of misadventures." She sighed. "I wish she were as smooth and beautiful as she was before. I tried to get rid of some of the holes once but ended up making more of a mess than anything."

She lifted her face to Rune, as an idea popped into her head. Perhaps *he* could—

"I'll see what I can do," he said before she could even ask. "I told you, I'm good with wood. With patience and skill I might be able to smooth away most of the imperfections." He placed the doll in the pouch at his belt. "I'll go and see if someone has tools in the village after we've eaten."

"Thank you."

Later that afternoon, for the first time, Rune took the little boy from her while she put herself to rights after feeding him. Holding her breath, Eowyn watched him cradle his son against his chest until the boy fell asleep. It was a heartbreakingly beautiful sight. Finally father and son were sharing a moment. Then, almost with regret, Rune put the baby in his nest of furs. When he turned to her, he was frowning.

"This is unrelenting work. Have you done anything other than take care of Rune these last few months?"

It was obvious from his scowling that the real answer—no, she had not—would not please him. Nevertheless she could not lie. "Not really," admitted, standing back up. "I was too tired most of the time to even think about going anywhere."

"As I thought." Rune grunted. "And do you miss having a man in your bed?"

Her heart skipped a beat at the very personal question. "Miss it?"

"Well, you just said that you haven't done anything other than take care of the babe recently, and I imagine that you didn't feel like pursuing men with your stomach heavy and full." He looked at her and shook his head. "So it will have been months at least since you've had a man in your bed giving you pleasure, maybe as much as a year."

He was right, it had been a year almost to the day since she had bedded anyone, since their night together, and yes, she had missed it. From the age of sixteen she had never before gone that long without a man.

"Well, how long has it been for you, I might ask?" she retorted, piqued to have her life so easily dissected.

"An eternity. Perhaps as many as two or three weeks."

She swatted his arm. "You are mocking me!" How dare the wretched man taunt her so when it had been much longer for her?

"I don't know how you did without for so long," Rune said in a low rumble that went straight to her core. "I know I could not. There is nothing more pleasurable in life than having a beautiful, warm woman under me."

Her heart missed a beat but she forced herself to calm. Then, before she knew it, she answered. "I would rather have a hard man above me. Inside me."

Was she mad to provoke him so? Rune's nostrils flared, proving she might well be. One does not poke a wild beast without repercussions.

"Now *that* is something I don't know anything about..." He pursed his lips. "I'm not sure I would want to find out either. I much prefer softness."

"Do you?"

His gaze fell to her heaving chest. "Absolutely. Wet, hot, welcoming softness. The perfect place to bury myself in, the perfect home for my... cock. I like to feel it slip inside again and again until my woman goes mad." After throwing one glance at the growing bulge between his legs, he stared at the place between her thighs. And that place instantly started to melt and quiver. None of her other lovers had provoked half as much reaction within her just by looking at her and talking about what they liked to do in bed. But really, the things he said...

It was shocking and yet, she didn't want him to stop.

Rune took a step toward her. They were now within touching distance and she had to crane her neck to look at him. Still, she didn't move away, could not.

"No, I've never felt the urge to bed a man, but I've often wondered how it would feel to be a woman. Perhaps you could tell me. What do you feel when a man touches you here?" he murmured, cupping her gently. "When I desire someone I get hard, blood starts pulsing in my shaft. How does it feel for a woman, I wonder? For you, Angel?"

The words were out before she could stop them. "I melt. I

burn." Just like she was now. She was certain he could feel it, even through the layers of fabric.

"Does it ache like it pains me sometimes, when the need is too strong? In the same way I'm desperate to plunge inside my lover's heat, do you need your little pussy to be filled?"

Oh. Lord. Had he just said that? How did he even know that word? His friend Magnar, no doubt. How had the man decided what words to teach him during their lessons? Only this morning she'd had to tell him the word for 'plate'! And yet he could name the most private parts of the body in crude terms.

"Rune. You have to stop talking right now."

And he had to stop touching her. His hand, warm and assured, was still wedged between her legs. Of course she could simply have walked away but somehow that was not an option. She was frozen to the spot. Her blood was singing in her veins and she was a heartbeat away from throwing herself into his arms.

"Why? Are you shocked? Can't we have a simple conversation?"

Oh, this was no conversation, simple or not, it was a seduction. It was torture! She closed her eyes and fought the need to moan, to squirm, to press herself tight against his fingers. Why wasn't he moving? Couldn't he tell she needed friction?

"You need to stop because you are making me... want you," she rasped. Surely he knew that already? Surely he'd seen the look in her eyes, noticed the flush on her cheeks, felt the heat of her core? Oh, yes, the devilish man knew full well what he was doing.

"I am making you want me? And what's the problem with that, exactly?" His voice, already impossibly husky, was now reduced to a purr. "We've already slept together. I think you'll agree we're past such shyness you and I, and we know we are good in bed together. You need pleasure, after being too long without, and you know I'm capable of giving it to you. So take what you need, make the most of the fact that I'm here, ready to give it to you."

He was going to kill her. He made it sound so simple. The offer was too tempting and his hand was... Dear God, he had finally started to move and his fingers were building her need to a fever pitch. This was so different from what he had done when he had come back from Denmark... This was no lewd advance but something utterly irresistible.

He was making her melt, reducing her to a puddle of need, and, even more pointedly, offering to give her pleasure, not just slake his.

She forced herself to stand still and not grind her hips against his hand, however much her pussy ached and she wanted it to be filled, just as he'd said. She had to be reasonable and refuse.

But somehow she could not utter the words.

Interpreting her silence as agreement, in one swift move Rune tumbled her to the fur pallet and settled himself over her. This gave her the jolt she needed to come back to her senses.

"No, we can't..." she whimpered. "Please, I don't want to fall with child again, it's too soon, I—"

"Hush, Angel, I know. But you won't."

Eowyn's insides collapsed in disappointment. She had expected more from him. He was claiming he wanted to give her pleasure but he was just like Ecberg, interested only in his release and unwilling to accept her refusal.

She pushed at his chest in disgust.

"It took you just one night to make me with child last summer, what is to say it won't happen again?" What sort of a fool did he take her for? She knew only too well one moment of pleasure was enough to change her life. "You are one potent man."

He grunted. Was he pleased at what he considered a compliment or frustrated that she was refusing him the relief he needed?

"As potent as I am, I think you will agree I cannot make you pregnant with my tongue." He gave her a wicked smile. "A man has his limits, Angel."

His tongue! She bit her lip in remorse for thinking the worse of Rune's intentions. Far from wanting to take advantage of her, he meant to pleasure her and leave it at that, forego his own pleasure. If that was the case then of course she could—

No. She shook her head to ward off temptation. He might well intend not to take her but there was no knowing how things would evolve once they started making love and desire flooded their veins. She wasn't sure *she* would not beg him to take her once he had her naked and panting. It was too risky.

"I don't think—"

He cut her off by coming to nuzzle at her throat. At the same time, one of his strong hands closed over her breast. She could not help a moan and almost asked him to rip her laces off and suckle her.

"You need not fear I will be overcome by need," he purred in her ear. If ever anyone had sounded like the Devil trying to lure her into sin, it was Rune in that moment. "Don't think, Eowyn. Just let me do this for you. You are due some pleasure. This is all about you. I promise I won't take you. It's probably too soon anyway."

It probably wasn't, she reflected. It had been three months since the baby's birth, surely she would be fine. But then all thoughts fled her mind because he said the most shocking thing she had ever heard.

"I'm dying to taste you. Come, sit on my face."

Seeing that Eowyn didn't respond, Rune rolled over to his back, desperate to have her accept his offer. He then lifted her by the waist and made her straddle his chest. She looked at him, a look of bemused arousal on her face. His whole body jerked in anticipation.

"You want me to—"

Apparently she could not repeat the lewd words. He had no such qualms. "Yes. Please, Angel, ride my tongue. I'm desperate for your sweetness. I haven't been able to forget the taste of you."

"Oh, Lord! You really say the most wicked things," she rasped, going all limp atop him.

Yes, he did say the most wicked things to her, because she was like no other woman he'd ever met, brazen and unafraid of her desires, because he knew it aroused her. As it did him. He had never been more ready for a woman in his life.

"Just for you, Angel. I do the most wicked things as well. Open for me."

Without waiting for her answer he slid down the pallet and positioned himself where he wanted, between her legs and under her skirts. His mouth was watering already but when her scent hit him, he could not resist. Slowly, he licked the wet folds waiting for him. Scorching heat met his tongue and he let out a groan.

Yes, finally, this was what he wanted.

A whimper reached his ears and he knew Eowyn would not stop him now. Drunk on his victory, he started lapping at her like a madman. Never had he felt more desperate to bring a woman pleasure. He licked, suckled and devoured her, wishing it could last forever. But her pleasure-deprived body was so primed it didn't take him long to make her erupt. When Eowyn's body started to convulse against his lips it gave him so much satisfaction he was certain his seed had shot straight out of him. He glanced down at his groin to make sure and let out a sigh of relief.

He had not humiliated himself, but he knew he would have to stroke himself without delay for fear of dying of unfulfilled need.

It had been so long since Eowyn's body had not exploded in pleasure. Too heavy with child to stroke herself the way she liked in the last weeks of her pregnancy, then too exhausted with her son to think about herself, she had not felt the blissful release for months. And of course she had not been with a man in more than a year, since that wild night with Rune.

No wonder this had been explosive.

Under her spread legs Rune was panting as hard as she was, as if he had reached his release at the same time. Perhaps he had... She stole a quick glance toward his lap and saw he was still as stiff as a fence post. Mm. No, he hadn't come, but he was dying to.

Too intent on pleasuring her, he had not even stroked himself. The urge to bring him the relief he needed was overwhelming and she didn't even try to resist it. Why couldn't she make him feel as good as he had made her feel? As he'd said, she knew they were compatible in bed.

And after what they had just done, she was past all shame.

She snaked a hand down his muscular chest and wrapped her fingers over his straining hardness. Even through the rough material she could feel it jerk in response. This proof that he desired her made her moan out loud.

"Don't!" he grunted. "You'll make me come in my braies." He sounded mightily aggrieved at the idea, as if he didn't want to be likened to an untried youth. A smile bloomed on her lips. He had nothing to fear, he was nothing like a green lad, but all virile male.

And in that moment, he was all hers.

"Oh, don't worry, I won't let that happen. I have a much

more satisfying idea for both of us," she purred, coming to kneel by his side.

She started to untie the laces holding her prize captive.

A strong hand clamped on her wrist. "What are you doing, Angel? I thought you didn't want to risk falling with child."

"I don't, but your seed will not make me pregnant if it's in my mouth, will it? You're not *that* potent."

A curse escaped Rune's lips but she wasn't going to let him get away with it so easily. He'd been ruthless with her earlier, ignoring her half-hearted protests and she had loved it. Now it would be her turn to make him think he'd died and gone to Heaven.

A devil in Heaven. Her smile widened at the thought.

"Here. Let me help ease your discomfort."

And hers. The heat between her legs was back, and she knew she would come again just from touching her swollen bud once Rune had reached his release.

She lowered her head.

CHAPTER SEVEN

A man was standing by the vegetable patch, staring intently in the direction of Eowyn's hut.

Rune walked up to him with slow, menacing intent. Something about the man's attitude bothered him, but he could not put his finger on what it was. It could have been the smile floating on his lips, the gleam in his eyes, the odd stillness, or it could have been simply the fact that he was here at all.

"What do you want?" He didn't try to sound friendly but the man didn't seem to take exception to the iciness in his voice.

"I came here to see Eowyn."

Yes, that much Rune had surmised. His heart started to beat faster in his chest. Surely the man wasn't one of her former lovers? But even as the question crossed his mind, he knew it would be the case. From what Eowyn had said, there would be dozens of them about, Saxons and Norsemen alike. This one, with his dark chestnut hair, was obviously Saxon, and he seemed confident he would be welcome.

Well, it mattered not what he thought. He was not going to see her, not when she was resting.

A memory of their lovemaking tore through his mind. After

she had drained every last drop of seed from his grateful body, he had not been able to leave it at that and he had pleasured her again and again, until she begged for mercy. The poor woman had fallen asleep with his finger still inside her, something that had both melted his heart and made him chuckle. Sigurd would be happy, he thought wryly, he who had ordered him to pleasure her until she passed out. Never before had he achieved such result. But then again Eowyn was like no other woman he'd met, a combination of breathtaking brazenness, and endearing spontaneity.

And she was his.

As was the child she had given him. It had taken him a while but he had finally seen, and accepted, that he could not pretend he didn't care about the little boy he would have to leave behind soon. Leave... Yes. Something would have to be done about that. He could not just go, abandon them, not now.

Now that he cared.

He sighed. Yes, Sigurd would be happy indeed. Hadn't the infuriating man foreseen this would happen?

You will leave with the last boat departing for Denmark, if you wish.

Well, Rune wasn't sure that was what he wanted anymore. But what else could he do? His life could not possibly be here, where he was made to feel like a stranger and an oddity on account of the way he looked. This would never change. He could learn to speak like a Saxon or even behave like one, but he would never look like one. So where did that leave him? He pushed the uncomfortable musings out of his mind. They could wait. For now he had a man to dispose of.

"Who are you?" he asked, coming one step closer to the man.

"I'm Albert."

Rune waited. Was this supposed to help him? It did not.

When he arched a brow in inquiry the Saxon chuckled, like a man certain of his right. Rune's heckles rose. The wretched man seemed to think Eowyn would welcome him with open arms—or rather open legs. Like that Ecberg. Well, it mattered not. If he said one word about taking her to bed, he would end up flat on his back as well.

"Albert? And who might that be?"

Another chuckle. Really the man didn't seem to take hints. Rune's attitude screamed menace and all the man could do was giggle like a child, a most disconcerting reaction. "I know I've been away for months but I think Eowyn might have mentioned me."

"She didn't, so could you be clearer?" Rune growled. The man was sorely testing his patience.

"I'm Eowyn's baby's father. We are to marry next month. There. Is that clear enough for you, Norseman?"

Oh, it was. Ice filled Rune's veins.

Eowyn was set to marry this man? At what point did the woman think it appropriate to inform him of the fact that she was betrothed to a Saxon and that the damned man, not Rune, was her baby's father, unlike what he'd thought, unlike what she'd claimed?

"Is she in?"

Albert seemed unaware of the magnitude of the blow he had just delivered. Rune cleared his throat. This was a nightmare and he was about to wake up, there was no other explanation. The alternative, that Eowyn had lied and wilfully misled him, was too painful to contemplate. Barely moments ago he had been making love to her, imagining they could have a future together, he'd been ready to accept his son and find a way to make this work despite the odds staked against them.

And now here he was, looking at a man who, in the next few

days, would get to have everything he'd thought to have for himself.

"She's gone to the Norsemen village to see her friend," he lied, speaking through clenched teeth. He had to get the man out of here before Eowyn woke up. Before he lost the battle with his reason and started beating the man out of all recognition.

"Frigyth? Oh. All right, then."

Oddly enough, Albert didn't seem put out. He didn't even ask who Rune was, even though with his bare chest it might have looked as if he'd just tumbled Eowyn into bed. Which of course, he had. He could still taste her on his tongue and there might well be red scratches all over his shoulders and back, testimony to the strength of the pleasure he had wrenched from her. For a moment he toyed with the idea of telling the man what he and his betrothed had been doing in bed that very morning, see how he liked it. Why should he be the only one feeling humiliated and in pain?

Albert spoke before he could open his mouth. "Well, I suppose I'd better come back tomorrow then."

"Yes. I suppose you had better do that."

EOWYN CAME BACK from her outing laden with mushrooms and herbs. As soon as she had deposited the basket onto the table, she went to the nest of furs to kiss the sleeping baby.

Rune emptied his third cup of ale, biding his time. He felt like a poisonous adder coiled under rocks, ready to strike the foolish wanderer disturbing his peace.

A soft voice reached him from behind. "Is everything all right?"

He didn't answer. Nothing had ever been further from all

right from the moment Albert had struck his blow but he'd been too stunned, too raw to confront Eowyn when she had woken up. Instead he'd watched with a bleeding, black heart as she hurried toward the forest. He'd guessed she had only gone foraging to avoid being on her own with him after what they had done and he had been happy to let her go.

He needed to calm down before they talked. Biting her head off would achieve little.

"I didn't expect to find so many mushrooms," he heard her say, her attempt at breeziness obvious. "I will have to dry some, I think, before they spoil."

What did he care about mushrooms? He had to stop her before this turned into a discussion about the best way to preserve food. She was embarrassed about their wild love-making from earlier, he could tell, and doing her best to pretend nothing had happened, but he was furious and he could not delay the conversation they needed to have any longer.

"Someone came to see you while you were out," he said, staring into the bottom of his cup. How he managed to keep his voice even, he would never know.

"Oh?" Eowyn didn't sound interested.

He turned around. As he'd suspected, her attention was wholly focused on their... Bile rose in his throat. Of course, he could not consider the little boy as his anymore. He had been fathered by another man, a man who was soon to replace him in his life, a Saxon who would sleep in Eowyn's bed, as her husband, before too long.

A man who belonged here, unlike him with his braided, fiery hair, his beard and his unnatural height.

"Who was that?"

"Albert."

This time Eowyn did look up, but he didn't elaborate. Let her wonder what the two of them had discussed, let her squirm, let her worry about what the man would think if he knew what they had done in bed that morning. But she only arched a brow in surprise.

"Albert? I'm not sure why he—"

Rune finally snapped. It was inevitable. He'd been able to control himself until now but if she was going to pretend she didn't know who the man was, then he did not see any reason to spare her from his ire. "Cut the pretense," he snarled. "I know you are to marry. He told me all about the little family you three are making together, told me he was your son's father."

Her dark eyes widened. "What are you talking about? Do you mean Albert, a man about a hand taller than me, with dark brown hair, handsome?"

Handsome! Was she trying to kill him? "I have no idea what you consider handsome," he snarled. "I thought he looked like a... mushroom myself."

She waved the comment away. "It has to be him, I don't know anyone else called Albert. But it doesn't make sense."

"Doesn't it? You mean you don't know the man, even though he knew your name and where you live, knew you were friends with Frigyth?"

"I... I didn't say that."

"You slept with him, didn't you?" He knew he sounded accusatory but he could not help it. "He's one of your numerous lovers."

Once again, Eowyn did not shy away. "Yes. But he's not Rune's father. That is the truth."

The truth, she said. And presumably he was to just accept her word? Rune swore at length. As it was something he could only do in Norse, he did not even try to restrain himself. Foul words escaped his mouth, without bringing him any relief.

"If you slept with him, how can you be so sure he's not Ru— the baby's father?"

She had the gall to look offended, even though anyone would have agreed it was a fair question. "I don't sleep with so many men that I don't know who might have made me with child or not. Besides, you know I went to the trouble of ascertaining your name so I could give it to the baby. Would I have done that if I had not known for certain you were the father?"

Rune was not so easily dissuaded. "Why would he think he is the father and you are to marry if you did not agree to it together?" The man's words had been anything but ambiguous.

I'm Eowyn's baby's father. We are to marry next month.

It didn't get much clearer than that.

"How would I know?" Eowyn threw her arms up in the air. "I barely know him," she added, slightly less brazenly. "We only slept together once."

"You slept with me just once as well," he pointed out. "And yet you claim it was enough to get you with child."

She winced at the word 'claim' but straightened her back. "I slept with him months before Rune's conception, if you must know. Babies do not stay in their mothers' wombs for twelve months or more!"

Rune still wasn't convinced. "It is your word against his. I have no way of establishing whether you slept with him twelve or nine months or even ten years ago."

"You don't have to establish anything, I'm telling you! You just have to believe me. But if you must, don't take my word for it, just look at your son." She gestured at the furs where the child was sleeping. "Rune looks just like you."

He clenched his teeth, refusing to glance in the direction of the child who'd just been taken away from him. "So you say. I don't see it."

Eowyn let out a snort. "You don't see his hair? Isn't it red enough for you? What else do you want to accept he is yours? For him to start babbling in Norse? Do you want to wait until he becomes a huge, pig-headed Norseman like you?" she exploded. "Albert is *not* the father, whatever he says. He cannot be. What we did..." Her voice trailed. "What we did could not have ended up in a pregnancy."

Rune blinked. Was she really saying what he thought she was saying? "By the gods!" He kicked a stone with his boot, sending it crashing against the wall of the hut. As if he wasn't suffering enough, now he had to imagine the bastard possessing Eowyn like a rutting animal. This was going from bad to worse. "I don't wish to hear what you two—"

"You asked how I knew for certain he was not the father! I'm telling you how. Albert and I never discussed getting married, and he did not get me with child! I cannot think what he means by this."

"It's not so hard to guess. Maybe he wants a wife who will let him take her in every way a man can take a woman!" he roared. Another stone was kicked toward the far wall, well away from the babe. "Evidently he liked what you did together so much he wants more. After what you allowed him to do, he's probably thinking there is nothing you would object to. Who knows, maybe he means to introduce you to some of his 'handsome' friends and have you service them while he—"

The resounding slap landing on his cheek did not surprise him. He knew he'd gone too far. But he was too hurt to care. Whatever he told her, Eowyn would emerge from this the winner. She would get to keep the child while he would have to leave empty-handed and mourn the loss of a babe he would never see grow.

Again.

All the fight went out of him at the thought.

Eowyn glared at the man standing in front of her, not even able to look her in the eye. With his head lowered, he had the gall to look like the injured party. After what he'd told her, it was hard to stomach. *She* should be the one allowed to feel bad.

"Not you as well!" She was bristling with indignation, hurt beyond words. Up until then Rune had never made her feel sullied for choosing to live her life the way she wanted.

When she had admitted to bedding more men than women usually did, he had not batted an eye. He had only nodded, agreed that it was her decision to make, even told her he would not judge her for doing nothing more than what he did himself.

And now, just because his pride had been hurt by that fool Albert, he was using her confession to hurt her back when she had done nothing wrong.

It was unbearable.

"Don't you dare try to make me feel like a whore now that you've heard something you don't like!" she erupted. "I did not hear you object to the fact that I welcomed men in my bed when you pounded into me last summer or when I took you in my mouth this morning!" Anger gave her the strength to utter the crude words. "And if you think for a moment that I do not know you must have had twice as many lovers as I've had, then you are a fool as well as a cruel man!"

He straightened back up, not a defeated opponent any longer, but every inch the formidable Norseman.

"This is not about lovers! I don't care that you bed other men and offer them pleasure in every—" The rest of the sentence was uttered in Norse. In his fury he could barely speak clearly. His accent had never been stronger. "It's about you lying about the identity of the baby's father!"

She recoiled under the attack. "I did not lie."

"No? A man who bedded you says otherwise. It would be foolish of me to dismiss his claim so easily. Why would he lie? Why would he try to trick me when he doesn't even know who I am? He's not an enemy, he doesn't have a score to settle with me, he didn't even see us together. He would have nothing to gain by pretending to be your baby's father. I have every reason to trust his word."

It was then that Eowyn understood. Indeed, this was not about her bedding scores of men. This was not about her at all. It was about Rune and his own issues, his mistrust of her, his inability—or rather unwillingness—to believe her claim that Little Rune was his. It was not that he had found it hard to accept she was telling the truth about their son when he'd seen her with the babe, it was that he didn't want to. He had doubted her from the start. That was why it had taken him days to warm up to the babe. Because he'd not believed him to be his son and he'd seen no reason to get attached to him.

It explained it all.

It was terrible.

She bunched her fists. "I don't know why you even bothered to come back here after your visit to the Norsemen village if you never believed Rune was your son. You could have gone straight to Denmark."

"I came back because Sigurd made me! I never wanted to stay but he made me. Without him I would be on my way home right now." His answer sliced through her as neatly as a cut from a sharp axe.

Everything crumbled inside Eowyn. To think she had once worried Rune would take their son away from her! But he didn't care, didn't want him, never had, didn't care about her either. He'd only been obeying his friend and trying to get between her legs while he was there, to compensate for his failure to bed her on the first day and restore his masculine pride.

And he'd succeeded. She'd surrendered to his seduction ploys all too easily, drawn in by his honeyed words and maddening touch. Self-loathing crashed through her. Was she just a wanton creature, governed by her urges, who couldn't see past a handsome face? Didn't she have any sense of pride?

"Get out," she said in a breath, too hurt to even raise her voice. It was her turn to be defeated. "Get out before I—"

"Oh, I'm going. No need to threaten me with another slap. I'm not sure I would survive it."

Rune slammed the door on his way out. Eowyn slid to the floor, numb to the bone. This day, which had started as in a dream, could not get any worse.

And then Little Rune started crying.

CHAPTER EIGHT

As he marched toward the Norsemen's village with the determination of a warrior about to charge the enemy, Rune could feel blood pulsing in his temples. How had everything gone so disastrously wrong?

Damn Sigurd and his ideas. Why had he listened to him?

Once again he'd had a child snatched away from him at the last moment, when he had started to love it. But this time it was a hundred times worse, it was not an anonymous babe he had never met. It was a little boy with the most adorable face, the sweetest smell and the most endearing smile, a little boy bearing his name.

He had been made a fool, an unpleasant feeling for anyone. For Rune, who had spent his youth craving to be seen for who he was, then his life trying to ensure he was not forced to act in a manner he didn't approve of, it was unbearable. That he had been blind to what was happening because of the lust he felt for Eowyn was bad enough, but he suspected there was more to his feelings toward her than mere physical desire, which made everything all the more pathetic. He had started to seriously wonder about what he felt for her and he did not like any of the answers he had found so far.

Now that he had been betrayed, he liked them even less.

He could not accept that he was nothing but a besotted idiot, governed by what his *heart*, and not his mind or even his loins wanted. For a moment he had thought he could have it all with Eowyn; a woman who fired his lust in bed and piqued his interest outside of it, a child he could love and the family both he and his parents had been craving for him to have. But he had been wrong, spectacularly so. There had never been any family, it had all been an illusion. The babe belonged to someone else and the woman was no innocent maiden waiting for love and marriage, she was a temptress who, by her own admission, did not want anything other than physical pleasure from the men she bedded.

He suspected that his heart had been broken by the discovery of her treachery.

That was why he was feeling so wretched. He did not feel betrayed and silly, as much as hurt.

Why had Eowyn lied to him, claimed he had fathered her baby? That's what he didn't understand. Had she been afraid of finding herself alone with a child to raise and wanted his support? Albert had said he'd been away for months. What if Eowyn had started to fear he would abandon her and never come back, despite their arrangement to marry? He wouldn't be the first unreliable man to shun his responsibilities. Had she thought to swap one bridegroom for another, one who pleased her in bed, one who wouldn't know better, who could not estab-lish the exact age of the babe and had no other choice but to trust her?

Had she premeditated it? No, she couldn't have guessed he would be back and her panic when she had seen him outside her hut had been genuine. She had not mentioned the child straight away because, of course, since he was not the father, he had no reason to be told. But then she'd had time to think and see that the Norseman's unexpected return could work in her favor. Was the little boy's name truly Rune or had she thought it a neat ploy to persuade him of her good faith?

Perhaps. And he had fallen for it.

He slammed his fist into the nearest tree, cursing himself for being taken in by a pretty face, beguiling manners and his need to be told he had a child. Pain exploded in his knuckles, the skin on his fingers split and drops of crimson blood fell on the grass at his feet. He ignored it all and punched the tree again, and again.

Damn Sigurd for placing him in that situation, damn Eowyn for crushing his hopes, and damn himself for being so easily fooled!

He set off for the village at a run. If he stayed here he would only reduce his hand to ribbons and that wouldn't change a thing.

He would still be alone.

The doll.

It was in Rune's pouch, the one attached to his belt. He had taken it with him when he'd left. Oh, no!

Eowyn knew she would have to go retrieve it. It was all she had from her beloved grandmother and she could not bear to be separated from it, to know it had ended up in the hands of a man who cared nothing for her, thought her a liar without honor, a schemer without scruples, a whore without feelings, a man who would only throw it away as soon as he remembered he had it in his possession. It might already be too late. She had to go now, before he either threw it into the fire or boarded a boat for Denmark, taking it with him.

She went to her friend Cwenhild, who had given birth a few weeks ago.

"Would you please look after Rune for me, feed him when he needs it?" she asked, handing over her son reluctantly. Parting from him was hard, but it would be better if he was not a part of this expedition. She would be able to travel faster without him in her arms and she didn't want Rune to see him anyway. He had forfeited all his rights over him by denying him so thoroughly. "I need to go to the Norsemen village. I will be back tomorrow."

"Of course."

Cwenhild looked at her oddly, but to Eowyn's relief, did not ask any questions.

Knowing she would not be able to sleep anyway, she set off in the middle of the night. The sooner she retrieved her doll and got back to her son, the better.

The first rays of the sun had not yet pierced the horizon when she came into view of the village but the sky was light enough for her to get a good view of the place. It seemed deserted. Then she spotted three boys drawing water from the well, the only sign of life for miles around.

She set off in their direction.

"Good morning."

"Good morning to you, beautiful," one of them drawled, eyeing her up and down. She knew what he was thinking even before his lips curled into a smile. Not that it was hard to guess. His gaze had landed on her breasts, as she could have predicted. They were more swollen than ever, in need for her son, and straining against her bodice.

"I was hoping you could help me," she said, crossing her arms over her chest to hide them from him. A bad idea. The gesture only seemed to push them further up. "I'm here to see Rune."

"Rune? Don't know anyone by this name."

No. He might not. Rune did not live here, after all. A thought struck her. She had assumed he had taken refuge to the Norsemen village, like last time, but after all, why would he have not gone into town? Or straight to the harbor? Was he this moment aboard a boat bound for Denmark? It was all too possible, if he thought nothing was holding him back here.

She would go see Sigurd and Frigyth. They would know whether Rune had come to the village or not. Why had she not thought of this before? She must truly be upset if she could not use her brain properly.

"You can call me Rune, if you like," another of the boys called out. "I don't mind."

His friends laughed. Eowyn mumbled her apologies and turned to leave. There was nothing to be gained from talking to them.

"Wait!" the third boy said. "I know who you are! You're that woman who's bedded the whole county, are you not? You must be, with that dark hair and that body. Looks like it's our lucky day, hey, lads!"

Eowyn's blood turned to ice. The three of them were younger than she was, barely older than sixteen or seventeen summers. Because of that she had not thought they would pose any real threat to her at first but now she was not so sure.

One thing was certain, she had better get out of here, fast.

"Please, I just—"

"Aye, apparently, it's our lucky day," the smallest one said. "I was told the wench had a particular taste for Norsemen. And isn't that what we are?"

"It certainly is. She can have her fill of us."

Still laughing, the other two started circling her.

Her scream got caught in her throat when they lunged at the same time and grabbed her arms. The third one, the one who had looked her up and down so lecherously earlier walked up to her. For all that he was so young, he was taller than her and already quite muscular. Panic seized her. If he really thought she was not better than a whore, he would not listen to her explanations or protests. He would just tumble her to the ground. He was young, but not so young that he wasn't capable of bedding a woman. She should know. Freodheric had been about his age when he had taken her.

Well, this one would not touch her, she would make sure of it. Before she could think, she lifted her leg and placed a well-aimed kick in his groin.

He let out a howl and wrapped a hand around her neck, forcing her face upward. "Don't think you will get away with that," he spat. "I will make you wish you had—"

"If I hear one more word out of you I will make sure *you* wish you had stayed in bed this morning."

The icy voice, colder than the early morning air, made Eowyn gasp in relief. Only one man she knew could infuse such lethal menace in softly spoken words. She let out a whimper as her legs sagged from under her. It was over. Whatever Rune thought of her, he wouldn't let anyone hurt her.

"I only wanted—"

"I know what you wanted to do, pup, I'm not an idiot. Stop talking now," Rune ordered, blood rushing through his veins. His fingers itched to seize the scoundrel by the throat and see how he liked it. "The fact that the hairs on your chin have not yet started sprouting is the only thing preventing me from giving you the ass-kicking you deserve but you might yet convince me that I am being too generous."

There was no need to say anything else. The thug let go of Eowyn's neck and his two friends released her at the same time. She stumbled backward. Immediately his hand was at her elbow, steadying her. Rune told himself he would have acted thus with anyone but he knew that it was not quite true.

He might have helped another woman, but he would not have been almost blinded by rage at the idea of her being manhandled.

Because this was Eowyn, he had almost throttled the three boys on the spot. He had to get out of there before he surrendered to the urge to do so.

Before anyone could say anything, he marched her back to the hut he occupied, bristling with ill-contained fury. That she had the nerve to come to him after what had transpired between them the day before both incensed and impressed him, and admiration was the last thing he wanted to feel toward her. It was bad enough he had been overwhelmed by rage when he'd seen her attackers circling her. Thank the gods he had not fled to the forest when he had heard her voice, as he'd first intended.

He would have to have a word with Sigurd later on and tell him about the assault. This was not the way to treat a lonely woman coming to their village. The three fools were old enough to start acting like men and men worthy of the name did not prey on defenceless women.

"What are you doing here?" he asked, closing the door behind him. He turned around and instantly regretted it when the sight of Eowyn made his pulse quicken.

No wonder the young pups had lost their minds. They would not have seen the likes of her often. Though she appeared pale and nervous, she was still the most beautiful woman he had ever seen. He gave an inward curse. Why did he think such things? The revelation of her treachery should have dampened whatever desire he felt for her but, infuriatingly, it hadn't. Worse, he knew it was not desire gnawing at his insides, it was something much more worrying.

It was recognition, longing.

"You have my doll," Eowyn said in a whisper.

Her *doll*? He blinked in disbelief. This was the last thing he had expected her to say to explain her presence in the village. She had walked all night, steeled herself to withstand his ire, placed herself in danger, been almost attacked by the three youths, and all this to get a toy back?

"You dared to come and confront me for a mere trinket?"

He saw her swallow the stinging retort already on her lips. Evidently she thought she had better not antagonize him while he had something she wanted in his possession in case he threw it in the fire out of spite. Did she really think he would do something like that? What sort of a monster did she take him for?

"It's not a mere trinket." He could tell from her flat voice that she was forcing herself to calm. "It is all I have from my grandmother and very precious to me. Please, can I have it back?"

"Of course, you can have it back. It is of no use to me." He put his hand in his purse to retrieve the little figurine he had completely forgotten about and handed it to her.

Once she had taken it she got hold of his hand, twisting it this way and that to examine his damaged knuckles. Rune knew he should ask her to stop but he could not. Her small, dainty fingers were soft as petals against his skin. When she looked at him, for the first time he caught a glimpse of emotion on her face.

"What happened to your hand?"

I punched a tree, that's what.

He shook his head irritably. "Nothing. Why should you care anyway?"

Eowyn swallowed. Although it had barely been a day since she had last seen Rune, she felt as if they had been apart for weeks. He stood taller, broader than in her memory, and a hundred times more intimidating. The blue in his eyes was not warm with mirth or hot with lust but cold with disdain. He had never looked at her in this way before.

And all this because of what Albert had said.

No, she amended ruthlessly. It was not Albert's fault, but Rune's. Albert was a fool, a delusional liar and he should never have claimed to be betrothed to her and the father of her child but he had not forced anyone to believe him. If Rune had not already been predisposed to doubt her, if he had not come to her only because he was forced to by a man he was not even friends with, none of this would have happened. Albert would have made his outlandish claim, Rune would have asked her about it, she would have explained what the situation was in a civilised conversation, he would have understood and that would have been the end of it.

Instead he had accused her of lying to him. He had chosen to believe a stranger over her.

It was his fault he was unhappy, no one else's, and she didn't see why she should make things easier for him.

"Why did you stop the boys at the well from taking their pleasure with me?" she asked, raising her chin. Say what he might, he could not be completely indifferent to her, for he had come to her rescue unprompted, and with surprising ferocity... If he was so angry with her, if he thought she deserved everything she got, then surely he would have washed his hands of her? She asked the question because she was desperate to hear she mattered to him in some way.

The blue eyes flashed. "I'm sorry, did I misunderstand? Did you want the fools to touch you?"

"No!" she cried out, unable to believe he'd made it sound as if she regretted his intervention.

"Then you know why I stopped them. I will not have any woman taken against her will, no matter what I think of her."

The last spark of hope died within her. He had not *wanted*

to protect her, she was not special to him in any way, he had only acted as honor dictated. She benefitted from his protection as any other woman would, and he didn't want her to be harmed, but she didn't have his respect, much less his affection.

Her heart broke anew, which was her own fault for asking.

"Anyway you should be glad to have appealed to them. You like Norsemen," Rune said in a sneer. "I know these were only boys but there were three of them. That might be enough to satisfy you if they took turns."

This attack was unwarranted, and it hit its mark, hard. Eowyn wavered on her feet and brought a hand to her chest like a woman mortally wounded.

"I will not bother you further," she said, her voice so low that she wasn't sure he heard the words.

She felt so weary, so dejected, so weak all of a sudden. Now that she'd gotten what she had come for, she had to leave, before she was sick. The pain slicing through her was one she feared she would never recover from. Her chest ached as badly as if it had been crushed with a blunt instrument. Rune was making her feel dirty and worthless, something no one, even the men and women taunting her throughout the years had managed to do.

Clutching the doll tight in her fist for courage, she walked out of the door. She had heard enough insults from him today to last her a lifetime. She had to go before she crumbled. Whatever happened, she would not give him the satisfaction of seeing how deeply he'd wounded her. He didn't deserve it.

As she neared the forest the sound of footsteps reached her ear.

Rune.

Instinct told her it was him, not Sigurd, or one of the three lads come after her. Had he changed his mind? Realized how cruel he'd been? So what if he had? It was too late, far too late.

He didn't deserve another moment of her time. She shook her head and tried to pick up her pace. In vain. Her legs could barely support her.

"Eowyn. Wait," she heard him say, his voice soft and gruff at the same time. No! She would not let him sway her with gentle manners now, not after what he'd had the gall to say to her. She wanted to get back to the only man she would ever allow near her from now on. Her son.

"Why should I wait?" she asked, not turning to face him. "You want to escort me back to my hut in case something happens to me? Don't worry about it. If the three boys stop me again I will be able to indulge my cravings for Norsemen without any guilt, as I will not be given any choice. Surely not even you would have the gall of accusing a violated woman of wantonness."

He cursed in Norse. "That's not what I—"

She never heard the rest of the sentence for at that moment her legs finally gave way from under her and she fell into a black hole.

CHAPTER NINE

"**B**loody hell, Rune, I told you to look after Eowyn and now you're telling me she fainted from exhaustion and misery?" Sigurd looked positively livid with rage.

Rune bristled. Trust the Dane to put the blame on him. But that wasn't what had happened. Or... Was it? Eowyn would have walked all night to reach him at dawn and not eaten a thing to sustain her. Upon arriving in the village she'd had a fright, courtesy of the three youths attacking her, and then he'd been unforgivably harsh with her. What if Sigurd was right? What if exhaustion and misery—misery *he* had caused— were the reasons behind her fainting fit? He could see no other explanation.

"I didn't say that," he answered less forcefully than he would have liked. He was not going to admit he had all but called her a whore, as he wasn't sure he would get out of the conversation unscathed if he did.

"Well, *I'm* saying it!" Sigurd roared. "What else could it be? Helga said there was nothing wrong when she examined her. You are going to make it up to her, do you hear?"

Rune's patience snapped. He might have been able to

handle the scolding if he had not felt in the wrong already. As he was starting to suspect he was, in fact, the cause of Eowyn's wretchedness, he found it hard to bear hearing it out loud. The Dane didn't know what he was talking about, had no right to judge him when he didn't know what had transpired between the two of them. He had no idea that Little Rune was not his, nor did he know that Eowyn was not his to protect, had never been his.

She belonged to that bastard Albert, the 'handsome' Saxon who was set to marry her. It was the man's responsibility to ensure her well-being, no one else's.

"Who do you think you are, that you can order me about thus? And who is Eowyn to you that you should be so hot to defend her? Does your wife know the interest you're taking in her? Do you think she would be pleased to hear how much you worry about another woman?"

This was a ludicrous accusation but he could not help it. His worry, anger and frustration had to go somewhere and it felt good to talk in Norse, without having to search his words, and be able to say exactly what he thought.

Sigurd came to face him, stopping so close their noses almost touched. "Be very careful what you say. If you insinuate that my interest in Frigyth's friend is anything other than honorable, you might find yourself having to sip your food through broken teeth for the rest of your life. You might as well know I am not renowned for my patience." The voice was calm, and all the more lethal for it.

"You don't say, *Beast*."

"I swear, you are looking for a fight."

"What if I am?" Rune suddenly realized that was exactly what he was looking for, or rather, what he needed. Just like the other day, after he'd found out about the babe, he wanted to use the Dane to free himself from all the pain and shock he had endured. The two of them would fight, he would exhaust himself, and then, with any luck, Sigurd would knock him unconscious. For a few precious moments, he would not think, he would not ache.

"Well, sorry, my friend, I'm not going to indulge you today, anymore than I did the other day," Sigurd grunted. "I could flatten you with one hand tied behind my back, of course, but you are not in that gang of boys anymore. You are going to face your responsibilities like a man this time."

Rune glanced toward the hut where he had left Eowyn. Had she woken up? Was she even still here? He wouldn't be surprised if she had slipped away unnoticed while he spoke to Sigurd.

The Dane shook his head. "Go to her instead of throwing pathetic glances her way. She needs you. I will tell Frigyth to join you at the hut in a moment. It's clear you have no idea what to do."

Rune didn't even think of answering and set off toward the hut. He had the sudden urge to see Eowyn, to assure himself she was well. How could he feel that way about someone who had hurt him so? It made no sense. He should be furious with her. He *had* been furious. And so he had accused her of being little more than a whore. He had used her honest confession about her life against her. And then he had distressed her so much he had made her faint. Whatever she had done she didn't deserve this, not when she was already exhausted from looking after a newborn child.

Yes... A child that wasn't his.

That was the whole problem.

Steeling himself, he pushed the door open. As soon as he entered, he heard Eowyn mumble. "Where is my son?"

He fell to his knees next to her. She still had her eyes closed and was writhing on the pallet, like someone in prey to a fever, repeating the question over and over. She didn't seem to know who was in the hut—or care. Had the healer given her a potion to help her sleep? It was more than possible. Long, sooty lashes were throwing shadows over her velvety cheeks. She was so beautiful! He sighed of despair. Was that all he could think, that she was beautiful? Yes. It seemed every time he looked at her, her beauty floored him, no matter what had happened.

"Where is your son?" he asked. She hadn't brought him with her but he knew she would not have left him on his own in the hut, but with someone she trusted.

She mumbled a name that sounded Saxon, and female. Canhild? He wasn't sure. "The hut next... the well... I need..."

Intent on reassuring her, he brushed her cheek with a light finger, but she swatted it away with a weak hand as if she didn't care to be comforted—or didn't want him of all people to touch her. He stood back up. It was clear she would not rest until she had her baby next to her. He would have to ask Sigurd and Frigyth, see if they knew about this mysterious woman who lived by the well.

"I will go and get your son. You stay here and try to sleep."

"Do you have a horse I could borrow?"

Rune burst into the hut and almost walked over little Eirik, who stumbled and fell on his bottom with a shriek.

"Can't you be careful, you devil?" Sigurd growled while Frigyth picked her son off the floor and kissed his cheek. "If you hurt any of my sons I'll make sure it is the last thing you do."

"Apologies. Do you have a horse?" he repeated. Why were they wasting precious time talking about children who were perfectly fine while Little Rune was away from his fretting mother? "Eowyn is asking after her son. She won't settle until she is with him. I will go back to the village to get him."

Sigurd nodded, finally catching on with the urgency of the situation. "Where did she leave the babe?"

"With someone called Carild? Cremhilde?"

"Cwenhild, her friend. I should have guessed. She just had a baby herself so will be able to feed him." Sigurd gestured toward the door. "I don't have a horse, no, but I'm sure Wolf will lend you Demon. Let's go ask—"

"Wait," Frigyth cut in. Rune barely repressed a groan. It seemed the woman was unable to keep his comments to herself, even when time was of the essence. How anyone could bear being married to someone like this was a mystery. She would drive him mad within a week. "Sigurd needs to go with you. Cwenhild has never met you. If you arrive with a face like thunder demanding to be given the child, she won't have any reason to comply and her husband Wulfric will throw you out. He's strong enough to do it."

"Of course," Rune mumbled. Perhaps he didn't mind her intervention after all. How had he not thought of that? Without her, he would have gone to the village only to come back empty handed.

Sigurd nodded and placed a kiss on the top of his wife's head. "You're right. What would we do without you, Birdie?" Then he turned back to him. "Let's go to Magnus. If we borrow his cart we can bring the babe back safely and quickly."

Luck was on their side. The blacksmith had just come back from a visit to the next village so his horse was already hitched to the cart. The two men jumped on it with a brief thanks. Urging the horse into a canter whenever possible, they made good time. At the village, Rune let Sigurd talk to Cwenhild, knowing he would only frighten her if he spoke to her. The woman was throwing nervous glances his way. Either she thought him the Devil, like her countrymen, or she was worried he would hurt her friend. He forced himself not to betray his mounting impatience, knowing they could not afford any delays. He wouldn't put it past Eowyn to have disappeared by the time he reached the hut.

A moment later, the baby in his arms, Sigurd climbed onto the cart. "I have him. Ride on."

They reached the Norsemen village just as the sun was throwing his last rays over the thatched huts. Rune hesitated when Sigurd handed him the little boy.

"What do I do with him?" he whispered to himself. The babe seemed smaller than before in his hands and he felt as if he had no right to hold another man's son.

Sigurd, damn his heart, mistook his reaction for fear of breaking the fragile babe. "Don't worry, you won't hurt him. I haven't broken any of my sons yet and you're not half as strong as me. The babe has nothing to fear with someone like you."

Frigyth, who, inevitably, had drawn up close, swatted her husband on the arm. "Stop being such a fool, Sigurd." Then she turned to him with a reassuring smile. Rune regretted his earlier condemnation of the little Saxon. Truly, he was warming to her and he could see why Sigurd might have fallen for her. She was both kind and sensible. "You'll be fine. Just take him to Eowyn. She will feed him. Even if she's sleeping, she has the milk. She will feel better for it, you'll see, mentally and physically."

Not quite sure what she meant by 'physically', Rune walked back to the hut, holding the child tight against his chest so as not to jolt him too much.

As soon as the door opened, Eowyn sat up. This time she was awake and alert. "Rune?"

He knew she meant the child, not him. In that moment, she probably didn't care about him and he couldn't blame her.

"He's here. But he needs to feed." The baby had started to

fuss and this was the most likely reason for it. He brought him to her.

Without a word Eowyn lay back down on the furs and bared her breast, preparing herself. Rune deposited the child next to her and averted his gaze. Though he had seen that same scene a dozen times over the last few days, today he felt like an intruder on this most intimate moment between mother and son. A heartbeat later the unmistakable sound of someone gulping greedily filled the room.

"Oh, yes, that's better," Eowyn whimpered.

Never had anyone sounded more relieved. Rune felt his own body relax, as if order had been restored. He positioned himself at the window, bracing his arms against the wall, waiting for the babe to be finished. Then he heard a voice, weak and tentative, behind him.

"Please, could you help me? I need to put him on the other breast."

"Hasn't he had enough?" Rune was dubious. By the sound of things, the babe had drunk three times his weight already.

"It's for me. I need him to suckle on the other side as well. I'm in pain."

"In pain?"

Only then did he see the stain blooming on her other breast, the one still covered by her dress. By the gods, the milk was coming out of its own accord. Not a man easily daunted, Rune shivered. That did look uncomfortable.

Appalled at the extent of her discomfort, he helped Eowyn turn to the side and placed the babe on her straining breast. This time he did not think of averting his eye or letting his unease stand in the way of doing what was right by her. She was in pain. He had to bring her relief. The rest didn't matter. He and his male sensibilities didn't matter.

"Come, little one. Do what you must to help your mother,"

he breathed in Norse, bringing the boy's mouth closer to his mother's nipple.

The babe complied only too readily. Rune could not help a smile. What a task that was... Suckling a beautiful woman to bring her relief. Would Eowyn push him away if he offered to help her next time she needed someone to suck the milk out of her?

Probably, and with good reason. He should not even entertain such outlandish ideas, especially when he should be furious with her.

"Why are you laughing?"

Was he laughing? He hadn't noticed. He cleared his throat. "It's nothing. How do you feel now?"

"Better. Thank you." She opened her eyes. "Thank you for going to get Rune."

And then, to his utter dismay, she started crying. His chest caved in because he knew she was crying because of him, because of what he'd told her, because of the way he'd treated her.

"I'm sorry," he murmured, kneeling by her side, resisting the urge to draw her into his arms. The last thing he wanted was to interrupt the baby's feed when he and Eowyn were suffering from having been kept apart for so long. "What I said this morning about the three boys... It was unforgivable."

"Yes. Unforgivable," she agreed, closing her eyes once more. A tear was glistening on her long eyelashes. He almost reached out to wipe it off. He never wanted to see her cry again, least of all because of him. "And yet here you are, hoping to be forgiven just because you acknowledged you made a mistake."

He frowned. "Am I?"

"Of course. Why else would you mention it?" Eowyn spoke in a flat tone that pierced his gut. This woman had the loveliest voice but right now there was nothing left of the tinkling joy in it. "In your arrogance, you are hoping I will say it doesn't matter, and I understand why you said it. Well I don't and I'm not going to pretend I was not hurt."

"I'm so—"

"The least you can do if you really are sorry, is let me finish what I'm saying!" she cut in ruthlessly. "First, I find out you never wanted to give me or our baby a chance, that you only came to live with me because a man who is not even your friend threatened you with retaliation if you didn't. Then when Albert showed up you chose to believe his mad ranting over my assurances. You do not know the man, yet you were ready to cast me and your son out from your life because of his foul lies. As if that was not enough, you refused to listen to me when I traveled all night to come to you. Instead of telling me *then* that you were sorry, you accused me of wanting nothing less than to get three boys between my legs to satisfy my rampant lust."

She bit her bottom lip to stop herself from crying but despite her efforts, another tear slid along her cheek. By the gods, he'd thought only moments ago he didn't want to see her cry again, and here she was, weeping with silent dignity because of his accusations. He should never have been so vile as to accuse her of wantonness.

In reality, his complaint was not with the way she chose to live her personal life, but with the fact that she had failed to tell him about Albert. He should only have expressed his bitterness on that topic, as it was fair he should take exception to finding out she had been betrothed all along and lied about the paternity of her son. But the rest had been unworthy of him.

"I think I need not say more," Eowyn finally said. "If you haven't understood by yourself by now that you acted like a monster, then you are past reasoning. And now you can leave. I would like to sleep."

Rune was stunned. Never had he been so thoroughly

dismissed or felt more sheepish. In truth, he'd had no idea he *could* be made to feel sheepish, or allow anyone to get to him thus. It was an unpleasant novelty.

"How can I show you I am sorry?" If she wasn't going to believe him when he said it or even allow him to express his regret, how was he going to manage to get the message through?

She shook her head. "I know not. You'll just have to figure it out yourself."

"Let me take the child at least. You need to rest."

"I do. But I will rest better with him by my side." Eowyn's hand landed on the small body snuggled up against her, the gesture so protective, so full of love that his chest constricted. The two of them were so beautiful together. "You don't want him. I do. You don't believe he's your son, but I know he's mine, I wrenched him out of my bleeding body by myself. He's staying with me."

A moment later Rune found himself outside the hut, staring at the mauve sky overhead. The sun had just disappeared below the horizon. Of the fiery globe that had illuminated the land mere moments ago, only a reddish glow remained, a pale vestige of what the glorious orb could do. Oddly, it put him in mind of Eowyn. The weepy, defeated woman lying in the hut right now was all that was left of the strong, vibrant vixen she had been only the day before. What sort of a monster was he to have had reduced her to this?

A Devil, that was what.

He had been called Devil time and time again and it had never affected him because he didn't understand Saxons' beliefs. Now for the first time he had an inkling of what their 'Hell' was like, and what sort of creatures inhabited it.

Men like him.

CHAPTER TEN

As soon as Eowyn woke up, she knew instinctively that Rune—Little Rune—was not by her side. Panic flared within her. Where was he?

She made to stand up but a growl stopped her in her tracks. "Stay where you are. He's fine."

She swiveled around to look at Rune—Big Rune she should say. Heavens, she really ought to think up nicknames for the two men. Them sharing a name was quickly becoming problematic.

Or... Perhaps it didn't matter, because if Rune didn't think the child was his then he had no reason to stay. In a few days he would go back to Denmark. As a matter of fact, she wasn't sure why he was still here.

Pushing these considerations aside, she looked at the two Runes. The baby was naked, gurgling and kicking his legs on a piece of fur spread on the floor. The man was squatting by his side, observing him with a frown on his face, like someone trying to puzzle out a problem. What on earth did he see in the delightful little boy that caused him such dismay? She saw nothing but loveliness.

But, of course, if he was seeing Albert's child, then he would have every reason to scowl.

"I told you I wanted to keep him with me," she accused, to try and hide the effect the sight of the two of them together had on her. For a moment they looked like any father and son sharing an intimate moment. How could the stubborn man not see what was staring at him in the face? The two of them belonged together. "You had no right taking him from me."

"Yes, well, I woke up to an awful smell if you must know, one coming from the boy squirming by your side. He was not ashamed in the least and smiled at me when I picked him up." Rune looked both impressed at the babe's courage and outraged at what he'd found in his clout. "Seeing as you were sleeping, I thought you wouldn't mind me wiping his rump."

"Not his rump!" she cried out. "I don't like that word, you make him sound like an animal."

"He didn't seem to object. Besides, I don't know why I'm telling you I wiped his rump when in reality I wiped all of him. You wouldn't believe the amount of shit that came out. I'm surprised there is anything left inside him."

He sounded so shocked that Eowyn couldn't help it. She burst out laughing. "Well, yes, it happens like that sometimes." This was just the sort of thing a new father would say as he learned to take care of his son. Then she remembered that Rune didn't intend to raise this baby he had fathered. He didn't even think Little Rune was his.

The thought sobered her and silenced the jest already on her lips. She could not behave as if they were a happy family when they were anything but.

After a moment, Rune turned to her and asked. "Now. Do you need to be sucked?"

There was such an expression on his face and he had worded his question in such a way that she swallowed hard. She bit her lip, certain that if she asked, he would do it himself. Could she... No. Of course not! This was not some of his wicked talk intended to make her melt. He was simply trying to win back her good graces anyway he could.

Good. Let him try. She would not tell him that his efficiency in dealing with Little Rune's dirty clout while she slept had impressed her.

"You mean 'suckled'. And yes, I do, so please bring the babe to me," she said briskly.

"Is it as painful as it was last night?"

"No. It's not as bad."

He grunted as if dissatisfied and turned to lift the little boy into his arms. Eowyn frowned. Was he... *concerned* for her? Surely not? He thought her a wanton liar, a despicable schemer. He did not care for her or her comfort, he was only trying to give himself good conscience.

While the baby fed, she mused on all that had happened in the last few days.

Where could she and Rune go from here? She wasn't sure. Was there even anywhere they *could* go? Could they recover from such a blow? He was convinced he'd been lied to and made a fool of, while she had been hurt and taken for what she was not.

How did people behave with each other after something like that? She had no idea.

Frigyth visited the hut later that morning, bringing a pot of stew and a loaf of bread.

"Here, you need to build up your strength," she instructed, ladling a generous portion of meat into a bowl.

"Thank you."

Rune's mouth started to water. The smell filling the hut was wonderful, rich with herbs and spice. The little Saxon clearly knew how to cook. His stomach rumbled so loud the two women turned to him at the same time. Frigyth laughed.

"Are you hungry perchance, Rune?"

"Starving," he admitted, accepting the bowl she was handing him with a nod. He still had not eaten anything that morning and there had been barely time to find a scrap of bread last night.

"I thought as much. Why do you think I brought the big pot?" She twisted her lip. "You Norsemen certainly need sustenance. Sigurd eats enough for two."

"I bet he does," Rune said, chewing on a piece of meat. It was as delicious as he had hoped, and the rabbit was succulent and tender. "Soon even your big pot won't be enough, with three sons following his lead. Eirik looks so much like him already."

"Mm." An odd expression crossed Frigyth's face. Before he could wonder if he had not unearthed a secret, she carried on. "Of course, Sigurd didn't father Eirik, you know."

He arched a brow. "He didn't? But... he..."

"He what? Loves him? Yes, he does." She swallowed, and for a moment looked about to cry. By the gods, what had he said? Eowyn last night, now her... Did he have a special talent for making Saxon women cry? "He does love Eirik. But he is not his son, not by blood anyway. When he married me I was carrying another man's child."

Rune stilled. "And Sigurd knew it?"

The tears were instantly wiped from Frigyth's eyes, replaced by blazing anger. "Of course, he did! Women are not vile creatures out to trick innocent men into accepting children they did not father!"

She narrowed her eyes and glanced toward Eowyn in the corner of the hut, her meaning clear. She'd been told about the encounter with Albert and all that had ensued and she sided unconditionally with her friend. Well, of course she did.

He took another bite of bread to avoid having to comment.

"Sigurd knew, and yet he married me." Her lip trembled again. "He now loves Eirik as his own, as you can tell."

Yes, that much was obvious. The Dane had not raised a hand to him when he had called him Beast or when he'd been spoiling for a fight—twice—but he had almost flattened him for accidentally causing the toddler to fall on his bottom, something that probably happened a dozen times a day anyway. It was clear he did love the boy as his own.

"And Halfdan?" he asked, crossing his arms over his chest. "Is he—"

Frigyth swatted him on the arm much as she did with her husband, causing him to flinch. Damn but she could hit! "Don't you dare suggest I was unfaithful to my husband! I just told you I married Sigurd when I was pregnant with Eirik. Moon is younger. So tell me, who do you think is his father? Think carefully."

He raised both hands in surrender. The diminutive Saxon was truly formidable. But not so formidable he would cower and keep his next question to himself. "And Elwyn?"

The boy was older than Eirik so she could not object to the question. She did not.

"Elwyn is not Sigurd's son by blood either. Or mine. We adopted him when we got married."

He resumed his eating, wondering what to make of her revelations. "Why are you telling me all this?" They barely knew each other and it was very personal information.

"Because I think you needed to hear it."

With those enigmatic words, Frigyth left the hut.

Rune stayed silent a long moment, lost in thought. Eowyn

was silent as well. She had not said a word during the heated exchange.

"Your friend is lovely," he said eventually, helping himself to more stew. "And a wonderful cook."

"She is," Eowyn agreed, dipping a piece of bread into the sauce at the bottom of her bowl. He could tell that seeing Frigyth take her defense had touched her. "I met her a couple of years ago when she came to live in the Norsemen village with Sigurd. Unlike others, she doesn't judge me for the way I live my life."

Others. There was no prize guessing who she was referring to. "You mean me?"

"No," she surprised him by saying. She had reduced the remainder of her piece of bread to crumbs, he noticed. Was she nervous? "When I told you about my lovers, you didn't judge either. At least, not until the other day." Dark eyes skewered him. "I mean other women. Men think they can bed me, but women think they have the higher ground over me, which is hardly better. Frigyth never made me feel dirty and has been a constant support. When I found out I was with child, she was there for me."

Rune swore to himself never to think badly of the little Saxon again. He'd been annoyed by her forceful manners at first, but then he had warmed to her. Hearing she had befriended Eowyn without question and been there for her when she needed it the most put a final seal on his approval.

Sigurd was a lucky man.

"She is like the sister I never had," Eowyn carried on.

"You don't have any sisters? Or brothers?" He realized he didn't know anything about her, other than she had been raised by her grandmother and had almost reduced her doll to wood chips during her childhood.

"No. You?"

Rune hesitated. Then he decided he might as well open up. One way or the other he needed to redeem himself in Eowyn's eyes, make her see he was not the monster she had accused him of being, even if he had been hurt by her deception. It was one thing refusing to be taken in for a fool, quite another unleashing his wrath onto her with no care for her feelings.

He wanted her to know he would not be used and manipulated, but he also wanted to make amends for the terrible insults he had thrown in her face. Talking about his childhood would be a good way to start.

"I am the youngest of a family of five but I grew up on my own. My parents had to watch as one by one their children were taken away from them. Grief nearly killed them. I was too young to remember any of my sisters but my eldest brother died when I was four summers. He went out mushroom hunting one day and he picked a handful of wrong ones along with the edible ones. Every single one of us was ill that night but Björn was particularly fond of mushrooms so he had eaten more than us." He gave a wistful smile. "He was twelve. In all the memories I have of him, he is laughing. I think he would have been a wonderful brother had I had the chance to know him."

Eowyn had stopped eating. Her eyes were unnaturally bright, filled with unshed tears. There he was, making her cry again. He cursed himself for choosing the wrong topic of conversation but there was no helping it now. He carried on.

"I grew up loved by my parents, as you can imagine. Nothing was too good for their only surviving child. As soon as I was old enough to take an interest in women, they let me know none too subtly they wanted me to start a family of my own so they could have grandchildren." He sighed. "I didn't see why I should be expected to replace the children they had lost so I rebelled, I'm afraid, and became rather unmanageable."

He was not proud of it, but he could not pretend otherwise. He had hated being seen as their only ray of hope, hated being introduced to all the girls in the village under some pretext or other with the obvious intent of making him fall in love.

"It was inevitable, I suppose," Eowyn said in a breath. Thankfully, she didn't seem appalled by his reaction to his parents' maneuvers. He took heart. Perhaps telling her about his past had been the right decision.

"Perhaps. Still, it caused them immense pain. They feared my recklessness would end up causing my death, not an unreasonable assumption, given some of the activities I got involved in."

"Was it then that you joined the gang of boys you told me about?"

Rune shook his head. "I had been with them from a young age, eleven or so. I had joined because I wanted to feel like a man, ensure myself some independence away from home. My parents treated me like a child, and a precious one at that. I wanted to free myself from their stifling presence. But as I was the youngest and smallest in the pack, I ended up having to keep my opinions and thoughts quiet on pain of becoming one of their targets. All this only stoked my need for freedom and recognition. Fortunately, as I grew up, it quickly became clear I would one day tower over them all. When I did, their behavior started to change. I finally got the respect I craved. I became their leader, and I went crazy."

Eowyn nodded. It was unfortunate but understandable. No child should live in such sad circumstances, no young man should have to deal with such expectations. His parents, lost to their grief, would not have realized the sort of pressure they put on their only surviving son by asking him to build a family and give them the children they had lost. They would have thought they wanted what was best for him.

Rune sighed. "And then, as if that was not enough, I bedded all the women who wanted me. There were a lot of them."

"I don't doubt it," Eowyn murmured. They would have tripped over themselves to fall into the strong Norseman's arms, just like she had done.

"I'm not proud of it but at least it got me out of trouble. Once I started to take an interest in girls, it allowed me to take my distance from the group of boys." He made a grimace. "About time, too. My head was starting to get too big for my skull, or however you say it. Too much power can do that to a man."

Eowyn could not help a smile. She already knew about his sense of humor and now she was now discovering a new side to Rune. The arrogant braggard was owning up to his past pains and mistakes, revealing a surprising vulnerability. It was a surprise, one that made it hard to hang on to her resentment of him because she was starting to suspect his reaction upon hearing Albert's declaration had deeper roots than wounded male pride. His views of family were skewed and his feelings toward children clearly complicated. Considering what his parents had put him through, his shock upon discovering he had fathered a babe he could never see grow had been more than justified.

Yes… Unfortunately for her, Rune's revelation made it a whole lot harder to resent him than it had been at first.

"So lust saved you from an excess of pride," she commented.

"Mm, so it would seem. Just as it saved you from a dull life."

She nodded. Indeed she had wanted to escape a dull and unfulfilling destiny. It had worked as well. Until it had landed her in more trouble than she could have anticipated.

"And you dare think less of me for taking as many lovers as I could when you did exactly the same?"

It was petty but she couldn't resist the pique. Only a few

days ago Rune had accused her of the worst kind of behavior. That he had opened up about his childhood and shown a side of him she could not have suspected didn't mean she had forgotten —or forgiven—his hurtful words.

He met her gaze unflinchingly. "I was a cruel fool for speaking as I did. I told you so already, and I will repeat it until you believe me. What you do with your body is your own choice. I mean it."

My, he seemed genuinely sorry. And... possibly aroused. The look he threw her seared a path all the way to her core. Though his eyes were blue as ice, they might as well have been made of fire for the effect they produced on her. Her whole body started to heat up.

She cleared her throat. This wouldn't do, it wouldn't do at all. They were discussing his past life, not trying to lure each other into bed. She had to resume the conversation. It seemed a far better idea than dwelling on the desire flaring between them. Infuriatingly, it seemed impossible for them to be in close proximity to each other without wanting to rip each other's clothes off.

"Did your relationship with your parents improve after you left the gang of boys?"

He rubbed a hand over his beard. "Yes. Marginally."

He didn't sound so sure. Either he was lying or there was something he was not telling her. Eowyn hesitated. A question was still burning her lips and there would never be a better time to ask it. With so many conquests, it was only a question of time before he got a woman with child. She knew he was not barren and he hadn't exercised any restraint with her. If he bedded all his lovers with as much ardor, he would have gotten dozens of them pregnant. Was *this* the reason behind his refusal to accept Little Rune as his? Because he already had too many children depending on him back home?

No. He had been shocked to find out about the babe, under-standably, but he had eventually accepted him. It was only when he'd been told Rune was not his son that he had balked.

She hesitated, not daring to ask the question but wanting to know. Rune was still looking at her with burning eyes, as if to will her to voice out loud what was on her mind. She opened her mouth.

Just then there was a knock on the door. She let out a little squeak and closed her mouth. The moment had passed.

Now she might never know what was eating at him.

Rune was grateful to whoever was behind the door for the interruption. He had revealed enough to Eowyn during their conversation, more than he had intended. How could he admit to her he had wilfully stopped himself from spilling inside his lovers just to deny his parents the grandchild they were so desperate for? His unmarried conquests had been grateful for what they thought was consideration on his part, but he knew his motives were actually of the most selfish sort and he didn't want to own up to them. And of course...

Of course there had been the gut-wrenching fear. He'd been afraid to become a father, only to have to watch as his child died of a fever, or in an accident or of anything else equally tragic. He'd been afraid of becoming his parents, a lost soul crushed by grief.

He could not tell Eowyn, or anyone, that. He could barely bear to think about it.

As if all that was not bad enough, he was also ashamed of his behavior the night they had slept together. He could not reveal that he had allowed himself full, glorious releases with her because he'd thought it didn't matter if she got with child. She was a Saxon, she lived so far away that he would never know about the consequences of their tryst, would not have to deal with any of it. He had simply spent the best night of his life with a wild woman, and he'd left without a backward glance, leaving her to cope with the aftermath on her own.

He'd been a selfish bastard, and she would be rightfully offended if she realized what had gone through his mind that night. Sigurd had been right to send him back to face his responsibilities. The Dane should have done more than to rant at him, he should have pummeled him to the ground.

As if he'd sensed his intervention would be welcome, Sigurd entered the hut. He nodded his greetings to Eowyn and came to face him.

"Wolf and I were wondering if you could come with us. The blacksmith's workshop is in sore need of repair. We promised we would help."

"Of course." He was taking the cowardly way out, he knew, but he was glad to have an excuse to put an end to his conversation with Eowyn. They had come too close to painful truths for his liking.

"I might be late getting back," he told her before leaving, glancing over his shoulder.

She didn't answer.

CHAPTER ELEVEN

"Thank you." Magnus raised his cup. "Rune, I'm glad you chose this moment to stay at the village. You were the man of the situation."

Rune nodded. It had not cost him much to help the smithy. Repairing a roof was no different to building a boat, as it turned out. His skill at joinery and carpentry had been put to good use. "You're welcome. You can sleep soundly now. The workshop will still stand the day your first grandson picks up a hammer."

"Grandson..." Magnus laughed. "You know, that might happen faster than you imagine. I asked Edith to marry me again the other day and I think this time she might well say yes."

At the announcement, instead of congratulating their friend, Sigurd and Wolf made a face. Rune arched an eyebrow. They didn't seem to think this union a good idea. When Magnus explained who his intended bride was for his benefit, he understood why.

"The tall, curvy widow living in the hut with the ornate door? Her late husband was a wood carver, that's why the hut is so lavishly decorated." He winked. "You must have seen her in the village. She's hard to miss."

Yes. Hard indeed, considering she made sure to throw herself into his path every time he went about his business. At first Rune had attributed their constant meetings to pure chance. But it had quickly become impossible not to understand she was stalking him.

"Mm," he said, noncommittally. He was not about to admit to the man that his intended wife was lusting after him. Magnus would think him either a vindictive meddler or a deluded lecher.

"She refused my first offer but I have hopes she will finally have gotten over her infatuation with Sigurd and now sees that I can make her happy."

Rune turned to the Dane with a slanted smile. The woman had been after Sigurd? Well, now, this was interesting. Finally a way to niggle the man! He'd been acting high and mighty for days, always telling him what was right and wrong, and making him feel like a child. "Does your little wife know about this—"

"She does, so don't you go about stirring trouble, Devil." The man threw him a furious glare. "You'll end up with a broken limb if you mention Edith to Frigyth."

Wolf, who'd stayed silent throughout the interlude, nodded. "Come. Let's go have a drink in my hut."

After thanking the three men again, Magnus went back to his forge. As soon as they were out of earshot of the blacksmith, the Icelander drew nearer to Rune while Sigurd strode ahead on his own.

"What do you know about Edith?" he asked quietly.

"What do you mean?"

"You looked distinctively uneasy when Magnus asked you if you knew her."

"Did I? All I recall is poking Sigurd, who snarled at me like the beast he is." Ignoring the attempt at distraction, Wolf merely waited. By the gods, the man was uncannily perceptive. He was also patient, the opposite of blustery Sigurd, and all the more efficient for it. It didn't take Rune long to see he would not be able to wiggle his way out of this. "Very well," he sighed. "It seems to me she may have gotten over her infatuation for Sigurd by bedding all the men she can find. Or trying to, at least."

"You mean she has made advances on you?"

"Yes." There was no point in lying. Only the day before she had asked him to lift her bucket out of the well and 'accidentally' brushed her breasts over his back while he pulled on the rope. The day after he had arrived at the village she had tripped and landed on her knees in front of him. The look she had thrown him from her very evocative position might have inflamed his senses if he had not at the time thought only of Eowyn and her cold welcome.

"Are you tempted to accept the offer?" Wolf asked.

"No." He did not even hesitate.

"Why not? She's a comely woman and she wants you. And it's not as if you owed anything to anyone, is it?"

She is comely, I suppose, but she doesn't stir my interest. And, odd as it may be, I do feel as if I owe my fidelity to someone.

Rune cleared his throat. Yes... The Icelander was too perceptive by half. He was going to make him admit to feelings he did not want to admit.

Sigurd called out to them. "Are you two coming, or not?"

Relief washed through Rune. He had been spared an embarrassing revelation.

"Coming, Beast, never fear."

Eowyn was awoken by a horse falling on top of her, stealing all her breath.

Once she had recovered from the shock she understood that

it was no horse, but a big, hulking Norseman. A big, hulking, *drunk* Norseman, judging from the smell hitting her nostrils.

"Rune!" she gasped. Had he forgotten she was in the hut with him, sleeping on the pallet? Thank God the baby was not next to her right now. He would have been flattened. She tried to twist away from under him. In vain, he was as heavy as... well, a horse. "Move, you big oaf! You're crushing me."

He instantly rolled off her and sighed. "Sorry, my love. I guess I'm rather heavy."

My love? The words sent an absurd burst of heat through her chest. "What happened to you?" she asked instead of dwelling on it. He was drunk, so the endearment meant nothing. He could have called her 'Mother' or 'Magnar' for all she knew.

"That beast, Sigurd, and his dog made me drink after the smithy went back home." He chuckled, as if that was the most amusing thing he'd heard in years

"Sigurd doesn't have any dogs. You mean his friend Wolf?"

"Yes, what did I say?" He sounded confused. "Wolf. A little cub, that one, with arms like tree trunks. I wonder if he's as big everywhere. Maybe I'll ask his wife. She will know. Lucky girl."

Eowyn could not help a smile. Apparently Rune was a happy drunk. She hadn't seen that whimsical side of him often. He was usually so forbidding, so intense... "They made you drink, you say?"

"Mm. They thought I would roll on the floor before them just because I'm younger. Well, I think they might be regretting it now."

"I think *you* will regret it in the morning," she mumbled under her breath. She wouldn't be surprised if he woke up with a pounding headache. She could well imagine that the quantity of drink needed to bring a man like him to his knees was enough to floor an ox. Mercifully, he didn't appear to have heard her comment. With a grunt he rolled over to his side, turning his back to her.

Then he started to stroke the log on the floor next to him. "What's that?" he exclaimed in shock. "Why have you gone so hard all of sudden!"

Eowyn pinched her lips together. Had he mistaken the piece of wood for her arm? Silly man. "That's not me, it's a piece of wood waiting to go into the fire," she explained. "I'm on your other side. Right here." With those words she placed his hand on her stomach.

"Ah, yes. Soft. So soft. That's you, my love." In the blink of an eye he had rolled over her again, this time taking care to rest his weight on his arms. Such thoughtfulness surprised her. Even drunk, he was more careful than most sober men, attentive to her comfort. "Come here. Let me feast on you."

Feast on her? This was slipping into something dangerous. Did Rune even know who she was? She doubted it. He would not have called her 'my love' if he did. He must be mistaking her for another of his lovers. Did he know what he was doing? Probably not, but he was definitely doing it. He fell on her like a man who'd been starved of women's company for years, kissing first her mouth then her neck then the swell of her breasts.

Eowyn whimpered, a natural reaction to the pleasure of his touch, then stiffened. She still had not forgiven him for the hurt he had caused her, she remember belatedly, she should be pushing him away, slapping him right now, doing anything she could to bring him back to his senses, not... melting in anticipation.

But she could do nothing but lie still and let him nuzzle her.

Her shift was pushed to the side and Rune started licking at her exposed nipple with a grunt of triumph. She cried out as pleasure exploded inside her then cried out again when he took it into his mouth and sucked on it deep, so deep she felt her milk burst through. She cried out again while Rune recoiled and started coughing.

"What the... I said feast, not *drink*! I've had enough to drink tonight, thank you very much! What even is this? It's foul!"

He shook his head as if he couldn't make sense of what had happened. Eowyn couldn't help it. She burst out laughing. This had to be the oddest moment of her life. And then... Then the laughter got stuck in her throat because Rune nudged her legs apart with his knee and positioned himself between her legs. He was as hard as the log he'd stroked earlier, ready for her. Everything within her leapt. Before she knew what she was doing she was moaning and rubbing against the length that promised her so much delight. This was wrong, forbidden, mad.

Delicious.

And she wanted more of it.

"Rune," she begged. "Please."

"I know," Rune rasped, nuzzling at her neck. "Need to come... badly... bursting..."

By now Eowyn's heartbeat had reached an alarming rate. The heat pulsing between her legs had spread to all parts of her body. She needed to come badly as well. She was bursting, just like he'd said, and already so close.

"Yes," she moaned, unable to resist the temptation of an orgasm that was just within reach. She had never been a woman to deny her sensual urges and it didn't get more sensual than this man. He would make her see stars if she let him. The temptation was impossible to resist. After all, if he didn't know who she was, it mattered not.

In the morning there would be no need to explain herself.

She spread her legs wider. "Rune, please, take me."

"Can't... not my seed... can't lose another child... here... you come for me."

He lifted the hem of her shift and plunged two fingers

inside her. Eowyn almost wept with relief. Yes! This was what she needed, to be filled. She was so wet the fingers slid right in, bringing her indescribable pleasure. Panting, she bucked her hips to meet his thrusts while he rubbed himself against her thigh with increasing urgency.

Everything happened at once. Her body disappeared in a burst of light, the place between her legs started to spasm uncontrollably, Rune shouted in Norse, a series of words that were evidently curses, and his shaft erupted, jerking between their two bodies, inundating her with the heat of his release.

Then everything went quiet. Her sensations reappeared one by one. The warmth in her body, Rune's weight pressing against her chest, the softness of the furs caressing her naked legs.

Rune slid to the side with a long exhale and was asleep within moments.

For a while, Eowyn didn't dare move in case she woke him up. She felt slightly disorientated, like someone waking up from a vivid dream, and unable to decide if all the colorful events had happened to her in truth or not. Then she looked at the man sprawled by her side, one arm flung in abandon above his head. A shaft of moonlight allowed her to see his face, so perfectly carved, his braided hair, tonight a muted bluish color so different to the usual fire. After the whirlwind they had just experienced, his immobility was all the more disquieting.

It was only once her own breathing had gone back to normal that she remembered what Rune had said in the heat of the moment.

...not my seed... can't lose another child...

What did he mean, 'another'? One of them might well be Little Rune, who had been exposed as Albert's child, or so he thought.

But who was the other?

CHAPTER TWELVE

His head was pounding hard but that was not the first thing Rune thought about when he woke up. It was the dream. It had been the most disturbing dream he'd had in his life, obviously brought on by an excess of drink.

He winced and rubbed the back of his aching skull.

He'd made love to the strangest creature he had ever held in his arms, nothing like his usual lovers, nothing like a human even. Its body had been soft and hard at the same time, its mouth had tasted of ale, its breasts—yes, breasts... so the creature had been female at least—had spouted liquid into his mouth when he'd tried to suckle them and it had had no sheath for him to plunge inside. As a result, he'd had to rub himself against its softness to reach his release.

Or... Perhaps it had been no dream at all.

Perhaps he had simply collapsed on top of the table where a blanket had been laid, which would explain the contrast between harness and softness. The liquid he remembered on his tongue might simply have been the drink he'd partaken of all evening. As to the creature under him having no sheath to plunder... Well, perhaps there had been no creature. Perhaps he had simply rubbed himself to orgasm against the table instead of using his hand to bring himself relief like a normal human being. This had to be a new low. He knew that when he overindulged in drink he became someone different, but he didn't usually dream of making love to a creature he could not even identify or come in his braies like an untried youth while he rutted against a piece of wood.

Yes. All in all, it had been a disturbing night. Rune didn't know quite what to make of it.

One thing was certain, his body had not let the strange nature of his imaginary partner deter it. He was covered with the proof that he had reached a powerful release. It was fortunate the table had not collapsed under his vigorous assault.

Feeling absurdly like a boy unable to control himself, he groaned. The humiliation! Now he would have to wash his clothes, seeing as he didn't have any spare ones, wash himself and, worst of all, explain to Eowyn what had happened. He sat bolt upright.

By the gods, *Eowyn*! He knew she was awake half the night with the baby. Had she seen him come in after his drinking session with the two Norsemen? Had she heard his drunken ramblings while she fed the baby? Had she seen him crawl over the table to make himself come?

It didn't bear thinking about.

Well, at the moment he was alone at least. Ignoring the pounding in his head, he stood up and decided to go to the river before Eowyn came back. That way he would not have to justify his decision. After all, it was a warm day, and people did wash. Perhaps she would not think twice about it.

Yes. Perhaps he would get away with it, Rune decided. With luck, Eowyn would not be any the wiser about his mad romp.

"How DOES it feel to be the only two Saxons in the village?"

Frigyth and Wolf's wife, Merewen, looked at each other and shrugged.

"It's not something we ever think about, you know. We've been made to feel at home here, no one sees us as different." Frigyth answered. "Besides, marriages such as ours will soon become the norm, I expect. After all, King Harold himself is the son of a Dane and a Saxon woman."

"Why are you asking?" Merewen's eyes twinkled. "Do you wish to settle here with a Norseman, perchance?"

Eowyn blushed furiously. She hadn't meant anything by the question. Or... Perhaps that was not quite the truth. After the events of the night before she had started to hope there might be hope of a reconciliation between her and Rune.

She shook her head. Why was she being so foolish? Even if she had entertained such thoughts, any sort of future between them wouldn't have been possible. Rune did not intend to stay here with a woman he didn't trust and a child he didn't believe was his, he would return home at the end of the summer, as he had told Sigurd, or earlier if he decided there was nothing for him here. The most she could hope from him was a visit every few years.

Lost to her musings, it took her a while to realize the conversation had moved on.

Merewen was laughing. "To think I was daunted when I found out my captor was called Wolf... What would it have been if he'd been called Beast or, heaven forbid, Devil!"

Frigyth giggled. "I can't imagine. You might have died of fright."

Eowyn stayed silent. She had never been daunted by Rune exactly. Even when she'd only known him as Devil, she'd been aroused. How could she have not? He was the most striking man she had ever seen, Norse or Saxon. Then he'd taken her to bed and she'd been fascinated by the combination of strength, gentleness and masculine confidence. How could it have been otherwise? He was an indefatigable, skilled and selfless lover. Then he had reappeared into her life and she'd been worried about what it would mean for her and Little Rune but still she'd been undaunted. When he'd chosen not to trust her word that he, not Albert, was the baby's father, she'd been angry, then crushed.

And now...

After what he had told her about his childhood and what had happened during the night she wasn't sure what she felt, or how to face him when she went back to the hut. They had made mad, passionate love last spring. Only a few days ago, fired by lust and need, they had done very wicked things together but nothing could compare to what they had done yesterday under the cover of darkness. The last two times they had both been fully aware of what they were doing, both willing. Last night, Rune had not known what was happening and with whom. This morning he would most likely not remember having done anything. He would be unaware he had pleasured her and revealed a part of himself she suspected he would have kept hidden had he been in full control of his capacities.

...not my seed... can't lose another child...

How would he react if he knew he had let slip such a secret? Not well, she imagined. What would he say if she told him he had made her come with fierce determination and come himself just from holding her? He would be mortified.

Perhaps it was better they never talked about what had happened.

"I feel rather tired. I will go back to the hut if I may," she told the two women. Suddenly an immense weariness invaded her. Between Rune and her son, she hadn't had much sleep the night before.

"Of course. Do you want us to look after Rune this afternoon? I could feed him when Moon has finished," Frigyth said, glancing at her son, who was settled at her breast.

"Yes. Thank you."

Merewen accompanied her to the hut and took the baby, assuring they would bring him back before nightfall. "He'll be fine. You just take time for yourself."

"I will, thanks. I might sit in the sunshine for a moment before I go lie down."

When she went to the side of the hut she came to a skidding halt. Rune was placing wet clothes over a rope he'd hung between two trees. But that was not what knocked all the air from her lungs

It was the fact that he was bare-chested.

This was a sight she had dreamed about for more than a year and thought never to see again. Not only were his back and chest exposed but he was also wearing wet braies, as if he'd just washed them and put them back on before they could dry. Wasn't the man aware that the way the fabric clung to his long, muscular thighs and perfect rump was thoroughly indecent?

She screwed her eyes shut. Not *rump*! She hated that word!

Then, unable to resist the temptation, she opened her eyes again. He really was magnificent. For the first time she had a glimpse of how her son might look as a grown man, all fiery hair and bulging muscles. It was impossible to imagine the sweet little boy as anything other than a baby, but considering who his father was, chances were he would one day be a stunning man.

The women in the county had better beware.

She cleared her throat, causing him to turn around. "Eowyn. I didn't see you."

Oh, but she had most definitely seen him! All six foot and

the rest of him, complete with muscles and sinews. His gorgeous hair was wet, falling in heavy coils over his shoulders. All this beauty was enough to make a woman's mouth water.

"Have you been to the river for a wash?" she asked, her voice more hoarse than she would have liked. But how was she supposed to think with a half naked man in front of her? One who looked like this?

He stared at her as if she'd asked what color his hair was. It was, admittedly, a stupid question. Why else would he be wet and in such a state of disarray? "Yes. I don't see what's so extraordinary in that."

"Nothing," she replied hurriedly. Why did he sound so defensive? Did he think she took him for a savage who didn't know the meaning of the word 'clean'? She didn't, even if she had once lied about him stinking like a goat. She knew full well he smelled delicious and tasted even better when she took him in her mouth.

Oh, what was she doing? Thinking of such lewd things would not help her hold on to her composure! She lowered her gaze and regretted the impulse when she saw the muscles of his stomach convulse

Rune stared at Eowyn, who was refusing to meet his eye.

Was she blushing? Yes, yes she was... A delicious color had crept up her cheeks. Please let it be because he was bare-chested and not because she knew the reason why he had needed to wash his clothes as well as himself... He would not bear the humiliation. But she had not given any indication she had witnessed his shocking display of drunken lust last night, so perhaps she was unaware of it?

One could only hope.

Whatever the reason for her shyness, he could not allow her gaze to wander too low on his body for fear she noticed how her scrutiny was affecting him. He had already started to lengthen.

"Where is Little Rune?" he asked to distract her from her contemplation. If anything was guaranteed to make all other thoughts vanish from her mind, it was talking about her son. As he'd predicted, her expression softened and she finally looked at him.

"Frigyth and Merewen offered to look after him this afternoon so I could get some rest."

It was only then that he noticed the dark circles under her eyes. She did look tired. He guessed the baby had kept her up most of the night, as per usual. "I can do that. You could have asked me." Apparently she still didn't trust him to look after the babe. It stung, even if he probably deserved it.

Her mouth quivered. "Well, you could ensure he came to no harm, I suppose. But you can't very well feed him, can you?"

"No." His heart sank. She had meant to tease him but she had only succeeded in making him see how inadequate he was. He rubbed the back of his neck wearily. "You're right. I'm utterly useless."

"Oh, I don't think we need to go that far. You have your uses."

He stilled, arm still up. Was she trying to seduce him? Had he imagined the glint in her eye or the suggestiveness of the comment because he wanted her to try and seduce him? It was all too possible. But then...

Then she looked at him and he knew he had not imagined anything.

She didn't move but he saw her gaze caress his naked chest slowly, taking in every inch of him, before landing on the place between his legs. His shaft instantly went hard as nails. His angel was one bold, irresistible woman. She licked her lips and he was reminded of all the things they had done together, of all the things he wanted to do with her.

The last of his doubts vanished. She *was* seducing him!

Why? Only days before she had told him in no uncertain terms that she didn't want anything to happen between them.

Because he wasn't sure how to deal with this new Eowyn, he decided to be honest. "Angel, if you're going to look at me like that, I can't be responsible for my actions. I want you too much. I might not be able to control myself for long." For good measure he glanced at the bulge barely contained by the tight, wet braies. He'd thought the warning would be enough to scare her away.

It wasn't.

She let out a low purr. "Perhaps... perhaps I don't want you to control yourself."

A growl, deep and possessive, started to build in his throat. He took a step forward, his body tensing to the point of pain, his mind scattering. Forget caution, forget everything; if she wanted him, then he would make sure she got him. And this time he *would* take her, slowly and thoroughly. Then, because once would not be enough, he would take her a second time, deep and fast. He would simply make sure to withdraw before he reached his pleasure. It would not be easy but he was no longer an excitable youth, surely he could—

"Rune!"

The man's voice burst though his thoughts, as jarring as a spear through the skull and just as welcome.

"What?" he barked at Magnus, who was standing by the fence, looking at him and Eowyn quizzically. By the gods, couldn't the man tell he was interrupting something of vital importance?

"What do you mean, what? We're waiting for you! Or have you forgotten you promised to help with the moving of the anvil?"

Well yes, he *had* forgotten all about it. And no wonder. After what Sigurd and Wolf had made him drink, he would not remember if he'd promised to sell his mother to pay for a new set of chains.

"I'm coming! Just give me a moment," he snarled, looking at his groin. He would *not* go meet the men with the proof that he had been on the verge of ravishing Eowyn tenting his braies.

He looked at her again and saw her bite her bottom lip. She had just realized how close they had come to tearing at each other's clothes. He could tell she was grateful to Magnus for having prevented it. His heart sank. She had been overcome by lust for a moment because she was a sensual woman, he was half-naked and she had gone without pleasure for months, but as she had not forgiven him for the hurt he had caused her, she would have regretted giving in to her urges if she had allowed him to take her.

"I should go..." she started.

"Yes. Go have a rest. You look about to drop from exhaustion," he rasped, willing his blood to stop drumming in his shaft. "I will go to the forge. Don't wait up. I'll sleep there tonight, so as not to disturb you when I get back."

It would not be comfortable, but still preferable to making a fool of himself again.

CHAPTER THIRTEEN

When he left the smithy's workshop the next morning after a night spent on the hard, dusty floor, Rune's mind was made up. Magnus was a good man, who did not deserve to be hurt and Edith was only going to make him the laughing stock of the village.

On the way to the forge the day before she had once again placed herself in his path, claiming she needed help straightening one of her pigpen posts. Rune had gone along with the pretense and hammered it back into place with a few well-judged blows, ignoring the way she'd licked her lips when she'd offered him a drink afterward. He had, however, asked her if she didn't know anyone else who could help her with such tasks. Simpering, she had replied that only a few men were capable of delivering the good pounding she wanted.

He had left without comment.

Once at the forge he had asked Magnus if Edith had accepted his offer of marriage. After all, if she had refused to become his wife then she was free to bed all the men that took her fancy. But the smithy had winked and said she had told him only the other night as they lay in bed that she was thinking of accepting his offer.

"You might well get to attend our wedding before you leave, my friend."

That had been enough to convince Rune.

He would expose Edith's behavior and prevent the smithy from making a colossal mistake.

The most efficient way to accomplish this was to lure the woman into the forge and allow Magnus to walk in on them as he finally allowed her to pounce on him. That would do the trick. If he merely warned Magnus, his friend might choose to give Edith the benefit of the doubt, or even think Rune was trying to keep the woman for himself. No, the blacksmith had to see with his own eyes how his intended wife behaved when he was not looking. If by an extraordinary stroke of luck he misunderstood the situation and thought *he* was taking advantage of *her*, then Rune would ask Wolf to relay their conversation of the other day. But he was confident it wouldn't come to that. One look at Edith and everything would be clear.

It struck him that people might have drawn comparisons between the widow and Eowyn and the way they chose to indulge their senses.

Except... In his mind the two women were nothing like one another. In the same way that one was fair and one was dark, their characters were complete opposites. Eowyn was not openly brazen, she was innately sensual, which was not the same at all. She didn't pounce on unsuspected, unwilling men, she lured in the ones who were already entranced with her. She was honest in what she wanted and she didn't go around whispering that her fence posts needed a good hammering or accidentally falling to her knees in front of strangers. And, most significantly of all, she was not going around seducing men while she was betrothed to another.

He stilled. No. Eowyn was not betrothed, not to Albert or anyone else, he was suddenly sure of it. When had he started to believe her? He wasn't sure. They had not even discussed anything related to Albert since she had come to retrieve her doll. It mattered not how or why he had come round to her version of the story anyway, all that mattered was that he would not accuse her of lying to him or hurt her ever again. From now on he would do everything right.

But first, he would help Magnus.

He started to wander around the village, guessing it wouldn't be long before Edith spotted him and claimed she needed someone to hammer at her front door or exposed her breasts on the pretext that she'd been stung by a bee.

"Rune. Just the man I wanted to see."

Of course, he was. He turned around but could not manage a smile. "Edith."

The woman giggled as if he'd paid her the most extravagant compliment. "I saw you walk out of the forge earlier."

Had she really? This gave him an idea and the perfect excuse to take her where he needed to have her. "Yes. I helped repair the roof the other night. Would you like to see it?"

Unsurprisingly, she beamed at him. "Absolutely."

Nodding, he led the way to the smithy's workshop. The sooner this was over, the better. The more time he spent in the woman's company, the more she grated on his nerves. He took care to close the door behind them, so as to give Edith the impression she could finally make her move. It was the first time they were out of the public eye and he hoped she would take advantage of the fact and pounce.

Then Magnus would see her for who she really was.

"Here we are. What do you think?"

Edith lifted her head. "My... That's impressive. I can see

you're not only strong but skilled with your fingers. A most promising combination."

Eowyn had told him almost the exact same thing the other day. It had aroused him beyond measure then. Now he could only grit his teeth to stop himself from wincing at the crude compliment. "Thank you."

"I feel as if I should lie on my back so as to better admire what you can do."

This was it, the moment he'd been waiting for. Rune tensed, wondering how best to approach this. He couldn't tumble Edith onto the floor and cage her under him. If Magnus caught them in that position, it would look as if he had initiated the seduction, which was not the impression he wanted to give at all. He had no desire of ending up locked in a fight with the blacksmith. Not because he was afraid of getting injured, but because then he would have to hold back so as not to hurt him, something that was not easy to do.

"Why don't you come straddle me instead?" he offered with what he hoped was an enticing smile. He usually found it easy to ensnare women but he could not muster the will to try to appeal to Edith. Fortunately it seemed she was already won over. "I don't want you to get hurt on the rough floor."

"Mm, so considerate." She placed a hand on his chest and came to press herself tight against him. "Are you always so attentive to your lover's comfort?"

Yes, of course, he was. What sort of men did she usually bed that she should wonder?

There was no time to give any answer. Without further ado she pushed him to the floor and settled herself atop him. Idly, Rune wondered why he did not feel the least ounce of interest for the woman. She was beautiful, determined, and grinding her hips over his groin in a most promising manner. Any sane man would respond to her, or at least his body would. But when she dipped her head toward him he turned to the side. She was not Eowyn, he suddenly realized. That was what the problem was.

His dark-haired angel was the only woman he wanted.

"No kissing," he said gruffly, not offering any explanation for his refusal. Edith only smiled, as if she wasn't interested in kissing anyway. He remembered how Eowyn had spent a long moment worshipping his mouth with hers the night he had come to her, before allowing him to explore the rest of her. It had built his need for her to a fever pitch.

This was another crucial difference between the two women. His Saxon angel had not given him the impression she was only interested in the part of him that lay between his legs. She had lavished her attention on every inch of his body.

"Very well," he heard Edith say. "Let's get straight to it then."

Sorðinn! Where was Magnus? He had not imagined the blacksmith would stay out of his workshop for so long. If the man did not arrive soon Rune would have to put a stop to this awful seduction. The woman really was brazen. They were in the workshop of the man who intended to make her his wife, at the mercy of anyone walking in on them and yet she was about to ride him with the determination of someone breaking a wild horse. That they were both fully clothed made little difference. She had bunched her skirts about her waist and lowered her bodice to expose the swell of her ample breasts.

How was he going to get out of this?

Finally, he heard what he wanted to hear, footsteps coming their way. Just at the right time. Edith was unfastening his braies with feverish fingers, her intent clear as crystal. Lost to the moment, she hadn't noticed their tryst was about to be cut short. He wouldn't even have to open his mouth, there could be no doubt about what she was about to do. Perfect.

The door creaked open. He waited a moment before

turning to face the smithy, even though the man hardly needed time to comprehend what he was seeing. Still, he wanted to make sure he hadn't done all that in vain. He wasn't sure he would have the guts to go through it all a second time. When Rune finally turned to face Magnus, all the air left his lungs.

Eyes ablaze, Eowyn stood in the doorframe.

WHAT THE *HELL*?

The curse exploded in Eowyn's skull at the same time as her jaw dropped open. Was she seeing what she thought she was seeing? Was Rune really lying on the floor with a woman sitting astride him? She could not make out his lover's features, since she had her back to the door, but even if he had not been betrayed by his flaming red hair, there was no mistaking the identity of the man staring at her with intense blue eyes.

So, yes, she really was seeing what she thought she was seeing.

Bile rose in her throat. Rutting on the floor of the forge with the first woman he could find, was that what he did while she looked after this son? Was he in league with the smithy? Had the repairing of the roof, the removing of the anvil, been merely excuses to allow Rune to slip away and meet his conquests without her being any the wiser? What was he playing at? Only yesterday he had almost taken her to bed. And now he was rolling on the floor with another woman. Had the two of them spent the night together? Was that why he had not come back to the hut last evening? And, fool that she was, she'd thought he hadn't wanted to disturb her sleep! She'd been touched. The pain of his deception pierced through her heart.

"Forgive me. I'll leave you to your task. I can see you're busy."

She ran back out of the forge, only to collide with Frigyth. Thankfully, Sigurd, who was just behind, steadied his wife before she could fall on her backside.

"What's the matter?" Her friend peered at her, concern etched on her face. "You look like you've seen a ghost."

No, not a ghost but the Devil, certainly, who cared nothing for her. "It's nothing... I—"

"Eowyn! Wait!" a deep voice called from inside the forge.

Oh, no. Eowyn took her friend by the arm and hurried toward the hut. "Please. I don't want to see him, or have to listen to his lies," she said under her breath. To think he had dared accuse her of wantonness! *She* was not the one rutting in full view of everyone, was she!

To her relief, she saw Sigurd stop Rune in his tracks as he bolted out of the door in pursuit of her. The Dane would have seen her upset and attributed it to him. Not that it was difficult, she was most probably white as a sheet. Her friend's husband would not let the treacherous liar anywhere near her, she could be certain of that. Grateful for Sigurd's help, she hurried toward the hut. Why, oh, why, had she chosen that moment to go to the forge? The purchasing of a new sewing needle could have waited! They had a perfectly good smithy in her village, he could have made a dozen for her. But, perhaps, despite the pain it had caused her, it was better to know where she stood with Rune before it was too late. Moved by his confessions about his childhood, stirred by their drunken romp, she had started to soften toward him and forget her resentment.

Well, now it was back with a vengeance. Anger and embarrassment at her stupidity consumed her insides like a great fire. How apt that a devil of a man should be the one stoking it.

Once she was safe inside the hut she let out a shuddering breath.

"What was that all about?" Frigyth asked, glancing through

the window. Eowyn guessed her friend would be able to see the two men from where she was. They were probably locked in a tense conversation, one where Rune tried to justify the unjustifiable. Or... Her heart sank. Why did she think he owed her anything? After all, there was no reason why he should be faithful to her. No. Perhaps not. But she'd thought he would have the decency to refrain from bedding someone less than a day after he had bedded her in a frenzy of need.

Except, of course, that he didn't know about what they had done... He had no memory of their mad romp. As far he was concerned, there was nothing stopping him from finding himself a lover. She was nothing to him, only a former conquest with a child by another man, and set to marry that other man. Rune was a virile male with natural needs. Why would he refrain from indulging his urges for her sake?

Oh, why was it all so confused in her mind? In the midst of it all, there was only one certainty.

"I don't want to see him ever again, he has—"

"Is that Edith coming out of the forge with her hair in disarray?" her friend asked. There was ice in her voice. "What is she up to now?"

"Nevermind what she's up to. I don't care about her!" The problem was not the identity of Rune's lover but the fact that he had one. Was the woman his only conquest even? It was far from certain.

Quickly, like someone ridding themselves of a task they found unpleasant, she related what she had just seen, fighting the nausea rising in her belly. Why was she so upset, she wondered? She and Rune were not married or betrothed, she should not care what he did. But apparently, she did.

Frigyth listened to it all with a cocked head. Then she twisted her lips. "It does sound bad, I will admit, but if it really is Edith who was with Rune inside the forge, it changes things," she said slowly, as if she knew her declaration wouldn't be well received. It wasn't. Eowyn had not thought her friend would take the man's defense. "That woman is trouble, mark my words. You had better listen to Rune's version of the story before you judge."

"It was pretty clear, I would say. Or are you saying this Edith is strong enough to subdue a man Rune's size? I doubt that. He could have sent her flying with a jerk of his hips if he hadn't wanted her. No. We both know he was lying under her of his own volition." She snorted. "The only thing I'm not sure about is whether I arrived before or after he came."

Had he spilled inside Edith, or had he told her he didn't want to get another woman with child, like he had with her? Had he given her one of his maddening kisses? Had he pleasured her before taking her? Had he used his—

A knock on the door interrupted the painful series of questions. "Go away!" Eowyn instantly cried.

"Eowyn." It was Sigurd's voice. "Rune is asking to speak to you."

How had the wretched man managed to persuade the Dane to let him through? She threw a helpless glance toward Frigyth but her friend shook her head, indicating she would not send her husband away.

"Sigurd wouldn't have taken Rune's side if there wasn't something odd with this story. I told you you should be wary of Edith. That woman is a snake."

The ice in her voice had turned to venom and Eowyn had the sudden conviction that her friend's dislike of Edith had something to do with Sigurd. One day she might ask her about it. Not now though.

"I don't—"

"Let Rune in. You need to get to the bottom of this and he deserves the chance to explain himself."

There was such conviction in Frigyth's voice that Eowyn was impressed despite herself. Was she making a mistake? She so desperately wanted to hear Rune had not gone to another woman while she was battling confused feelings for him...

"Very well. Let him in."

Frigyth gave her hand a squeeze. "If he doesn't convince you of his good faith then you have my permission to ask Sigurd to pummel him to the ground. He will be only too happy to oblige you and I might well help him."

With those comforting words, she left. A moment later Rune walked in, his attitude unusually subdued.

Eowyn glared at him and lifted her chin in defiance. He would not get to see her pain or her doubts. "Let me guess. It's not what I think."

He sighed and fell onto the stool. "It's not. But I can't expect you to believe me after the way I doubted you when Albert claimed to be Little Rune's father."

This threw her. She hadn't expected him to look so defeated or to admit so blithely he didn't believe Albert's mad ramblings anymore. True, he hadn't said he now trusted her claim he was the baby's father, but it was progress of sorts.

This lack of vindictiveness convinced her Frigyth might be right. Something was odd. Rune was arrogance and self-confidence personified. He would not be so subdued if he didn't wish to establish the truth.

In the end, curiosity won.

"I'm listening."

Relief flashed in Rune's eyes. He cleared his throat, as if trying to find the best way to explain himself. "Edith is set to marry Magnus."

This was the last thing she had expected him to say. "Well then she's lucky *I* was the one to walk in on you, not him!" she sneered.

"Yes, but I'm not. It was my intention for him to walk in on us, you see. That's why I took her to the forge. Foolishly, I had not imagined anyone other than Magnus might come in."

This was getting weirder and weirder. "You wanted him to see you bedding his betrothed?" Eowyn clarified. Was that some sort of male pride thing? Did he mean to prove to the blacksmith that he could seduce his woman if he wanted to? Her opinion of Rune would not improve if it turned out he had not gone to Edith out of lust but to settle a score with another man. It might even sink another notch.

Rune sighed again, like a man realizing he was making a mess of his explanation. "The other day when we repaired the roof Magnus told us he intended to marry her. But I think he would be better to stay well away from the woman."

"Why?"

"She's been after me from the moment I arrived in the village. I know you will think it is awfully convenient, but it's true." Eowyn didn't say anything because, contrary to what he feared, she did not think of doubting him on that score. A man like Rune would turn heads anywhere he went. In fact, she would be surprised if Edith was the only woman in the village lusting after him. "I didn't know she was as good as engaged then, of course, but then Magnus told me as much and Wolf confirmed she was famous for seducing all the men she could find."

This did not make his behavior any clearer. "How is you giving in to her advances going to help Magnus, exactly?"

"I chose to lure her into the forge, thinking that he couldn't fail to see her pounce on another man and finally understand he had better set his sights on someone else if he means to marry."

Eowyn stared at him, unsure what to do. She didn't know whether to laugh at his hare-brained scheme or send him out with a curse for thinking she would believe such an outrageous story. But the expression on his face was all the proof she needed to know he was telling nothing but the embarrassing truth. Had he been lying he would have blustered his way through in typical arrogant fashion and expect or even demand she believed him. Instead, he was mortified to have to admit that he had thought his stupid plan might work.

"Rune, you do realize that if Magnus had entered the forge instead of me, he would have seen you two locked in an intimate embrace. What do you think that would have achieved?" she asked in the same tone she would have used to speak to an unreasonable child. "He doesn't know you, has no reason to trust your word. Why would he believe your absurd claim that the woman he wants to marry had been the instigator of the seduction? Why would he give you the benefit of the doubt, even? You're a mountain of a man, far too strong to be subdued by anyone, much less a woman. Had he walked in on you, Magnus would never have concluded you were being used against your will by a predatory female. He would have thought exactly what I thought, that you were so eager to get between the woman's legs that you did not stop to consider where you were."

Rune ran his hand through his hair. He still hadn't braided it since he'd washed the day before, she noticed. Why she should think of such a thing right now was beyond her but here she was, wishing she could weave her fingers through the fiery locks. "I guess... It wasn't my best idea."

"I guess not." Her lips quivered at his obvious discomfiture. "Why would you even want to meddle in Magnus' affairs? What is it to you who he marries?"

"I like the man." Rune shrugged, as if he could not quite explain the urge and was coming to regret it. "And I know what it's like to live with someone and discover too late you should never have trusted them. I guess I wanted to spare him that pain."

Her heart skipped a beat. Was he talking about her? He could be, considering what had happened with Albert and yet somehow she sensed he was referring to something different, something linked to what he had unwittingly revealed the other night. She had already started to suspect there was more under the surface with this man. The arrogant, carefree façade might well be just that, a façade. What painful secrets were lurking under it?

Eowyn took in a deep breath.

Could she take the plunge and decide to trust Rune was telling the truth? He was right. It was just like it had been for him with Albert. She had to accept that his version of the story was the right one of her own volition, as there were no proof of it, and he could not *make* her believe him. For the first time, she got a glimpse of what he must have felt when he'd heard about her supposed treachery. Why would he have immediately concluded that the man was lying? Albert had asserted he was betrothed to her and it was all too plausible. After all, the two of them had been lovers, were of an age to get married and no one made such extraordinary claims unless they were true. Hearing that the woman they had just bedded and the child they had been told was theirs belonged to another man would have been a terrible blow for anyone. No wonder Rune had reacted badly.

She had only thought he was rutting with Edith and already the discovery had been a knife to the heart. Rune had had to deal with the loss of all his hopes of a family, which was a hundred times worse.

In the end it all came down to trust and she was now convinced he was not lying about what had happened with Edith. He had been a fool, nothing more. Mentally she addressed her thanks to Frigyth and Sigurd for insisting she listened to his side of the story before judging. Sometimes it seemed there was more than met the eye.

"You're saying you only wanted Magnus to come to his senses and see the woman for who she really was?" she said slowly.

"Yes!" A most emphatic answer. "It had to look as if she was the one who had pounced on me. Why do you think I took her to the forge? Why do you think I made sure she was the one straddling me?"

Mm. Privately Eowyn thought this proved nothing. She knew all too well this position was one he favored. The man liked his lovers to ride him. Then again, he also liked to take them from behind or lie next to them, or have them sit on his—

She shook her head. Was this really the time to relive all they had done together? No. She had better focus on the task at hand.

"And you will do whatever it takes to persuade him she was the one at fault, even if it doesn't present you in a favorable light?"

"Yes." This time there was a hint of hesitation in his voice. This, more than anything else, convinced her he was telling the truth. He seemed worried to hear what she had in mind but determined to redeem himself whatever the cost to his dignity.

She afforded a smile. It seemed she was going to get a small revenge after all.

"Well, then, I'm going to see Edith and you are going to make sure Magnus overhears our conversation."

CHAPTER FOURTEEN

"Oh. It's you."

Edith sounded less than happy to see Eowyn, Rune noted from his hiding place behind the fence. But the widow's coldness could be explained by the fact that Eowyn had interrupted their tryst in the forge earlier or that she knew—or rather thought—that the Saxon shared Rune's bed. Ah, if only that could be the case... He dreamed of having the dark-haired angel in his bed, writhing under him, but that possibility had never appeared more remote. Too much resentment lay between them. At least, if she believed he had never meant to bed Edith, it would be a step in the right direction.

Which was why he was here, crouching behind a rickety wooden fence.

He glanced at Magnus kneeling by his side. The smithy seemed unsure what he was doing here, spying on the two women's conversation, and no wonder. Not to worry, it would soon become clear. They could not see anything but they could hear them well enough.

"Yes. It's me," Eowyn answered calmly. "I'm afraid we didn't have time to talk earlier."

"Well, don't blame me for it. You were the one who fled like a scared bird when you saw me and Rune together."

At this, Magnus threw him a furious glare. Rune raised a hand and gestured that they should carry on listening. Thankfully the man didn't protest.

"Yes, I was shocked, I will admit. I don't mind confessing that I had once hoped to get Rune for myself," Eowyn said. Though he knew that was a lie destined to get Edith to blurt out her desire for him, Rune could not help his heart from leaping at the words. "But I see that you are making more progress than I am."

Edith gave what could only be described as a satisfied simper. Rune hoped Magnus at least would see it as such. Then she spoke and there was no room for misinterpretation. "Yes. I think I am. He's ripe for the plucking, I'd say."

He did not glance at his friend, guessing he would be shocked by the declaration.

Eowyn spoke again. "I had better warn you though. Rune is... not all he appears to be."

"What do you mean?" Edith sounded both dubious and worried. "Are you saying he favors men?"

There was a pause, far too long for Rune's liking. What was Eowyn waiting for? She should be denying the accusation! Magnus looked at him uncertainly, as if wondering whether to stay where he was or edge away from him. Damn, this was not how he had imagined this conversation would go. Or... Perhaps he should have.

You will do whatever it takes to persuade him, even if it doesn't present you in a favorable light?

Was that her plan? To lie and spread rumors about his supposed preferences in bed? How would that help anyone?

"Well, no, he doesn't favor men, not that I know of anyway," Eowyn finally answered. Rune tensed up, not at all appeased.

What sort of a weak denial was that? Before he could burst through the fence, she spoke again, her voice little more than a mischievous whisper. "But... He is impotent. You will only be disappointed with him as a lover, I'm afraid."

Sorðinn! Impotent! Was the woman insane? By his side, Magnus smirked. This was a nightmare. Rune clenched his fists, resolving to make Eowyn pay for this humiliation. He didn't doubt that by morning word of his supposed inadequacies would have spread through the village, courtesy of the disgruntled widow.

"Really? Mm, mind you, he was limp as a worm when I straddled him," Edith said. "Well, if that is the case I suppose I had better find someone else to see to my needs... Pity. In all other ways he is quite the man. It just goes to show you cannot trust a pretty exterior."

"Forgive me but I thought... I heard you were about to marry Magnus?"

The snort that answered the question would have been a blow to any man's pride. Rune should have pitied the smithy but, selfish bastard that he was, he was glad to see the smirk finally wiped off his face.

"Oh, he did propose, twice in as many years, actually, and he is the richest man in the village, so I am giving his offer the consideration it is due," Edith was saying. "But I don't know if I want to tie myself to one man, and one whose skill in bed is adequate at best. He's too gentle, and I prefer a good—"

The smithy vaulted over the fence before Rune could do anything to stop him. A moment later he had dragged Edith with him to the forge and Rune found himself alone with Eowyn.

He nodded toward the hut, indicating she should follow him and, to his relief, she complied without a word. He stayed silent, holding on to his simmering anger until they were safe from prying eyes and ears.

"So." He crossed his arms over his chest to try and calm down. "I'm impotent, am I?"

The infuriating woman only shrugged, as if having the whole village believing such a thing of him was no issue. Which was not his opinion at all. "It seemed the easiest thing to say. I needed her to admit she had been the one instigating the seduction and make plain her intention of bedding other men than Magnus. She did both. I think it was a success."

"A success. For whom, I wonder?" he asked through gritted teeth. Not for him at any rate. "Not only did you spread slander about me, but you forced Magnus to listen as the woman he's chosen to marry told you that he did not satisfy her as well as her other lovers and was only worth considering for his money."

Eowyn winced, feeling sorry for Magnus. She hadn't expected Edith to slight him so cruelly. No man should have to hear such declarations. "I know, it's awful, but it's not my fault if that's what she thinks," she defended. "It is as you said, he doesn't deserve to be tied to such a woman. I had to make him see she would only make him unhappy."

"And that couldn't have been achieved in any other way than to lie about my ability in bed?" Rune was mightily aggrieved, as she had expected. She merely smiled.

"Would you have preferred I agreed to her suggestion that you favored men?" she asked, fluttering her eyelashes. "I suppose it would have worked just as—"

"No!" he barked. "But your lie was not very believable, I would argue. Tell me, how could an impotent man have got you with child?"

She stilled at the implication of what he had just said. Was he… Had he finally accepted the paternity of their child? Something in her chest expanded. Hope. She refused to dwell on it.

He might just be trying to rankle her because he hadn't like being called impotent.

"But you didn't get me with child, remember?" she breathed, wanting to see his reaction. "Albert did. If you are stupid enough to believe such nonsense, why wouldn't Edith, who doesn't know me, believe it?"

Rune clenched his teeth. She'd hit her mark. Well, good. If that was what it took to make him see sense, she would hit again. "I swear you will—"

"In any case," she cut in, "Edith might not even know I have a child. We are not acquainted, and you saw she did not question my assertion. She did say you'd been 'limp as a worm.' Or did you not hear that part from where you were?"

"I did hear, thank you. My ears are in perfect working order. As is the rest of my body."

A smile bloomed on Eowyn's lips. He was vexed indeed. The mighty Dane piqued in his virility... It was a sight to see. "Perhaps you weren't lying when you claimed not to be interested in her," she mused, arching a brow. "That could be one explanation for your limpness, I suppose."

"It is the *only* explanation for it!" The words were little less than a growl. "I'm glad that humiliation will at least serve to convince you I was telling the truth about not wanting to bed her."

Eowyn was enjoying herself now. Rune was not so amused, however. He pinched the bridge of his nose in an attempt at calm and she heard him mutter something in Norse. Probably something along the lines of 'You will be the death of me.' Her smile widened.

"But you know..." she said sweetly. "An inability to perform is nothing to be ashamed of. It can happen to every man."

"Perhaps. But I am *not* impotent and could make love to you right here, right now."

He grabbed her wrist and forced her hand to land on his shaft to prove his point. There was no need. She knew all too well the man was as potent as could be. Why, even drunk he had been as ready for her as a stallion for a mare. And, of course, he had made her with child in only one night. There was nothing wrong with him, and no woman of sense should question his ability to perform in bed. He was hard as steel under her palm.

Her throat went dry and she tried to swallow. Touching him so intimately, feeling his pulsing heat was creating havoc within her. Perhaps she should not have provoked him so.

"Feel this, Angel?" he purred, leaning in to speak in her ear, overwhelming her senses with his scent, his heat, his strength. "I could not get hard for a woman actually straddling me and yet I am aroused simply from arguing with you. Explain that if you will."

Eowyn took her hand away as if it had been burnt. It was the only way she could stop herself from stroking him. Right now she was battling the urge to kneel at his feet and take that glorious length into her mouth. She was a heartbeat away from lifting her skirts and begging Rune to put an end to the torturous need that had not left her since he had reappeared in her life.

She could do no such thing, of course.

That wretched sensual nature had always been her problem, getting her into all sorts of trouble. But she could not let it rule her life anymore, not when so much was at stake, not with a man who would only use it against her.

"I can't explain it," she whispered, speaking with her mouth in the crook of his neck. Dear God, he smelled good. Of wood and spice and man. "Any more than I can explain the way my body responds when you're near. But that doesn't mean anything. I've known all along that we are compatible in bed. It doesn't mean we should base anything on it. Straw will always catch fire when you bring it close to a flame. It is the way of things. But fire destroys what it touches. I don't want to be destroyed."

Physical pleasure was not what she wanted from him. She could get that from any man. Well, maybe not all men, but most. But trust, support, and affection she wanted only from one person. The father of her son, the man who should have been overjoyed to meet Litte Rune and want to be in his life. Want *her* to be in it too.

"You think I destroyed you?" Rune sounded appalled. Perhaps she'd been too forceful in her choice of words.

"I don't want you to want to tumble me into bed as you did last year, when we were strangers, and then leave, never to come back," she explained. "What was good then is not good enough anymore because now we are not strangers. We have a son together. I don't want you to just desire me, I want you to trust and respect me. I want you to..."

I want you to want me. In all the ways a man can want a woman, not just for my body.

Silence stretched in the hut. Dusk was slowly descending, blurring the world around them. They remained entwined a long time, Rune bent over her, Eowyn breathing in his wonderful scent. After a while she forced herself to move. This conversation had not gone how she had wanted or ended the way she had anticipated and she was more confused than ever.

"I need to see to Rune."

The little boy had not made a sound. They both knew she was fleeing when she bent over the furs to take her son into her arms.

In the morning Rune's tresses were still cascading over his shoulders in a ripple of copper. It was a striking sight and Eowyn's fingers itched with the need to touch him. How could she satisfy that urge? One way would be to allow him to pleasure her with his mouth in the same way he had the other day. Then she would be able to clutch at him, weave her fingers through the silken mass to anchor him in place while he devoured her. Another, less scandalous way, would be to braid the flowing hair for him. Dare she ask—

The words left her mouth before she could think. "Do you want me to braid your hair?"

Rune stared at her with all the disbelief this question deserved. Eowyn bit her bottom lip. Why, oh why, had she spoken? Why did she want to do it, even? Only the day before she had told him she didn't want physical intimacy from him and she had meant it. Why was she now offering to do such a thing for him? He could be forgiven for being confused, or even worse, for thinking she was trying to seduce him. She wasn't.

Wasn't she?

"If you don't want to, it's not a—"

"Yes. Please," Rune rasped as he sat on the stool. "Braid my hair."

Everything within her melted. His voice was so hoarse, the light in his eyes so bright he might as well have ordered her to spread her legs for him. How was she going to withstand the intensity of the moment?

"Very well."

She could not back down now, or rather, she didn't want to. If she was not to make love to Rune, she owed herself that small gratification. Tentatively, she reached out to take a lock of hair. It was just as soft and sleek as she had imagined. And the color! The sun coming through the window caused a myriad of shades to ripple through it when she wiggled her fingers, making it appear almost alive. It truly was wondrous. She could have played with it all day.

But she was supposed to braid it.

"I'm afraid to—"

"Don't worry. There is no chance you are going to hurt me with those delicate hands. Do what you must."

She did exactly that. She did what she must, not what she wanted. If she had done what she wanted, she would have buried her face into his hair and let the soft strands caress her skin. She would have played with it as she had liked to play with stream water as a child, and feel it ripple between her fingers. She would have rubbed her cheek against it and inhaled the wonderful, comforting scent.

Instead she simply braided it.

As she worked, various sounds escaped her lips unbidden, as they often did while she fed Little Rune. Soon they coalesced into a song. She carried on, braiding and humming at the same time. Singing helped her to keep her desire at bay. By focusing on the song's lyrics it seemed she could stop her mind from imagining the different places on Rune's body she could brush with her fingers. Too many of them held an interest. His collarbone, his hands, his mouth, his lower back, his forearms, his—

Drat, there she was, doing it again. She had better start singing louder.

All too soon it was over. Eowyn drew back to observe the result of her handiwork—and her heart sank in her chest.

"Oh, no. You look ridiculous!" she cried out. "The braids are a mess."

To her shock, Rune burst out laughing. It was a sound she had never heard before, one that tugged straight on her heartstrings.

"Well. They do feel a bit loose," he said, running a hand over the braids at his temples. She had attempted to reproduce the way he usually wore them, tight against the scalp and following the curve of his ears.

"A bit loose..." She shook her head in consternation. That was a generous description from what she could see. But, of course, Rune could only feel them. "Any looser and they would flap like a dog's ears."

He laughed some more. "Angel, it's not a problem. I expect you haven't often braided men's hair, that's all." No, she hadn't. Men's or women's hair for that matter. Or even her own. She always wore it loose, liking the feel of it around her shoulders. "It requires practice. In truth, I knew they might not turn out so well. Not to worry. They can always be undone. I don't have to be stuck with dog's ears all my life."

She bristled. He had allowed her to tend to his hair like one indulged a child, all the while knowing she would not manage a satisfactory result?

"Why didn't you say anything sooner?" she accused. "Why let me waste my time and yours?"

The laughter died in Rune's throat. How could he tell Eowyn nothing could have made him put a stop to the moment? To have her run her delicate fingers through his hair, brush his scalp, hum and sing to herself as she worked and simply stood next to him, bathing him in her delicious, clean scent had been heavenly, as the Saxons might say, anything but a waste time. He had so feared she wouldn't want to have anything to do with him after what he had made her go through these last few days...

He was relieved she had not noticed how her proximity had affected him. It had been an inspired idea to sit on the stool and hide his lap under the table because if she had taken but one glance at the hardness straining his braies, she would undoubtedly have stopped her ministrations.

"It was not wasted time. I thought I would give you a chance to get the hang of it," he said in a rasp. "How else are you supposed to get better?"

"Well, I thank you for the opportunity to practice but I did not achieve anything remotely satisfactory." She planted her fists on her hips. "I cannot let you go around the village looking like this. They will have to come undone."

Yes, that was precisely what he had been hoping to hear. He clasped his hands over his aching groin and nodded, anticipating more of the delicious torture.

"If you would do the honors?"

Without a word Eowyn applied herself to the task. Rune closed his eyes and allowed his body to enjoy the moment and his mind to drift. To his delight, she started singing again. Her voice was truly magical, transporting him to another place. Just like before, it was over all too soon. It took him a while to realize that she was standing by his side, as if waiting for him to open his eyes.

"Show me," she whispered when he finally did.

"Show you what?" The words came out as a croak.

How much your presence affects me? How I want to kiss you? You don't want to know, Angel. It might frighten you.

"How you braid your hair."

"Oh, that." Relief washed through him. For a moment he'd feared she wanted to be shown how hard he had gone. He wouldn't put it past the vixen. But she only wanted to be taught how to braid his hair, something he could have done in his sleep. "If you want. I will need a... little rake if you have one."

Eowyn smiled. He knew she loved it when he needed help with her language. "A comb, you mean? Here."

Rune was certain the braids would not be his best. With Eowyn's gaze fixed upon him he hadn't been able to focus on the task. But at least now that she was not touching him any longer, his hardness had softened somewhat. He could finally leave his seat.

"Better?" he asked, coming to stand in front of her.

"Much better."

The expression on her face told him that the result of his efforts wasn't as bad as he'd feared. She clearly thought him splendid, but he knew he was nothing compared to her. She was the most stunning woman he had ever laid eyes on. Her eyes in particular, of a brown so deep he could almost not distinguish the pupil in the middle, and her hair, black as the blackest night, fascinated him. He had never seen hair and eyes like hers before. They had evidently been inherited from her mysterious father, come from distant, exotic lands. Rune mentally addressed his thanks to the man. Where was he now? Was he still alive? Did he know he had a daughter here in East Anglia or had it been like it had been for him and Little Rune? Had the foreigner left the country not knowing he was leaving a part of him behind?

The best part?

He imagined the man's pride at meeting this wonderful woman he had fathered. Would Little Rune one day grow into a man Rune could be proud of? Would he even be there to see him at such an age?

He frowned. Why was he torturing himself with these questions he didn't have the answer to when he was as good as holding Eowyn in his arms? He should make the most of the moment, enjoy the unexpected truce they had established. Touch her.

Yes. He most definitely should touch her.

But how? After their discussion from the previous evening, he could not ask to make love to her. If he took such liberty, she would only refuse.

"Maybe one day I will braid your hair," he said, not resisting the urge to bury his fingers into the heavy, silky mass calling out to him. Perhaps he could get away with stroking her hair, since he could not touch her body. "I have never braided black hair before."

His hand came to cradle the back of her head and he started to massage it slowly. It fit into his palm perfectly, and felt so fragile, so feminine. He blinked. Since when was he fascinated by the back of a woman's skull? Not, not any woman's skull. *Eowyn*'s skull, which was not the same at all. Everything about that woman fascinated him, the hollow between her collarbones, the color of her lips, the shape of her nails even.

"I..." Her lips parted on a silent sigh and he felt the weight of her head settle more firmly into his hand. "Yes, I would like that. But not today."

No. Not today. He wouldn't be able to stand it, not when his manhood had gone hard again after a brief respite. He had to get out of here, for fear of making her lewd propositions she didn't want to hear. Intimacy was one thing, uncontrollable lust quite another. She'd told him only the day before she didn't want him to tumble her into bed. He could not stop his body from reacting to her, but he could find the strength not to bother her with it. He would be the one dealing with the desire roaring through his veins, she would not be expected to offer him relief.

He cleared his throat and took a step back, releasing her.

"So, now that I'm presentable, shall we take a stroll? It's such a fine day it would be as shame to waste it inside." Not giving her the opportunity to refuse, he strode over to the baby. "I'll carry him. You take a basket, see if we can find some fruit along the way."

They took the road to the south a moment later. Rune had never explored that side of the village before. For some reason the landscape seemed less welcoming to him. As they progressed through the fields, he felt Eowyn's demeanor change.

"What's the matter?" Was she too thinking they should have gone to the other side of the village, toward the town?

For a long moment she didn't answer. Her eyes were glued to a point in the distance. Had she spotted some danger? He couldn't see anything. Finally she spoke. "The farm... It's over there, beyond that hill." She shivered. "I hadn't realized it was so close to the Norsemen's village."

No wonder she had become quiet. The place where she had gone after her grandmother's death would hold bad memories for her. And good ones as well, presumably, courtesy of her young lover.

"What became of your friend?" Though Rune hated himself for being jealous of the man, he could not help it. He was not a good man, so he was jealous.

Eowyn came to halt and said with terrible bluntness. "He's dead."

There was such pain in her dark eyes that he drew her against him with his free arm and brought Little Rune closer so she could kiss him. He knew she would get comfort from her son's presence. "I'm sorry. Do you want to tell me?"

He felt her nod against his chest, but she stayed silent. It mattered not. There was no rush. He just held her and waited for her to be ready.

"About a year after Freodheric and I started sleeping together, the woman's son came to visit the farm. He was a nasty man."

A nasty man. Cold invaded Rune as all sorts of possibilities, each more horrifying than the last came to his mind. Had she been hurt? Had her friend died defending her against a rapist? Eowyn had placed her cheek against his chest. He knew that, placed where she was, she would be able to hear his heart pumping hard. He didn't care.

"The man took an immediate dislike to Freodheric. Probably because he was always trying to help others, doing what he could to alleviate the younger children's burden." Rune's heartbeat eased marginally. As awful as this was, it didn't appear as if the man had focused his attention on her. It was something, he supposed. "He started to demand more and more of him. We had always been overworked but now Freodheric barely had time to sleep. He became so tired he could barely see straight."

Rune knew for certain he was not a good man when his first thought went to what that would have meant for their love life. The exhausted youth would not have been able to bed her if he could not function properly. He gritted his teeth, appalled at his heartlessness. What did it say about him that he was glad the poor sod would not have been able to lie with Eowyn because he'd been treated like cattle? Never had Rune felt more ashamed of his feelings but there it was. He was jealous of a dead man. Not only had this Freodheric given Eowyn her first kiss, shown her pleasure and a glimpse of happiness, he had most probably gained her love too.

Yes. And he was now dead. He could not lay claim to Eowyn's love any longer. She might well choose to gift another man with it if that man turned out to be worthy. Could he be that man?

Rune stilled as the answer hit him square in the chest. No. A man like him, arrogant, jealous, selfish, would never be chosen.

"One day Freodheric was sent to help repair the water mill. The wheel had stopped working and someone had to swim under it to try and unclog it. It was bitterly cold and he was already exhausted. There was no way he could have survived the ordeal. I think the man knew it, that's why he sent him." She shuddered against him. "They brought his mangled body back to the farm that night. I retched when I saw what was left of him. The mill... The mill had started working again, of course, but, too numb with cold, too weak, he had not been able to get away from the wheel in time."

"Oh, sweetheart." Rune felt like retching himself. This was a horrific story.

"I could not show my shock. No one knew about us. Freodheric kept telling me it was a good thing, as it meant the man would only start paying me more attention if he knew, but I should have said something before it was too late, I could have —"

"No. There was nothing you could have done except place yourself in danger by betraying the connection between you. It was best you did not draw unwanted attention to yourself, your friend was right. He did what he could to protect you and you honored his efforts by staying safely hidden from the man's lust." What that bastard would have done to a beautiful young woman to punish her impertinence did not bear thinking about. "Freodheric sounds like a good man to have made your safety his priority."

"He was."

Another silence.

"After that, I fled. I was now old enough and being with Freodheric had shown me that there could be more to life than what I had at the farm." She spoke in a whisper, either due to the pain of the memory or because she didn't want to disturb the babe, who had fallen asleep in his arms. "I owed the vile woman and her son nothing but I felt I did owe it to Freodheric to try and make a better life for myself."

"He would have been proud of you." Rune was surprised to see that no bitterness came to mar his reassurance this time. He meant it. The youth would have been proud to see her flee from her miserable fate thanks to the strength he had given her.

Eowyn let out a heart-breaking sob and went limp against him. He had the impression she had not allowed herself to grieve at the time of her friend's death. She would have been too busy planning her escape, too desperate not to betray any untoward intimacy between them. Then once she was free she had most probably forbidden herself to think of him, for fear of collapsing if she did. She had not dared linger on her pain, not wanting to be overwhelmed by the horror of it all.

But she hadn't forgotten. In every man she'd bedded she would have tried to find a bit of the first man she had loved. It was more than pleasure she had tried to find in their arms, it was the illusion that Freodheric had not completely left her.

"He was only seventeen."

"I know." He tightened his hold around her, feeling quite helpless. "I'm sorry," he said, talking into her hair.

"He's dead."

"Yes."

"He said he would be here for me, keep me safe and he's dead."

"I know," Rune repeated. "But I'm here."

He knew the moment Eowyn drew back from his embrace that he had said the wrong thing. She wiped her tears from her cheeks and glared at him. "Yes. You're here but you don't want me, do you, so what good is that going to do? You don't want *us*."

Rune didn't know what to answer. All he knew was that in this moment he wasn't sure that was the truth.

CHAPTER FIFTEEN

"I want to go back home," Eowyn announced the following morning.

After their discussion about Freodheric's death they had returned to the hut in tense silence. Rune had spent the best part of the evening at the forge, trying to earn Magnus' forgiveness for his meddling. To his relief, the smithy had agreed he was probably better off knowing about Edith's true nature now than five years after their wedding and they had parted as friends.

When he had entered the hut in the middle of the night, he'd found Eowyn asleep, one hand curled by her face. She had looked so peaceful, so innocent. For a moment he had just watched her breathe, not moving a muscle for fear of disturbing her rest.

The baby had started fussing not long after. As Rune had approached, a horrid smell had assaulted his nostrils. Not hungry then, rather dirty and uncomfortable, and no wonder.

"You little Devil," he'd murmured under his breath. "Come. Let us wipe your rump."

The memory of what he'd found in the clout made him

smile. Would he ever get used to the amount of waste a baby produced? Probably not. It really was astounding.

When Eowyn cleared her throat he remembered she was still waiting for an answer.

"We can leave whenever you wish," he said, helping himself to another of the oat cakes Frigyth had given them the night before. Damn, but Sigurd's wife was a good cook. "If you feel strong enough to travel?"

She looked at him fixedly, as if he'd offended her by calling her weak. It had not been his intention. "I have been strong enough for days. But I will feel better in my own home."

"Of course."

Perhaps Wolf would agree to let them borrow his horse for the journey? He knew Eowyn was no weak female, but he also knew she was a tired new mother who had fainted only the other day. He would see her travel in comfort.

Rune took one last bite of oat cake and opened the door. Outside a fierce wind was blowing, causing wispy clouds to chase each other in a lead gray sky. In the last few days, the weather had taken a turn for the worst and autumn was now well on its way. The color overhead reminded him of the skies at home and a sudden, unexpected pang of homesickness hit him. Could he ever feel at ease in a place so far away from home? He wasn't sure. Things were no different from the previous year, the Saxons still viewed him with suspicion. Why he was even asking himself that question wasn't clear. He was going back to Denmark soon enough, wasn't he?

Feeling suddenly nauseous, he ran to Wolf's hut.

Eowyn was tying the blanket Frigyth had lent her to carry her meagre possessions back home on her back when Rune walked inside the hut a moment later, his face unusually grave. Why? What had happened? The answer hit her like a bolt of lightning. He didn't want to watch her go.

Because, well, since she was leaving, this was goodbye.

She was about to walk out of his life, possibly forever.

She hadn't realized that by going back home, she would effectively be putting an end to their time together. She had only wanted to ensure she was in her own house, surrounded by her own comforts. But that meant leaving Rune behind and now that she thought about it, she wasn't sure that was what she wanted. Still, she would not humiliate herself by asking him to accompany her. The last time he had only gone to her because someone else had forced him to. If he came to her, it would be because he wanted to, not because he felt he had to.

And after their conversation of the previous day, when she had finally dared to say out loud the painful truth, namely that he didn't want either her or Little Rune in his life, she wasn't sure he would want to return to her village. Wasn't he supposed to leave for Denmark soon anyway? A few days would make little difference.

No. This was goodbye, that had to be why he looked so grave.

She steeled herself for the moment.

"Are you ready?" he asked.

Nodding, she took her son into her arms and walked through the door—only to come to skidding halt.

"I cannot ride him!" She looked, appalled, at the enormous stallion tethered to the fence in front of her. Rune had said he was going to get a horse, but she had not imagined he would get one like this. She would never be able to ride him. "I thought you meant... well, a mule or some such animal."

He shrugged. "I don't know what a 'mule' is but I'm not having you walking all the way back to your hut when you've barely recovered your strength. Wolf agreed to lend us Demon so we can get you back home without you overexerting yourself."

We.

Her heart missed a beat. "You're coming with me?"

"Of course."

"But..." Emotion threatened to engulf her at the same time as relief swept through her. This was not goodbye just yet.

"But what?" Rune asked. He sounded so perplexed, seemed to think it so obvious he should accompany her that she wasn't sure what to say. She had done him a disservice for thinking he would be only too happy to wash his hands of her and her son. But he had never meant this parting to be final. He had not meant it to be a parting at all.

He was still frowning, waiting for her answer. She could not tell him she had thought he would send her and Little Rune on their way without a backward glance. She felt ashamed enough to have thought it.

"Demon cannot carry three people," she said instead.

"Humpf. Considering that one of those people is no longer than my arm and the other one weighs little more than a child, I'm sure he could manage. But he won't have to. I will walk next to him. You and Little Rune will sit on him. And you will give me that blanket, I will carry it. I don't want you to be uncomfortable."

Her stupid, stupid heart, already beating unbearably fast, began to thump in her chest. Such thoughtfulness had to mean something. But what? Well, at least if he came back home with her she would have some time to try and work it out.

She handed the baby to Rune and climbed onto the watering trough so she could place her foot on the stirrup. No way would she be able to climb onto the stallion without some sort of help and right now she could not have borne to feel

Rune's hands around her waist. Her body was already alarmingly hot.

Once she was settled she held out her arms to catch Little Rune. "I'm a bit nervous riding with him in my arms," she admitted, looking at her son. "Demon is enormous. What if he bolted?"

Rune gave the horse's rump an affectionate pat. "Demon *is* enormous but I've rarely seen a more placid animal. An impressive size doesn't always mean danger, it can also give immense satisfaction, as I think you well know." He threw her a meaningful look, one that scorched her all way to the soles of her feet. Oh, yes, she did know. "Besides, I'm holding the reins. You'll be fine. After all, who better to tame a demon than the Devil himself?"

He winked and Eowyn feared for a moment she might fall from the saddle.

At her nod, they set off and soon her fears were allayed. Demon indeed seemed placid and Rune, as per usual, was confidence and skill personified. The horse's gait never wavered, despite the wind howling around them. After a moment though, the rolling motion became problematic.

"I'm sorry, I need a moment of privacy," she whispered, wincing in embarrassment.

The hut was still too far away, she would never make it there in comfort. Rune brought the horse to a stop without any comment, for which she was grateful, then held out his hands to take the baby from her while she dismounted. But Demon was so tall she staggered when she touched the ground. Instantly Rune steadied her. For a moment he held her against him, one arm around her waist and the other cradling the baby. The posture had become quite familiar in the last few days. It struck her that they would appear to any onlookers as a happy family.

Her heart gave a jolt and for a moment she forgot all about her need to relieve herself.

Rune cleared his throat and, recalled to her senses, she took a step back.

"I'll hold the baby while you see to your needs," he offered, looking as ill-at-ease as she felt. Had he thought the same thing as she had?

"Let's place him on the ground for a moment," she replied. "It will do him good."

Doing her best to behave naturally, Eowyn placed the blanket on the mossy ground and lay Little Rune on it. After being in her arms for so long, he would relish the opportunity to kick his legs.

"I won't be long," she muttered, before disappearing behind a bush.

Eowyn was standing back up to straighten her skirts when she heard the crack. Instinct had her lift her head up to locate the cause of the noise. It was her mistake. The falling branch hit her next to her eye, causing a burst of pain to explode in her skull. While she groaned, rubbing at her temple, another, smaller branch, fell at her feet. Overhead, the trees were swaying in the fierce wind, scattering leaves and branches everywhere. It was as if the forest was breaking apart.

She froze. Just a few feet away was her baby. Her fragile, helpless baby was lying on a blanket, waiting for a branch to fall and flatten him. Oh, what had she done?

She ran.

CHAPTER SIXTEEN

"*Sorðinn!*" Rune watched as Eowyn stumbled into the clearing, looking wild, dishevelled—and bleeding. "What happened?" he asked, rushing out to her.

Had she been attacked? He hadn't heard a thing, but she was definitely injured. There was a cut just above her eyebrow and blood was oozing down her cheek. She seemed unaware of it, however, only focused on one thing.

"Rune!" she cried out, looking to the blanket on the ground. She hadn't even glanced at him, not seen that he was holding the child. "I need to—"

"He's here," he said, stopping her with a hand at her elbow as she ran past him. "With me."

She stopped and saw the little boy cradled in his other arm. Her body turned to molten wax, her gaze, so wild and glazed when she had burst into the clearing, instantly sharpened.

"Oh, thank God," she said in a sob. "Thank God!"

The little boy was gurgling away, totally oblivious to her distress.

"The wind caused a few little branches to fall on the ground," Rune explained as he handed her the child. It was obvious she would not calm down until she held him. She needed to feel him, to know he was safe. "So I thought it was best if I didn't leave him lying on the blanket. It was too dangerous."

"Yes." She nuzzled at her son's neck, reminding him of an animal sniffing at its cub. "That's why I ran back here. A branch fell on me, hit me on the head while I was putting myself to rights. I thought... I thought it could happen to Rune and I—"

Just then there was a crack and a branch as thick as his arm fell on the blanket, in the place where the babe had been lying mere moments ago, scattering bits of wood everywhere.

"Oh..." Eowyn sagged against him, evidently thinking the same thing as he was. If he had not thought to move Little Rune when he had, he would be dead by now. "Oh, no!"

"Hush. You have him. Nothing happened," he told her, speaking with his mouth in her hair. "He's safe. You have him."

It took a while for her to stop trembling. In truth, he was unsettled himself. It had been a narrow escape. If he'd left and relieved himself as well, if he'd not seen the leaves fall on the blanket and thought to move the babe... How would he have felt if he'd had to watch as his son was killed in front of his—

Rune stilled. Had he just thought of the little boy as his son? Yes. He had. And he was proud to have been there for him.

Eowyn lifted eyes shiny with unshed tears to him. "Thank you. You saved his life."

"I... I know." He had. His mother had given him life and he, his father, had just saved it. The three of them were now linked by an indefectible bond. They were a family.

From now on, nothing would be the same and they would have to find a way to deal with it.

"Let's go," he murmured.

"Yes."

As they rode on, Eowyn remained silent, mulling over what

had just happened. Rune had saved their son's life, not in a daring deed of bravery, not while defending him against people intent on hurting him but simply by acting as a responsible, attentive parent would. It seemed even more significant. For a man who doubted the paternity of the child, he was being extraordinarily considerate, toward both her and Little Rune. She steeled herself against the impulse to beg him to stay and take care of them for the rest of their lives.

He had hurt her deeply and she couldn't start weakening her resolve just because he had done what he should have done in the first place. She wouldn't make it too easy for him, even if she was starting to wonder whether she would manage to hold on to her resentment for much longer, or even if she should. He might be able to redeem himself more quickly than she had imagined. The man was impossibly compelling and had not put a foot wrong since he had gone to get Little Rune from Cwenhild's hut. Well, except for his ill-advised romp with Edith... But that had been foolish more than anything else, and nothing to do with her.

The memory of their fiery moments together made it harder for her to resist the appeal he exerted over her. She wanted him, there was no denying it. Her blood heated at his proximity, her breath hitched every time she set eyes on him, her heart started to drum whenever they touched.

As if that was not enough, she had glimpsed a vulnerable side to him during their time at the Norsemen village. And, of course, there had been the secret he had unwittingly revealed whilst drunk... This had been the *coup de grâce*. Had the man been all about arrogance and bluster as she'd first thought, she would not have found it too hard to keep him at bay and guard her feelings. Now she knew he harbored a painful secret and she couldn't help it; she wanted to know more, wanted to help if she could.

And now she owed him her son's life...

How was she going to bear the separation? It was best not to wonder. First they had to get home safely. That was the priority. In spite of the wind howling around them they made good time and reached the hut as the sun hit its zenith. On her lap, Little Rune was getting increasingly agitated.

"We arrived just in time, it would seem," Rune said, taking the crying baby from her while she dismounted. "He needs a feed. I can't say I blame the boy. I'm starving myself."

In her relief to be home, Eowyn couldn't help a smile at the comment. The man was constantly hungry and, for some reason, she found that endearing. "You're lucky Frigyth gave me some dried meat and oat cakes, for I fear I don't have much in the hut, save some honey and flour."

He grunted. "I'll get what I can from the vegetable patch while you feed the baby. I'm sure I will find something."

"Probably, but it will require cooking. The meat is ready now."

Not waiting for an answer, she entered the hut and settled herself on the furs.

Once her son had drunk his fill and fallen asleep, Eowyn stayed with him on the pallet, loath to let him out of her sight. She had almost lost him this morning. For a long moment she kept staring at him, fighting the tears wanting to escape her stinging eyes.

As odd as it was for someone who had taken precautions against falling pregnant for years, she had always wanted children. But she had also wanted a father with whom to raise them. That was why, considering what had happened to him later on, she was glad Freodheric had never gotten her with child during their time together. A year of lovemaking had failed to make her womb quicken. It might be that her friend had been barren, because the proof that she, at least, was not, was lying next to her. Or maybe they had just been lucky, there was no way of knowing. Either way, and even if Rune was set to leave soon, she wouldn't want things to be different. She was now mother to the most precious little boy and the idea of losing him was more than she could bear.

A moment later, Rune entered the house with a handful of onions and a chunk of cheese.

She arched a brow. "I know I planted onions but I don't remember sowing cheese seeds."

He gave a slanted smile. "I went to see Cat and Dog."

"Who?" She frowned. Then it came back to her. "Ah, yes. My neighbors, Gedla and Athelred. What did you do this time? Offer to straighten the walls of the hut?"

"Nothing so drastic. I said I would split their biggest logs for the fire this afternoon. Oh, and I also told them you needed sustenance as you were feeding a babe. Always worth appealing to a woman's sensibilities, I find. They cannot resist me."

No, unsurprisingly. "So the cheese is for me, not you?"

"Well... I was counting on your generosity. Perhaps you could share."

"Of course." It was then she realized she was famished as well. Now that they were all safe inside the hut, her body reminded her that she did indeed need sustenance. She left the pallet and sat in front of the feast Rune had assembled on the table. They ate in companionable silence.

"We will need to clean your wound," Rune told her once the food had gone, looking at her temple.

It did sting, even if she was not worried about it. "Is it very bad?" she asked, suddenly self-conscious. With her hair disheveled by the wind and her cheek crusted with blood, she would look a fright.

"Bad enough, even if it doesn't seem to be serious," Rune

grumbled. "But nothing should have come to mar the perfection of your face."

It could have sounded like a compliment destined to soften her up in his bid to earn her forgiveness, but she knew he was telling the truth. In that moment she was certain he thought her the most beautiful woman he had ever seen, blood or no blood.

"Do you think it will leave a scar?"

"I will tell you once we've cleaned it. Do you want me to—"

"No," she cut in. She didn't want to have him hovering over her, engulfing her in heat and wood scent and maleness. "I can clean it myself quite easily."

Rune glanced over to where Little Rune was sleeping and nodded. "You don't have a cot for him?" he asked, crossing his arms over his chest.

"No. When he was born my friend Cwenhild lent me hers, but she gave birth herself a month ago so she took it back. I haven't yet found another one but this seems to work fine." The baby was peacefully asleep, his little fists balled up. "And he spends most of the time by my side at night anyway. I like it that way."

"Mm." Rune didn't sound convinced but he didn't press her further. He stood up with decision. "I will go get some water at the well, so I can see to your wound."

Had he heard her refusal earlier? Probably. And then, in typical arrogant fashion, he had chosen to ignore her. She lacked the strength to refuse his offer a second time, because in reality she did want to have him hovering over her, engulfing her in heat and wood scent and maleness. Heart in her throat, Eowyn stayed where she was and waited for Rune's return.

It didn't take him long. All too soon, he was standing in front of her, a wet piece of cloth in hand.

"Tell me if it hurts, all right? And I will stop."

Dear God, how could it hurt? He was so tender she could

scarcely credit it. How could a man his size be so gentle? But right from the start the Norseman had surprised her. You expected him to crush you under his bulk when he lay over you, but she had never registered his weight when he'd bedded her. You feared his grip would leave a bruise but she had not seen a single mark on her skin in the morning after their night of passion. Rune was all about control.

Carefully, he kept wiping her face.

"I'm sure it must be clean now," she breathed. She had no way of checking but she could not have bled that profusely. Her dress wasn't even stained.

"Yes. It's clean." Still he didn't stop brushing her cheek.

"You can stop."

"I know."

"Thank you." He stopped. Eowyn placed a finger over the cut on her temple and before she knew it a tear slid down her cheek.

"Hush, Angel," Rune said gently. "He's safe. Nothing happened in the end."

How had he known she had been thinking about what could have happened to their son? "Yes, he's safe," she repeated. How would she have borne it if he hadn't been?

"I swear when I saw the branches fall next to him my heart stumbled." Stumbled. She couldn't help a smile at his mistake. "Is that not the correct word?"

"Well, no," she admitted. "But all the same, that's exactly what it felt like. My heart stumbled as well. Or tripped," she specified.

"Ah. I see."

This was one aspect of their conversations she enjoyed the most. She liked helping him improve his knowledge of her language, so much so that she often wanted to ask him to teach her a few words of Norse in return. But every time she thought she'd mustered the nerve to ask, she ended up backing down. For a reason she could not quite explain, it felt like a very intimate, personal thing to ask. She gazed into Rune's eyes. Blue, so blue. She looked at his hair, roaring fire, at his skin, pale cream, at his body, pure strength.

He was the opposite of her in every way, and yet he completed her, in the same way his body filled hers and her softness welcomed his hardness. Together, shadow and light, they had created the most perfect little boy.

With each passing day she could feel her resistance crumbling. He had asked what he could do to earn her forgiveness and she hadn't had any answer to give him. She had even been certain such a thing would prove impossible. And yet... He was doing everything right, without even trying.

Without extravagant gestures he proved he cared for Little Rune, even if he didn't believe him to be his son. The way he looked at her betrayed more than simple lust. He took care of her also, and even if he didn't trust her, he wanted her to be comfortable and safe. At this rate it wouldn't be long before she told him she had forgiven him for the hurt he'd caused her. And from then on there was no saying what she might do.

Or rather, she could guess all too easily.

Sharing her life with a man who took such great care of her and their son, who made her feel cherished by day and explode with pleasure at night would be a dream come true. The three of them were a family for all intents and purposes, they lived, ate, slept together, looked after each other. And if they behaved like a family... Didn't that mean they were one in truth?

Was she ready to face the implications of that? More importantly, was Rune? He had no intention of staying here and she didn't think it right to demand such a sacrifice from him. Why should he leave his life in Denmark behind? But how could he see his son grow from another country?

It was an unsolvable problem.

"Let us get you into bed," Rune decided, taking in the way Eowyn was swaying on her stool. It was still early but she had gone pale and dark circles shadowed her eyes. So much for ensuring the journey had not been too strenuous for her... "You look exhausted."

"I am." She shook her head. "But I'm not sure I will be able to sleep. I need something to drown the voices in my head, telling me I could have lost my son today."

He frowned. That wouldn't do. She had barely started to regain her strength. The last thing she needed was to lose more sleep while she fretted over what might have happened to Little Rune.

"Come here. You need to sleep." Without waiting for her agreement, he whisked her off her feet and brought her to the pallet, where he settled himself next to her. "Put your head against me," he instructed, drawing her into his arms. To his intense relief, she did not protest. Either she was too tired or she found his proximity as soothing as he found hers. He hoped it was the latter.

Once she was draped over him with her head pillowed against his chest he started to speak to her in Norse. She wanted to drown the voices in her head? He would do that for her, give her something to focus on instead, something that would lull her to sleep so she could stop thinking and get the rest she needed.

"Mm," Eowyn moaned, the sound causing Rune's groin to leap to life. He had anticipated this reaction so he didn't even bother to worry himself about it. By now she would have noticed he was hard more often than not when she was near. She would also have seen that he didn't act on it. "Yes, keep talking. I can feel your chest rumbling against my ear. It's... soothing."

Knowing she couldn't understand him, Rune opened his heart.

"Angel, I'm so sorry for everything I did wrong. I know you won't believe me but I truly am. And I have no idea how to prove it to you or earn your forgiveness for calling you a lying whore, forgiveness I'm not even sure I deserve. But I will find a way, if it's the last thing I do." He hesitated, then decided to tell her the whole truth. "And I thank you for the gift of my son. I had lost hope of ever holding a child of mine in my arms but now, thanks to you, I have known that joy."

By the time he had repeated the heartfelt words twice, Eowyn had fallen asleep.

CHAPTER SEVENTEEN

Eowyn woke up more rested than she had been in weeks. There was no prize guessing why she had slept so well. Rune had held her all night, only leaving her to get the baby when he needed feeding, then joining her back on the pallet once he'd cleaned him and rocked him back to sleep.

It had been wonderful.

But now she was embarrassed. Accepting that desire flared between them every time they were together was one thing, dealing with this kind of intimacy quite another. Rune was conveniently stirring the fire when she got up, which allowed her to avoid his gaze. She saw that he had brought in a selection of vegetables from the patch. Her stomach started to rumble at the sight. She seemed to be constantly hungry these days.

"I'll go to the well to get some water," she mumbled. "We will need it for the pottage. I won't be long."

Outside, the wind had stopped. It was a beautiful, sunny day, one of the last they would enjoy before autumn set in. Placed on the fence, in the sunshine to dry, was a row of immaculate clouts. Her embarrassment crept another notch. Rune had been doing everything while she slept, oblivious to her surroundings. Her thoughts went back to poor Cwenhild, whose husband Wulfric worked tirelessly to provide for his family but did not think it his responsibility to help with the babes in any way.

The more she came to know the magnetic Dane, the more she saw he was a man like no other.

The sound of wood splintering reached her when she approached the hut. What was happening now? Was someone fighting in there? She had only been gone a moment, surely Rune had not picked a fight with anyone? Or... She knew her house was not the sturdiest. Was the roof about to collapse? No, not again! Her son was inside! He had avoided getting hit by a branch the day before but if the whole hut fell in on itself, then even Rune's arms would not be enough to protect him.

Dropping her pitcher to the ground, Eowyn rushed to the door. Inside, she found Rune groaning on the floor amidst what appeared to be the remnants of her only chair. Of course, the hut was not falling to pieces, what a ninny she was for even thinking such a thing! Her chair had simply given out under the hulking man's weight. Before she knew what she was doing, she burst out laughing. Maybe it was the relief of knowing her son was safe, maybe it was just a normal reaction to the scene. She laughed until tears streaked down her cheeks.

"I'm all right," Rune grumbled. "Just in case you were wondering, you know."

"I'm sorry," she said in a gasp. "Only, for a moment I thought... I-I thought the house was falling down. Forgive me."

"No. Not the house. Just this rickety old chair, me and my sore rump."

Rump.

This time she didn't remonstrate. The word was oddly

comic applied to him. Then she pictured said rump naked, in all its muscular glory and her throat went dry.

"Yes," she breathed. "Just you."

Which was more than enough for one woman. More than enough for her.

"Are you going to help me or are you going to carry on laughing?"

"No, of course." She held out her hand. Rune took it with a side smile that gave her pause but before she could wonder at his intent, he had jerked her off her feet, forcing her to land on top of him.

"So you find it funny to be on the floor, do you, Angel?" he purred in her ear. Another jerk and she found herself flat on her back, caged under a huge Norseman. Dimly, she noticed that he had taken care to avoid all the pieces of wood scattered on the floor when rolling her over. Typical. Her heart melted at the same time as her body. "Tell me, do you feel like laughing now?"

No, she certainly didn't. Her whole body had gone liquid with anticipation. What did he mean to do? As if she didn't know... Something hard was poking at her thigh.

"Rune, please, don't do this," she whispered, her heart fluttering against her chest like a trapped bird.

"Do what?" He didn't move but his eyes, usually so blue, had gone almost dark.

"Use my body against me." She swallowed. There was no point in pretending she wasn't affected by his proximity. He knew all too well what he was doing, otherwise he would not be here on all fours, straddling her, overwhelming her with his masculine presence. "You know I want you. I won't be able to resist if you touch me. But it's not... It's not what I want, not really. Not when I am not sure I have forgiven you or where we could go from here."

Rune clenched his jaw. He had not expected her to be so

blunt, she could tell. But she had no other choice but to rely on him to protect herself because she could feel her body on the verge of surrendering and she knew she lacked the will to push him away.

A moment later he had yanked her back to her feet.

He was looming over her, a look of pained hunger on his face. It evidently cost him every ounce of self-control to respect her wishes. "I will go and see if I can repair that chair while you make the pottage. I think it's best if I leave the hut. Don't you?"

Yes, much better.

With a curt nod, he strode through the door.

"THE DAY IS TOO nice to be spent inside," Rune decided the following morning as they broke their fasts. To her relief, he was behaving as if nothing had happened the previous day, as if they had not nearly made love on the floor in a blaze of lust after having spent the night in each other's arms.

It was getting more and more difficult to behave as if they were not battling feelings that threatened to overwhelm them. That was why she seized his suggestion. If they were outside in full view of everyone, she might be able to better resist the urge to throw herself at him and beg him to stay here forever.

"What do you suggest we do?"

"There must be a river nearby."

"Yes, of course. Don't tell me you mean to build a boat to sail on it?"

"Mm, there's a thought..." Rune smiled. "But no. Building a boat is a grand enterprise, you know, it's not something you can impervise."

"You mean improvise." She smiled.

"Yes. It cannot be made in one day. And the most important

part happens even before you start. It is selecting the right wood, or rather, the right tree."

"The right tree?"

"Yes. To get the right planks, solid but pliable, hard but smooth. It's difficult to explain but just like a person's strength comes from within, each tree has a different... inside. Not all are equal. But you know when you see one that will give you what you need. You just know."

She swallowed hard. "I see."

She did see. Indeed you just knew when you met what you needed, especially if they were staring at you from their great looming height.

As soon as they had broken their fasts, they left. As he had the other day at the Norsemen village, Rune insisted on carrying Little Rune. She guessed he was only trying to spare her the discomfort of walking while holding a baby that was getting heavier by the day but she could not help but hope part of him was starting to accept that the little boy was his.

"You know, that is why I came here last summer," he told her as soon as they passed the last village house.

"What do you mean?" Lost in thought, she had no idea what he was referring to.

"Because I'm a boat builder. One of the boats I had built was to be used by the merchants to come here. I seized the opportunity to sail with them, to see how it fared in the high seas."

"Isn't the crossing over from Denmark dangerous?" She was surprised anyone would join such a hazardous expedition just to see how a boat handled the voyage.

Rune shrugged, as if it didn't matter if it was. "I suppose it could be, depending on the weather and the sailors' skill. But we cannot live our lives never doing anything that could be dangerous, can we? It would be dull beyond belief. I'm not even sure it is possible. Danger could be anywhere. A man in my village was so afraid of being attacked by strangers he surrounded himself with menacing hounds, and never left the village. What was the result, you might wonder? He died one day exiting his hut, when he slipped on his dogs', er..." He paused, as if to find the right word then shook his head, as if he could not. "Shit. He would have been better seeing the world, I think."

Well, now he'd told her. But as she happened to agree with him, she did not take offense. Besides, he was right. Disaster could strike anywhere. Hadn't his brother Björn died from eating his favorite food? Hadn't Little Rune almost died from being placed on a soft blanket?

She shivered and pushed the horrid thoughts from her mind. "Were you satisfied with the way the boat fared then?"

He threw her a smile that set her heart aflutter. "Very, as it confirmed what I had started to suspect."

"Which is?"

"That I'm the best boat builder in the country."

Eowyn burst out laughing. Really the arrogance of the man! That was what made his smile so blinding, she supposed, because he never doubted himself. "The best. Is that all?"

"The best," he confirmed without even slowing down.

Suddenly she didn't doubt it. No one would be his match. In any way. "Did you build the boat that brought you here this year as well?"

"No."

"Why did you come then?"

This time he did slow down, and looked at her intently. "I don't know. But when I was asked whether I wanted to join the expedition, I just said yes. It felt as if it was the only thing to do."

Her heart skipped a beat. Could she dare hope she had

something to do with his decision? The way Rune was looking at her certainly seemed to suggest it.

"You must now be wishing you had stayed behind."

He glanced at the child in his arms. There was such a depth of emotion swirling in his eyes that her chest constricted. "No. I don't."

After that they stopped talking. Soon they reached the river bank, and found a sunny spot next to a scattering of rocks. Eowyn lay on her stomach on the mossy ground, using her bent left arm as pillow. By her side, Little Rune was gurgling happily.

It was a perfect moment. The sun was warming her back and the babbling of the river soothed her mind. She could feel sleep creep over her, as her grandmother always used to say. It drew her in irresistibly.

"I'm falling asleep," she mumbled, surprised she should feel sleepy after the restful nights she'd had of late.

From his place on the boulder, Rune let out what sounded suspiciously like a chuckle. "So I can see. It's not a problem, you've earned your sleep. I'll make sure Little Rune doesn't disturb you, at least not until he's hungry. Then I won't be able to do anything."

She gave a lazy smile. Indeed. "I'm afraid it won't last long before he is."

"No. So you had better make the most of it." He walked over to her, and brushed a finger against her cheek. "Sleep, Angel. I'm here."

"WAKE UP, EOWYN."

A groan escaped Eowyn's mouth. Already! It felt as if she had been asleep a mere moment and she couldn't even hear any crying. But she knew Rune wouldn't have awoken her without reason. "Bring him here," she sighed, reaching out for her bodice.

A strong hand covered hers. "No. Don't."

He sounded adamant she should not bare her breast. What was going on? He usually didn't bat an eye when she uncovered herself. Was it because they were outside that he objected?

"Get up," he whispered, already helping her up to her feet. "Someone's coming."

The urgency in his voice cleared the remainder of the sleep from her mind. Someone was indeed coming their way. Three people to be exact, three men with a determined stride.

"Trouble?" she asked, giving Rune's hand a squeeze.

He didn't answer but his face hardened. It was clear he anticipated trouble. She glanced at Little Rune asleep at his feet. Rune had positioned himself in the best place to protect him. In that moment he looked like a wolf guarding his cub. She was certain that if he'd had fangs he would be baring them. No one was getting to her son.

Except... except Rune was on his own and there were three men.

She squared next to him. No, he was not on his own. She was here as well. Weren't she-wolves just as fierce as their male counterparts, especially when it came to defending their cubs? Yes, they were, and so was she. The three men would harm her child over her dead body. Of course they could just be people out for a stroll on a nice day.

That hope was dashed as soon as they opened their mouths.

"Well, look at this. It would seem that the Norseman thinks he can steal the best women from under our noses. For shame," the man tutted in her direction. "Don't you prefer to have one of your kind between your legs?"

"He looks like the Devil himself," another man piped. "Look at his hair!"

"Don't move, just ignore them. Stay next to me," Rune growled, his eyes not leaving the men.

Eowyn was trembling. This would end badly, she could tell. Then the third man, who was also the filthiest, spotted the baby, which was little wonder. Little Rune had woken up and was starting to squirm.

"Look at that, the Devil's spawn." He took a step forward, causing her to tense up and Rune to inhale sharply in warning. "What's the matter, wench? Don't you like real men? Come, let me fill your belly with hot Saxon seed. You'll feel the difference, I can promise you."

The moment Rune moved she knew that the man who'd just spoken would end up flat on his back, unconscious, just like Ecberg the other day. A heartbeat later she was proven right.

"Hey, that's my brother, you filthy dog!" the first man who'd spoken roared.

"Well, then you should teach him to mind his tongue."

"I will sooner send you back to where you belong."

A scream escaped Eowyn's lips when he launched himself at Rune. How was he going to get out of this? The Saxon was as tall as he was, built like a boulder and no doubt just as solid. This was bad enough, but he was also holding a dagger in his hand. She would have screamed in warning if at that moment the last man had not grabbed her by the waist.

"Seeing that Osmund is out of action," he rasped in her ear, "I will be the one showing you what Saxon men can do."

"Rape women, you mean?" she spat.

"A feisty one, hey? Even better. I like a good fight."

Oh, he would get one, she would make sure of that.

Eowyn crouched down and closed her fingers on the gravel and sand at her feet, grabbing a handful. She wasn't as strong as the man or as skilled as Rune in getting rid of her opponent but she liked to think she was resourceful and determined and she was not going to just stand there and wait to be raped.

With a cry of outrage she threw the dirt into the man's face. Momentarily blinded, he flinched. "I'll make you pay for that, you'll see if I don't!"

Before he could straighten back up she kicked him straight in the knee, sending him reeling backward. He tripped on a root and fell flat on his back. A heartbeat later, having disposed of his opponent, Rune was straddling him, pressing one strong forearm against his throat.

"You want to see what Norsemen can do now?" he growled, his voice dripping with ice. "Or have you had enough with being shown what Saxon women can do?"

With his throat being squashed, the man could only utter a garbled sound. Before Rune decided the answer was not to his satisfaction, Eowyn placed a hand on his shoulder. "Don't kill him," she whispered.

"Why not?"

She wasn't sure what to say to that. Why was she even taking the defense of the man who would have raped her? Maybe because he had not touched her, in the end. "Please," was all she said.

Rune grunted and seemed to release the pressure marginally. He was still glaring at the man, though. Lowering his face to him, he spoke, each word laced with menace. "Now. Your friends will take a while to wake up, I imagine, so I suggest you do not wait for them and you disappear from my sight before I decide that I have been too kind with you."

The man didn't need to be told twice. He scrambled to his feet and fled without a glance at his brother or his friend.

Finally, Rune got up and turned to face her. His eyes were burning with a low fire. "Are you all right, Angel? He didn't touch you?"

"No. He didn't have chance," she replied fiercely.

"Yes, I saw what you did. You did ever so well defending yourself." A gentle hand came to cradle her cheek. "You're a marvel, you know that? Strong and brave, like no woman I've ever seen."

"I..." Her throat was dry. There was so much intent in the blue eyes she could barely breathe. "I need to feed Rune." Fully awake, starving, the baby was crying at the top of his lungs. "I cannot bear to hear his distress."

"Me neither."

Rune was not lying. There was something visceral about the need to bring the child comfort. Of course, he could not see to his needs in the same way his mother could, but that didn't mean he found it easy to deal with it. He glanced at Eowyn's breasts and gritted his teeth. He had to get her somewhere else before she opened her bodice. "Let's go to the forest. I don't want the men to wake up while you feed him."

And see you.

He didn't finish the sentence but she nodded as if she understood what he meant, and agreed wholeheartedly. "I don't want to be ogled by those vile men."

Cradling Little Rune against her chest she followed him to the cover of the trees. The baby obliged them by drinking his fill as fast as he'd ever done. As soon as he had finished they set off for the hut.

Only once the door was closed behind them was Rune able to relax. Then he heard Eowyn cry out. His heartbeat instantly picked up. What now? Just when he had started to think they were safe...

"What is it?" Had she spotted a threat through the window? Had the two men woken up and followed them home? Had she discovered that Little Rune was hurt? All sorts of possibilities, each more disturbing that the last, flashed through his mind.

"But you...You're bleeding!" she cried out. "You've been cut! Why didn't you tell me?"

He looked to his left thigh where there was indeed a cut inflicted by the Saxon's blade. Focused on getting Eowyn and Little Rune to safety, he had failed to notice it.

"I'm all right," he said gruffly. "It's nothing, just a skin wound."

"It's *not*! And you mean a flesh wound."

He smiled. Apparently she was not so upset that she forgot to teach him her language. Another woman might have swooned at the sight of blood. Not his Angel. She still remembered to share what she knew with him.

"It's a scratch, nothing more, I will just clean it. There will be no need to knit it," he added, unable to resist the temptation.

"Stitch it you mean," she answered, just as he had hoped. "I don't think—"

"I do. Stop fretting." He placed both his hands over her shoulders and looked at her straight in the eye. "Angel, I'm so sorry. Please forgive me."

"Whatever for?"

He ran a hand through his hair. "Going to the river was a stupid idea. I should never have taken you to there. I placed you and the babe in danger."

Under his palms he felt Eowyn stiffen. "Listen to me, you did nothing wrong. Why should you not have taken us to the river?" She flared up with an anger he knew was not directed at him and that warmed his chest. "It wasn't a stupid idea, it was kind of you to suggest we enjoyed the sunshine in a beautiful spot. It wasn't your fault those vile men targeted us. Why shouldn't you be able to walk around without being insulted? Why should they think they have the right to rape me just because they don't like who I take to my bed? Why should my son be called a spawn of the Devil just because he has red hair?"

This only made him feel worse. Her son was only being called the Devil's spawn because of the way he looked, and the way he looked was all down to him. Had she had a child with a Saxon, her baby would not be singled out for his red hair, and she wouldn't be mocked for opening her legs to a Norseman.

It was just like it had been for her mother.

Eowyn didn't say anything but he knew this would be playing through her mind as well. Her and Little Rune's coloring made it obvious that their respective fathers was not someone the Saxons deemed acceptable. Would Eowyn end up like her mother, unable to deal with it all, and take her own life? No, surely not. They weren't even sure that was what had happened to the woman. Besides, his Angel was too strong, too brave, she loved her son too much to abandon him.

"I'm so sorry," he said, clenching his fists. He had not only left her alone to deal with a newborn child, he had placed her in a position to be mocked for her choice of lover and in danger of being shown what 'Saxons were capable of,' to quote the words of the bastards who had wanted to assault her.

"You have nothing to worry about, do you hear?" Eowyn said, coming closer to Rune. She could not bear to see him feel guilt over what had happened. "It's those men who should be sorry. I hope the way you dealt with them will teach them a lesson."

"You and I both. Gravel. So simple. You are one amazing woman, you know that? Brave, strong, unashamed of your needs and feelings." He lowered his head to her, his eyes ablaze. "I feel humbled next to you."

Humbled? The change of mood took her by surprise. A moment ago Rune had been about to kiss her and now he was baring his soul to her. Besides, humble was possibly the last word she would have chosen to describe Rune. Apart from repulsive, maybe...

"What do you mean?"

"You never shied away from your feelings from a very young age, going to Freodheric, living your life the way you wanted at the risk of being mocked or even hurt for it."

"Well... I don't know if that makes me brave exactly."

"It does, because it shows you were not afraid to be yourself, even as a child."

"And you were?" She found that hard to believe from the master of confidence.

He hesitated and she knew he was about to confide something he was not proud of. "I told you about the gang of boys in the village." She nodded. "I thought that being the youngest, rather small and thin, exempted me from doing what was right, provided me with the perfect excuse not to take responsibility for my actions. So instead of standing up for what I believed in, I followed their orders. To protect myself, I allowed others to suffer at their hands."

Suffer. Eowyn's heart started to beat faster. Surely he was not saying... "You didn't—"

"No," Rune cut in. "We never killed, or even seriously injured anyone. But that doesn't mean we didn't hurt people. I did everything the wrong way around at that time. I pretended to be a man to please the boys when secretly I was happy to be just a child. All the while I resented being coddled by my parents, when I should have been grateful for their love. It was all stupid and I regret it now."

She was touched that he would open up about something so personal, and reveal a side of him he was not proud of. She placed a hand on his forearm, thinking he was being too hard on himself. He'd been just a child.

"You did what you needed to avoid being hurt, there's no shame in that."

"But there is, and you know it." He ran a hand across his bearded jaw. "One of the people we teased was Sigurd."

"Frigyth's husband?" Eowyn did not try to hide her surprise. But after all, she knew he was a Dane and it was clear from his accent that her friend's husband had not spent his childhood here. Still, it seemed an odd coincidence that the two men should know each other. "You grew up with him?"

Rune sighed. "He's a few years older than me but yes. He was an orphan, living alone in the woods behind the village. We called him Beast. Of course now I see how appalling that was, mocking a lonely child thus when we should have befriended him." He shook his head. "So you see, I cannot help but being impressed by you and your honesty. You were never afraid to act as you truly wanted, all the while knowing it could land you into trouble, while I tried to win people's approval by doing things I'm ashamed of now."

Eowyn's chest felt impossibly tight. The air between them seemed thicker, hotter. Of its own accord she could feel her body edging toward Rune. He thought she was brave enough to act as she wanted, but she wasn't so sure. If she had been, she would be in his arms right now, and to hell with the consequences.

"Don't be ashamed of who you are," she whispered in his ear. "You're not half as bad as you seem to think. If *I* can see it, it must be true."

Rune cleared his throat. "I have something to finish. Will you be all right on your own in the hut a moment? I won't be far."

"Of course." Though she would have liked him to stay, she guessed he was trying to do the right thing by her. She had seen the desire flaring in his eyes and appreciated his efforts to hide it from her.

He was doing what she'd asked, and though in this moment

she wasn't sure it was what she wanted anymore, she could only try and help him.

As soon as he was gone she applied herself to the task of making bread. She needed something to occupy her hands, so as to stop them from ripping at a certain Norseman's clothes. It barely worked, but at least that evening she had a veritable feast prepared, which was just as well because she expected Rune to be famished, as usual. Just as she was wondering whether she should go hunt for him, he walked back inside the hut.

"We are ready to eat," she told him, trying not to focus on the fact that he had rolled his shirt sleeves to the elbow. Right now she was contemplating taking a bite from his strong, muscular arms.

"So I see. It smells wonderful in here." His gaze landed on the table. "I'm starving."

She couldn't help a smile. "When are you not?"

"Mm, when I've just eaten, maybe?" He twisted his lips in consideration. "Come. I have something to show you."

Before she could say anything, he took her by the hand to lead her outside. It was such a spontaneous, almost childish gesture, that her heart—well, her heart stumbled rather than tripped.

On the bench was an object she had never seen before.

She recognized the carving on what was now the head board of a cot. Two days ago it had been on the back of her only chair. "Is it what I think it is?" she asked, her voice full of awe.

"Yes. As soon as I started to rebuild the chair I saw that it would never be sturdy enough, not for a man like me anyway. It was shocking workmanship, really. But at least it gave me most of the wood I needed to make a cot." He rubbed the back of his neck like a man in prey to doubt. "I hope you don't mind. I will make you another chair to replace the broken one, I swear. You have three stools anyway so I though you would not—"

"Rune." She stopped him with a hand over his arm. His naked arm. The skin was warm, the muscles underneath hard as steel. She almost groaned out loud. "I love it. And I thank you for the thought. And the beautiful cot. And..."

And the rest.

Most of all the rest. Had he realized what he'd said? He wanted to ensure there was a chair sturdy enough to hold his weight in the hut. Why would he need that if he didn't mean to stay with her, at least for a while?

He had heard her say she hadn't had time to see about a cot the other day and had set about rectifying the situation without her having to ask anything.

"Thank you," she repeated, moved to tears.

"It's not a problem. Now let's go eat," Rune said in a rasp. "I'm ravenous."

CHAPTER EIGHTEEN

"Tell me about the day Rune was born."

Dawn was near and in the firepit, the fire had dwindled to a few embers. The baby was settled against Eowyn's breast, feeding greedily, as was he was wont to do. Rune had just changed his dirty clout and gone outside to rinse it out, as had become his habit. Eowyn could have cried at the matter-of-fact manner he was taking charge of even the most unpleasant tasks night after night. The contrast with his behavior during the first few days, when he didn't even dare glance at the babe, was hard to believe.

She didn't doubt anymore that he had come to care for his son, and she was certain that that he'd realized it himself. Only the other day by the river he had looked like a man ready to kill to defend Little Rune—and her. Then he had made a cot for him. Earlier he had brought her a cup of ale, arguing she could only be thirsty after feeding a babe.

As she drank the ale gratefully, she wondered what all that meant for the future? They could never be a family, what with them living so far apart. So did he mean to stay for a few months instead of leaving in a few days? But was that a good idea? Wouldn't it make the final parting even worse?

She pushed the questions out of her mind. For now, she would tell Rune what he wanted to know.

"He was born just before spring, at the end of an exceptionally cold winter. It had been snowing the day before. When my pains started I found the door of the hut blocked by snow. I didn't have the strength to dig my way out and go to the midwife."

"By the gods! You gave birth to him all alone here, in the cold?" Rune was appalled.

Eowyn gave a small smile. "Well, what choice did I have? He was ready to be born, there was no stopping him. It was slow, agonizing, but eventually he came out, so small, so beautiful, so... perfect. I could not believe it. I spent the first few days staring at him, unable to comprehend how I could have made such a perfect child. I still look at him at night, when he sleeps next to me, and wonder at such a miracle." She ran a light finger over the baby's cheek. "He's the most precious little boy I've ever seen."

There was a silence. Then Rune knelt down by her.

"I'm sorry you had to go through all this on your own. It shouldn't have happened that way."

"I'm not sorry. I can't imagine my life without him."

"No. It's obvious you two belong together."

Little Rune had finished feeding and was asleep against her, his downy cheek pillowed against her naked breast. She never thought of covering herself when she was in Rune's presence. He had a way of making her feel at ease. After a while, though, all the ale she had drunk started to play havoc with her.

"I need a moment outside," she said, covering herself again.

Rune nodded and helped her up. When she came back in the hut, she didn't feel like going back to sleep. The sun had pierced the horizon and gold light was streaming in through the window. A new day was dawning. It would be glorious. But Rune looked sombre.

"What is it?" Eowyn breathed.

"I thank you for saying you don't regret falling with a child you never wanted, despite the circumstances of his birth."

"I don't regret it, even if my body's different now. This I didn't see coming, I will admit."

Rune crossed his arms over his chest in a gesture that had become familiar as he allowed his gaze to wander over her. "How do you mean?"

"It's..." She glanced down at herself and blushed in embarrassment. Why had she even mentioned it? Because she was a fool, that was why. The expression on Rune's face, however, made it clear she had better answer his question. "Well, there are scars and lines on my hips and stomach. I'm not sure they will ever fade away. It's not very—"

Before she could finish her sentence, he kissed her. Or rather, he put his mouth over hers. This was no fiery prelude to lovemaking, and all the more inexplicable for it.

"What was that for?" she asked, feeling rather dazed. As swift and chaste as the kiss had been, it had quite overwhelmed her.

Rune shrugged, as if the reason for the move was quite obvious to him. "I had to stop you as I didn't like where that sentence was going. Besides, if you must know, your new figure is rather an improvement. Not that there was any problem before. You are every man's dream, have always been."

One heated glance at her breasts made her blush. She had noticed men did not seem to mind her new fullness. Ecberg had even told her as much the other day. "I was not talking about these," she murmured. "But rather my thighs, my hips. They—"

"Eowyn. Are you trying to make me kiss you again?" Rune

chided, raising her chin with a crooked finger. "I wouldn't mind if you were. I could kiss you all day."

"N-no, I wasn't." Or was she? She couldn't think straight with his mouth hovering over hers and his body so close.

"Then I suggest you stop talking about your thighs and hips. Or is that a trick to have me lift your skirts so I could have a good look at them and tell you what I see? I will do it, if that's what you want." His eyes darkened. "But I have to warn you. I won't stop there. If I lift your skirts, I will end up burying my face between your legs and devouring you."

Dear Heavens. Only a moment ago they had been talking about the way pregnancy had changed her body. How had they ended up talking about him devouring her? How could he say such shocking things out loud? And how did she like it so much? It made no sense.

"It's fine," she managed to say.

"So we are agreed. You have nothing to worry about. You are more beautiful than ever."

Well. That was precisely the opposite of what she had been trying to say, but she could not point that out, at the risk of finding herself flat on her back, with her skirts bunched up around her waist and Rune's wicked mouth at her core making her regret her words and dissolve in ecstasy.

That could not be allowed to happen until matters were clarified between them, no matter how much she wanted it, because it would change everything, so there was no other choice but to pretend to agree. She nodded.

"I promise I have no idea what Albert means to do by pretending he is the father of my child and spreading the word that we are to marry. It simply isn't true. I told you, we barely know each other and he never even alluded to his intent before leaving the village. I swear it is the truth. Please, you have to believe me."

She stared at Rune as the words exploded out of her mouth. She hadn't meant to tell him that, had resolved never to beg. He would have to choose to believe her without any help or explanation from her. But things had evolved between them since their awful argument, and he had just kissed her, told her he thought her beautiful. And after what she'd heard the other night she couldn't bear for him to think she had willingly led him on.

...not my seed... can't lose another child...

Rune pinched the bridge of his nose like a man in pain. She could tell he was loath to discuss Albert. But they had to, they had skirted around the matter for too long. Suddenly she wanted him to know the truth, so he could begin to trust her. She needed them to move past that obstacle, so they could start thinking about the future in earnest.

"There is something wrong with him," she started explaining. "That is why I only bedded him once, his attitude seemed odd even at the time. It's difficult to explain but I think he suffers from delusion. I know you are going to think I'm only trying to—"

"No, I'm not," he cut in, eyes piercing. "I believe you. He acted too odd for a man supposedly promised to you, too disinterested. When I said you weren't at home he didn't insist, when he saw I was half naked and in your garden he did not ask who I was or what I was doing here. He should have taken exception to it at the very least, but he kept giggling. And there was this strange emptiness in his eyes."

She nodded. Seeing that he finally believed her was a relief. "As I said, it is impossible I could carry his child anyway." Heat invaded her cheeks. Rune would not like being reminded of what she and Albert had done together, but he needed to know everything. "Not only because of... what we did, but because I made sure I would not fall pregnant."

"How do you mean?" His voice was gruff, but at least he seemed prepared to listen to her.

"You can imagine that for a woman in my situation, avoiding pregnancy was paramount. I didn't want to end up with dozens of children by different fathers so I took plants to ensure I wouldn't fall with child. For years and years, it worked."

There was a pause.

"But if that was the case, how did you fall pregnant with Little Rune?"

Eowyn gave a little smile. She'd guessed he would ask her the question next. Rune was anything but stupid. "I fell with your child because a few weeks before we met, I had stopped taking the plants I took to try and prevent conception."

"Why?"

She shrugged. "Everything was starting to unravel. I had thought I could live the life I wanted, indulge my senses, and for a while it worked. Then word about my ways started to spread and things quickly became uncomfortable." She stared at her hands. "I had wanted pleasure, and I got it. I regret nothing, I just didn't expect to have to pay such a high price for it."

"Price?"

"At first I was the one to choose who I bedded and when. After a while that freedom disappeared. You saw for yourself that men like Ecberg took it for granted that I would welcome them back without question. That might be understandable, since I had welcomed them in my bed once, but then others I had never met before started to make lewd propositions to me."

"Is making lewd propositions the only thing they did?" Rune asked in a growl.

Eowyn gave a little smile. "Yes. I am not quite the helpless female, I am not above kicking and biting when need be."

"Mm, no, or throwing dirt in people's face." His eyes softened. "You are quite a resourceful, fierce woman, Angel."

"Thank you. Still, it quickly became clear I was fighting a losing battle and would end up getting hurt if I didn't amend my ways. The next man to come knocking on my door might not be so easily deterred. So I decided to stop bedding men, at least for a while, to see if it helped calm things down."

There was another pause. When Rune opened his mouth, she had already guessed what he would ask her.

"Why... Why did you have me that night if you'd decided not to bed men anymore?"

She bit her bottom lip. "Because I couldn't *not* have you. As soon as I saw you, my wretched blood came roaring to the surface. I wanted you more than I had wanted any man. And I thought... Well. You said that you were only here for a few days. I thought I would never see you again. You would not be back a few weeks later, demanding more, or spreading word about my wild ways, at least not here. I thought I didn't have anything to lose."

Rune rubbed a hand over his face, feeling utterly ashamed of himself. "But I did come back, assuming you would welcome me in your bed without question, and I did demand more."

He remembered his words to her clearly, his appalling, appalling words.

I've got an itch to scratch.

How was that better than Ecberg saying his balls were full to the brim? It wasn't. No wonder she had sent him away with a lie about his smell that day. In fact she had been surprisingly measured. She should have hit him in the groin.

"I did everything wrong with you, didn't I? From the very start."

He'd gone to her because he'd heard from Leif that she was ripe for the taking and he'd wanted to see it for himself, he'd made her with child during a night where he had indulged his senses selfishly, and left her to deal with it on her own. He'd then come back with his manhood erect and the swagger of a victor, talking about his masculine urges, all the while knowing it would not lead to anything, knowing that he would bed her and leave her once again. When a deluded fool had claimed to be her betrothed he had not given her the benefit of the doubt, he'd accused her of lying, of being little more than a whore, and he'd left.

How could she even bear the sight of him after all that?

"I know I overreacted to Albert's declaration. It is no excuse, but I was too shocked, too hurt to react otherwise when he claimed to be your baby's father."

"Hurt?" She didn't sound angry, rather hopeful, as if she had been waiting to hear he'd had a good reason all along.

He did. At least, he thought he did.

Taking in a deep breath, he decided to be honest. She already knew about his childhood in the gang of boys, but she deserved to know the whole truth, needed to know what had happened afterward and why he'd reacted the way he had.

"Little Rune was the third child to be taken away from me."

Eowyn instantly started to protest. "He's not been taken aw—"

He stopped her with a raised hand. "Please. This is not going to be easy but I want to be honest with you."

He had asked what he could do to make her forgive him. Well, this was one of the answers, he was suddenly sure of it. Bare his soul and make her understand why he had been so harsh toward her. It might not excuse anything, but he knew Eowyn well enough by now to know she would appreciate being told the truth and take his honesty into consideration when she judged his behavior.

She nodded, indicating she would listen without interrupting.

He started to pace around the hut to gather his courage.

"A few years ago I got involved with a woman who was new to my village. It was the first time anyone had managed to hold my attention for more than a couple of days. I had overgrown my rebellious phase and had started to choose my lovers more carefully. Astrid and I spent the whole summer together and at the end of it she announced she was with child. I was overjoyed."

Eowyn's whole body went cold. There was such bitterness in Rune's voice she knew the story would have a terrible ending. Had the woman died in childbirth? She had been terrified this would happen to her the day Little Rune was born and unfortunately it was all too common.

"What happened?" she asked when he stayed silent.

Rune stopped his prowling and came to plant himself in front of her.

"She lied. She had asked around about me and got it into her head that I was about to abandon her, not an unreasonable assumption given what she would have been told about my past behavior, I will admit." He shook his head as if regretting not having been able to reassure the woman. "For months she made me believe I would be a father, finding excuses not to be with me when she bled. I saw nothing, but obviously after a while it became impossible not to notice that her body wasn't changing. One night I asked her questions. She confessed everything and made it appear as if it was my fault she was not yet with child."

He stopped. Eowyn placed a hand on his forearm.

"I'm sorry." She could not imagine the pain of hearing such a betrayal, of having your hopes crushed, of being denied a child you had started to love. Now she knew who he had been thinking of when he had wanted to spare Magnus the pain of betrayal.

"After that I did leave her. I could not be with someone who had lied to me thus, hurt me thus. Because...Well, I had been looking forward to the little babe I thought would be mine in the spring."

Of course he would have. Eowyn waited, heart thumping hard. Rune had mentioned another baby... What other loss had he suffered?

"After a while I met another woman who managed to make me believe it was possible to trust again. A few weeks after we first slept together she came to me crying, saying she had missed her courses. At first I was dubious, as you can imagine, but her attitude was so different to Astrid's that I gave her the benefit of the doubt. She seemed worried I wouldn't stand by her rather than proud to have captured me, if that makes sense. When she started to be sick in the mornings I had no choice but to believe her. Soon, her stomach started to swell. I found myself hoping once more, and happy. But once again, it was not to be." Rune clenched his fists. "She miscarried the babe in the fifth month, and..."

An immense cold invaded Eowyn when his voice trailed. "She died herself?"

Slowly he shook his head. "No, but it was a close thing. She refused to see me when I went to see her. The midwife who tended to her told her she might never be able to bear children again after the ordeal she had suffered. I think she did not want to be a burden to me." He braced his arms on the wall, bracketing the window. "Whatever her reasons, once she had recovered her strength, she disappeared. I could never find out what happened to her. Like with your mother, I often wonder if she didn't take her own life."

"Oh, Rune, I'm so sorry." Such heartache!

"It killed me, both times, and it killed my parents, both times." He spoke in a voice full of anguish, his back still to her. "That is why when Albert claimed to be the father of the little boy I had come to see as mine, I didn't stop to think. I left before

I could get any more hurt. We had just made love that day and I knew I was getting attached not only to the little boy but to you as well, you who had lied to me and led me on a merry chase, just like Astrid. Or... so I thought. I hope you understand. Not forgive, but understand at least."

She did, because it all made sense now.

He'd reacted the only way he could have, he'd wanted to protect himself. Animals in pain lash out, she had seen it many times. Rune had done the same, reacted on instinct. He had not paused to think but how could he have done otherwise? Who in their right mind would lie so blithely about being the father of a child? He would have had no reason to doubt Albert's word, especially after having seen Ecberg coming on to her and hearing about her life. He'd known she'd had numerous lovers. Having been betrayed once by a woman he'd trusted and perhaps even loved, he had been more than ready to believe another capable of the same treachery.

He had not given her the benefit of the doubt, it was true, but she was not exempt of all fault either. She hadn't stopped to think there was something odd in his reaction or tried to see things from his point of view. Of course he would have been devastated to be told that a child he had come to love would never be his! She might have reacted the same way in his place. If anything, it proved how attached he'd become to the little boy. If he'd not cared a fig, he would simply have accepted Albert's claim that Little Rune was his and left without asking himself any questions.

"I'm so sorry."

Hearing the tears in Eowyn's voice Rune turned to face her. She was crying. For him. He couldn't bear it.

He placed a hand on her cheek. "Look at me, Angel. I'm the one who is sorry. I made you pay for the betrayal of a woman you don't even know and the pain I'd been through before we met when I should have listened to you, given you the benefit of the doubt at least. It won't happen again, I swear."

Suddenly everything was clear in his mind. It might have been clear from the start, only he'd wilfully ignored it, too scared by the implications.

He was not scared anymore.

"Tomorrow I will go to the port."

"The port?" Eowyn froze and he cursed himself for his bluntness. She thought he was sailing back to Denmark, she thought he was leaving her, unable to deal with it all.

He was not. Quite the contrary.

"I'm going to tell Sven I won't be on the boat when it leaves. I will be staying here if you will have me."

"You..."

She evidently didn't know what to say and in truth he wasn't sure what he was offering either. Except he knew they could not work anything out between them if he left for Denmark. He had to take that first, necessary step to show her he was ready to make a sacrifice for her and their son.

Yes, their son. He had a son to love and protect now, and a woman he wanted above all others. He would not make anymore mistakes where they were concerned. He was going to stay, he was going to fight for this family. And this time, he would win.

"I'll be staying, and I'll do whatever I can to persuade you that I mean to look after you and Rune."

Eowyn didn't answer, she seemed utterly at a loss by this reversal of their situation, as well she might be. Only a few days ago he'd told her he had only come back to her because Sigurd had forced him.

He set off for the forest, knowing there was one thing he could do to make her believe him. For that, he needed a piece of wood.

CHAPTER NINETEEN

I n the morning, Rune left.

Unable to stay in the hut while he got ready, Eowyn went to the vegetable patch. Fortunately for her, weeds had flourished in the last few weeks, ensuring she had enough work to keep her hands, if not her mind, busy. She went down on all fours, remembering how Rune had found her weeding the day he had come back. Here she was today, weeding again, when he was leaving. They had gone full circle.

Whatever happened next would have to be new.

He came to find her a moment later, a bag slung over his shoulder. Her heart skipped a beat. Why was he taking his belongings with him if he intended to stay here? He'd said he would only go to speak to his friend Sven to tell him of his intention to stay in East Anglia.

"Have you—"

"I will be back," he assured her when he saw her eyeing the bag warily. "I promise. This contains presents I sculpted for my parents. Sven will inform them of my decision to stay behind and tell them about Little Rune."

Something in his eyes dimmed and Eowyn's chest squeezed

at the same time. He was choosing his new family over his old one. Her and Little Rune's gain would be his parents' loss. "They will be devastated," she said in a breath. Not only would they feel as if they had lost their last surviving child but they would be denied the chance to meet the grandson they had hankered after for so long.

"Yes, they will be sad." Rune did not try to pretend otherwise. "But I know they want what's best for me. And after all, there is nothing preventing me from visiting from time to time."

She nodded, unsure what to say. He was giving up so much, all without any assurance of anything. Could she be so selfish? Should she not tell him to leave? Could she bear to watch him go?

Rune straightened to his full height. His decision was made. Nothing she would say would change a thing now. "I will be back. Tonight if I can locate Sven immediately, but most probably tomorrow. Will you be all right on your own until then?"

She gave a wan smile. "I managed for a whole year without you, you know. I'm sure I can survive one night."

"Of course." He hesitated. "If anyone comes sniffing around for—"

"I will kick them in the groin, I promise, and tell them they stink for good measure."

"As long as you do. And then when I come back you tell me who they are and *I* will deal with them. Never fear."

She could not help another smile. "Thank you. And, Rune... I promise you I will do some thinking of my own while you're gone."

It was only fair she would have an answer for him regarding their future when he came back. He was giving up so much for her and Little Rune without any guarantees, she could not leave him dangling for months, while he awaited her decision. He nodded, as if he understood all she was not saying and was grateful for it.

"I'll go then."

"Yes."

He didn't move a muscle. She could tell he wanted to kiss her but didn't dare take the liberty. In the end she was the one who lifted her head to him. The kiss was brief, but felt like a goodbye.

When she saw his tall silhouette disappear through the trees Eowyn knew a moment of panic. What if this was the last time she saw him? What if he had lied to her and he didn't intend to come back? What if Sven's boat left today for Denmark, with Rune on board?

No. She forced herself to be rational. If he'd meant to abandon her, he wouldn't have opened up about his painful past, he wouldn't have tried to reassure her, he would simply have vanished during the night, while she slept. She was getting herself all bothered for nothing. This was not good bye, it was the space they needed to think clearly and decide what they wanted.

She would get back into the hut, eat something and try to calm down. Tonight or tomorrow at the latest, Rune would be back, as promised. And then they would talk.

Her heart stopped as soon as she opened the door.

On the table was a little sculpted figurine. A man. A Norseman, as evidenced from his beard and braided hair. Although the wood was of a uniform, rich brown color, she knew the hair was meant to be red. Devil red.

It was Rune, his height and shape perfect to compliment her woman doll, the doll she had always seen herself as.

At his feet were a handful of what looked like wooden beans. Upon closer inspection Eowyn saw that tiny faces had been carved at one end. They were not beans but swaddled newborn babies.

He had replaced the little doll's original partner with himself, and added children, transforming the couple into a family.

Eowyn fell onto her stool and started crying. The wretched, wretched man! He had found out how to show he was sorry and earn her forgiveness after all... She should have known from the start she was fighting a losing battle. He had decided to stay behind without any guarantee she would ever accept him into her life, what else did she want? What else did he have to do for her to see that this man, if she let him, could give her all she needed?

Well, she would stop being so stupid right now. She had promised Rune she would do some thinking while he was gone. She had done better than that, she had taken a decision. The right decision. Tomorrow he would be back and as soon as he walked through the door, she would throw herself into his arms and tell him she—

"Eowyn!"

The voice calling through the door almost caused her to drop the figurine. Rune? Was he back already? Her heart leapt in her chest and she chided herself. Of course it wasn't him. He did not have a woman's voice. She slipped the doll man and his babies into her pocket.

"Cwenhild, heavens, you made me jump!" she chided, opening the door.

"You have to leave! You have to hide." Her friend rushed in, not returning the greeting. Eowyn frowned. Hide? Why? "Rune..."

Her heart missed a beat at the name. "Which one?"

For a moment her friend stared at her in incomprehension, as if she could not believe she would even ask the question. But perhaps she didn't know the tall Norseman's name. "Er... Your son?"

"What about him?" Cwenhild's agitation was staring to worry Eowyn.

"I went to the market in town this morning and I overheard three men talking together, saying to whoever would listen that they knew of a dark-haired Saxon woman who had consorted with the Devil and had borne him a child." Cwenhild shook her head. "By the time I left, a sizeable crowd had assembled around them and the grumbling had grown louder."

Three men. Three men looking for revenge for the attack by the river, no doubt. For days she had feared this would happen. After the humiliation they had suffered, the Saxons would want revenge on her and Rune. If the men were spreading word about her son being a 'spawn of the Devil', then there was no telling what they would do if they got their hands on him. Only one thing was sure, it would be awful, and she would do all that was in her power not to let it happen. She didn't think they knew where she lived, but if they started where they met the other day it wouldn't take them long to find her. There weren't many dark-haired women living with ginger Norsemen around. If they were assembling a mob to get to them, they would be here soon enough.

There was no time to lose.

"You have to help me," Eowyn told Cwenhild urgently. They would have to make it appear as if her son had never existed in case people came sniffing around. Of course the ruse would only delay proceedings, but she didn't see what else she could do and anyway, soon Rune would be back. He would help her.

Perhaps they could flee together and find a new place to live...

Forcing herself to focus on the moment, she assembled all

her son's clothing and stuffed them into the cot Rune had made the other day.

Then she looked around in despair. Where would she go? Not to the Norsemen village, as that was the first place the mob might look for a red-haired giant, not to the forest, which was too dangerous for a woman on her own, not—

Cwenhild placed a hand on her arm. "Give me the babe. I will go to my sister's in the next village with him. I can feed him and keep him out of the way until you find a solution."

Yes, it was the perfect idea. Except... "Are you sure? It's a risk. If they find you with—"

"I'm sure. I will keep his hair covered with a hat, and no one will know he's not who I say he is. Why would anyone visit my sister's house anyway? She has never even met you. No one will make the connection between you two."

"Thank you." Eowyn squeezed her friend's hand. "I don't know how to—"

"We can discuss that later. For now we need to go."

"Yes. Take the cot. I will carry Rune."

Heart in her throat, Eowyn lifted her son into her arms. Being parted from him would be excruciating, but there was no other choice. She had to put his safety above everything else.

LATER THAT AFTERNOON Eowyn watched through the window as three men approached the hut. There it was, the mob baying for her son's blood. In truth, she was surprised not to see more people. Still, three determined men were more than enough to hurt a woman and an innocent babe. Thank heaven Cwenhild had warned her in advance and she had been able to get Little Rune to safety.

Bracing herself for the confrontation, Eowyn flung the door open—and froze.

"Albert?"

The tallest man in the group, he was looking at her with immense satisfaction. What was he doing here? He could not be the instigator of such villainy, could he? If he really thought the baby to be his, then surely he would not call him the spawn of the Devil or want him killed? She waited, heart in her throat.

"Eowyn, good day to you. I have this day presented my case to the local reeve who agreed you should honor your promise to me. We are to be married without delay."

She blinked. Married? Was that why he was here?

Relief flooded through her. The men hadn't come to accuse her of consorting with the Devil, or some such nonsense, they weren't here to take her baby from her. It was all that mattered. For a dreadful moment she had feared they would take her to be burned and hound her son to kill him. Anything was better than that.

Then she frowned, realizing what she'd been told. How on earth had the reeve decided to pander to Albert's whim? Since when did such important men deal with private affairs? Hadn't he seen the man was not talking sense? And how was she going to get out of this?

"Please follow us into town," the man nearer to her said. His patience already seemed at an end. Evidently he resented having been sent on such a fool's errand. She could only agree with him. This was ridiculous. She would never marry Albert, no matter what anyone thought. "Edmund of Chorley intends to question you."

Hope surged through her. If the reeve wanted to question her, she would be able to present her version of the story. It would not take her long to convince him they were wasting his time. Unless... Had Albert bribed him? Blackmailed him? He was smiling like a man sure of his victory. She knew he suffered from delusion but his confidence was unnerving.

Was she going to be married by force this afternoon? Surely not, surely if she didn't give her agreement during whatever travesty of a ceremony they had planned, the union could not be valid?

She stared to the forest beyond. Oh, would that Rune chose this moment to reappear! Alone, she didn't stand a chance against three men. But with him by her side, she had nothing to fear. They would be flat on their backs before they had time to blink. It wouldn't be the first time he'd disposed of men in such a way.

"Do I have a choice?"

The answer, coming from the man in the middle, was delivered without any attempt at mitigation.

"No."

CHAPTER TWENTY

"I hope all goes well for you here," Sven said, shouldering the bag Rune had just given him.

"So do I, my friend."

Luck had been with him. As soon as he'd reached the port, he'd found Sven, who was overseeing the last preparations on his boat before leaving. The Dane had been surprised by his decision to stay behind but had agreed to deliver the bag and the message to his parents.

"You're a braver man than I am, settling so far away from home," he commented.

"Mm. I'm not sure this has anything to do with bravery."

No, but what was it about ? Foolishness? Desperate hope? Love? His heart started beating hard.

Yes, perhaps this was about love.

Rune slapped the man on the shoulder before taking his leave. Having found his friend so quickly meant he would be able to go back to Eowyn tonight, which he hadn't dared to hope. With luck, tomorrow morning he would wake up with her in his arms. He would roll her over and settle himself above her, then he would kiss her and finally, *finally*—

No. He could not afford to get carried away just yet. First he had to get back to Eowyn and hear what the result of her thinking was. She'd promised to have an answer for him when he came back and he knew she would be true to her word.

A group of men started grumbling when he walked past. One of them spat on the floor. One word reached his ears. *Devil*. Unsurprisingly. He ignored the men and walked on. Foolish Saxons were not worth him wasting his time over. As he left the bustling sounds of the port behind, his mind started to whir. Had he taken the right decision in staying in a hostile land?

Yes.

The answer left no doubt in his mind. He could not leave now, he could not give up, he had to try to win Eowyn over. It was a gamble, undeniably, but it was the only way to act. And besides, he did feel hopeful.

Because his angel desired him. Alone, it would not have been enough to play in his favor, but he knew lust was not all she felt for him. In the last few days she had started to look at him differently. At first, after his awful accusations, he had truly thought he had irremediably lost her. But as they revealed more about each other he had started to hope lust could turn into something more between them. She would have seen his change of attitude toward Little Rune. He had to trust that she would take that into account. There was something between them, maybe not quite what she wanted, but surely enough to give her pause and allow him time to win her around.

And then, of course, there was the man doll he'd made for her, and the babies. The little figurines and the message behind them might well be the weapon he'd needed to break through the last of her resistance. He dearly hoped so because he'd given all he had. If she threw them in his face then he had nothing left.

He took the path to the village with a heart full of hope. Before tonight he might have a family of his own.

IT WAS NOT A CELL, exactly, but neither was the room welcoming, and there weren't any windows. Eowyn stared at the wall opposite her without blinking. This didn't make any sense. If the reeve believed Albert's claim and intended to see them married, then why was he keeping her here, under lock and key? Why weren't they in a chapel right now? Why was he not questioning her as promised? And why would he even bother with such a private affair? How had he taken Albert's claim seriously? Anyone could see that the man was deluded. How long had she been in here? Where was her son now? Was he safe? The endless questions swirled in her mind, making her head spin.

Then there was the sound of chains being dragged over stones and the door swung open.

A tall, middle-aged man with a slight paunch walked in. The reeve. She instantly knew from his demeanor that this was no ordinary person. This man was an unmistakable figure of authority. Hope soared through her. If she could appeal to him and make him see that she and Albert had never agreed to anything, she would be fine. After all, he didn't know them, why would he believe one over the other?

"I would like to—"

He raised a hand, interrupting her. Evidently he would be the one conducting this conversation. She waited. Antagonizing him now would be a mistake.

"I think you know why you're here, but in case you don't, let me explain. My nephew told me you promised to marry him a couple of years ago, before going back on your word. In addition, he claims to be the father of your child."

Eowyn's heart sank to the pit of her stomach. Edmund of Chorley was Albert's *uncle*? Now she understood everything. That was why he was abusing his position to force her into a marriage she didn't want. For some reason she could not fathom, he wanted to please his nephew.

Well, she was not going to make it easy for him. This was her life they were talking about and she had truth on her side. She straightened her spine, readying herself for a fight.

"I swear Albert and I never agreed to get married. Why would he have left me for two years if we had intended to marry? And he is not the father of my child, he cannot be. We haven't seen each other for almost two years and my son Rune is only three months old! They look nothing like each other. You have to believe me."

Edmund waved a hand dismissively. "Oh, I believe you. The man's a fool, always has been. I have seen you and your babe in town a few times. As you say, the boy is quite distinctive, is he not? How could he be Albert's, with hair that color? You are both very dark. No, the father of your child is obviously a Norseman."

Relief swept through Eowyn. If he believed her then he would not force a marriage between her and Albert. Then her heart started to beat frantically again. If he didn't think Little Rune was his nephew's child but a Norseman's, then did he believe him the spawn of the Devil, like the men Cwenhild had overheard this morning? Was that the real reason why he'd had her brought her here, to have her liaison with a Norseman exposed and her punished for it?

If that was the case, then she was facing a greater danger than she had first thought. Instead of forcing her into marriage, the reeve might well kill her for consorting with evil. And Little Rune would suffer as well... Was that why he had alluded to her son's distinctive hair color? To make her see that she had better comply with his wishes for fear he would hurt them both in retaliation?

If she had to agree to marry a man she didn't want to spare her son, she would do it. Anything was preferable to seeing her child hurt. Even if she married Albert today, Rune would find a way to help her later on. They could disappear to Denmark with their son. No one would find them there.

Heart in her throat, she waited.

"Besides..." Edmund came to stand in front of her. "We all know where a man's seed is supposed to go to make a child. All but Albert apparently. If what he told me is true, then he cannot be the father of your baby, now, can he? It seems to me you are a most open-minded woman, allowing your lover access to every part of your luscious body."

Eowyn's heart stopped beating for a moment. Had she imagined the hint of lust in the man's gaze? Probably not, but it was best to behave as if she had.

"I am grateful for your understanding," she breathed, doing her best to appear demure.

He snorted. "I bet you are. I could have you married off to my fool of a nephew, but I will not. I could have you killed for consorting with the Devil, just to appease those idiots who came to see me yesterday, but I will spare your life. I have better things to do to you than kill you." He gave a smile that chilled Eowyn down to the spine. "On your knees. I think my magnanimity deserves a reward, don't you?"

"A-a reward?"

"All I ask in return for my help is that you do what only whores seem to want to do. Albert, the fool, delighted in telling me all about your skills at pleasing a man. It got me quite aroused, I must tell you. So I think it's only fair you help relieve the ache."

"Please. I—"

"Kneel," he snapped, his fingers already at the fastening of his braies. "And put your heart into it, so I can feel how grateful you really are."

Eowyn almost retched. "No."

"You will do as I ask if you don't want this to turn into an ugly business."

It already was an ugly business! Eowyn's eyes darted around the room in panic. How was she to get out of this? Even if she called out for help, no one would come. Who would take her defense against the reeve? No one. She was on her own.

The knock on the door behind her caused her to cry out.

"What is it?" Edmund barked, his hands hovering over his braies.

"A riot, on the market place. Your presence is urgently required."

"Damn it all to hell, can't a man know a moment's peace!" Edmund spat on the floor and planted his stare into hers. "We'll finish this... conversation later. I hope to find you in a more accommodating mood then."

A moment later Eowyn was alone, standing on shaky legs. Before she could rush to the door, she heard a chain being bolted. Although she already knew she would be locked in the room, she tried the handle. Nothing moved.

She fell to the floor in a heap.

CHAPTER TWENTY-ONE

In the end it hadn't been enough.

Baring his soul, making the figurines, taking care of the baby as his own, agreeing to leave his old life and his parents behind, trusting Eowyn would see sense, none of it had been enough.

Rune stared at the empty hut without blinking. Eowyn had decided she could not forgive him after all, and left before he could come back from the port. He could not doubt it, because not only was the fire pit cold and she not in the hut, but their son wasn't here either. Even his cot had disappeared. She had not just gone out for a walk, she had left for good. In fact, it was as if neither of them had ever existed.

They had vanished, leaving a gaping hole in his soul.

Why had he left her alone? Why had he given her time to think? He should have guessed she would take advantage of his absence to flee. What a fool he really was. The last few weeks had been a series of bad decisions, ranging from the ludicrous—pretending to bed Edith in the forge—to the unattainable—hoping he could earn Eowyn's forgiveness.

Blind with pain, he rushed to Cwenhild's hut. Would

Eowyn have told her friend where she'd gone? Most probably. Would the woman share the information with him? He doubted it. She would have been ordered to keep her destination secret. Still, he had to try. But Cwenhild was nowhere to be seen. Her husband told him she and the children had gone to visit her sister.

Rune set off for the Norsemen village at a run. Sigurd and Wolf were his last chance. They might know where Eowyn and his son were. Night had already fallen when the familiar thatched roofs appeared at the edge of the forest. He went straight to Sigurd's hut, and was relieved to see the Dane open the door.

"Rune. What are you doing here at this—"

"Have you seen Eowyn?" he cut in, trying to peer inside the hut. Was she hiding here, trying to build up the courage to leave?

"No. Why?"

"I thought perhaps she'd come to see Frigyth?"

He knew even as he asked that it would not be the case. Of course, she hadn't come to see her friend, she would have guessed it would be the first place he would come looking for her. If she had wanted to disappear, the Norsemen village was the last place she would have gone to.

"We haven't seen her for days," Sigurd confirmed. "In fact, Frigyth was telling me earlier that she wanted to pay her a visit soon. Is anything the matter?"

"No. Nothing." Rune gritted his teeth. He could not tell the Dane that Eowyn had vanished because of him, because of what he'd done. He might well get a beating for it, but this time it would not help. "Could I sleep in the hut tonight if it's still empty?"

"Of course." Sigurd frowned. He wasn't fooled, he had

guessed something wasn't right but Rune cared not. He could think what he wanted.

"Thank you. Oh, and one last thing. Do you know where I can get a cask of ale?"

Tonight he would drink until he forgot he'd known a dark-haired angel called Eowyn.

Sigurd narrowed his eyes. "Go see Björn, Rorik's son. He will have what you need."

In the morning Rune woke up outside the hut, face down in the mud, having no recollection of how he had ended up there. All he knew was that the pain in his head would clear away sooner than the ache wreaked in his heart by Eowyn's departure and the loss of Little Rune. That particular injury might well take a lifetime to heal.

With difficulty, he stood up. He could not stay here, where he would find only pain. With her gone, he had no reason to. He started the long walk back to the harbor with a numb heart. To think only the other day he had walked the same path, filled with hope for the future. Now he felt hollow inside.

As luck would have it, he arrived in time to board a boat sailing for Denmark. It had to be a sign that going back home was the right thing to do. The merchants agreed to take him with them without a fuss. A boat builder was always someone useful to have onboard and they accepted his meagre offer of coin for the passage.

While he waited for the men to finish loading the boat, he tried very hard to convince himself he'd made the right decision. He would forget Eowyn once he arrived back home and he was surrounded by friends and family once more. Of course, it was in vain. He would never forget the sight, the smell, the feel, the taste of this woman, however far he fled. Meeting her and their son had changed his life forever. He would never be the same man ever again.

His gaze landed on a figure draped in a moth-eaten cloak.

"I can't wait to leave this country," the man was telling his companions. "The people here are nothing but savages without honor."

Rune arched an eyebrow. He had not seen anything during his stay to suggest that the Saxons were savages. The three men who had assaulted him and Eowyn by the river had been thugs but the majority of the people he'd met had been as expected, no better or worse than Danes, even if they seemed to view him with suspicion.

"How do you imagine we are better than them?" he growled, drawn despite himself into the conversation. Anything was better than obsessing about Eowyn and all he had lost.

"Because we worship the true gods of course, and do not believe in any of their nonsense!" the man said, as if talking to a simpleton. "Did you know the people here believe in only one god who, from what I understand, doesn't even have any hammer or weapon of any sort and whose enemy is a creature made of fire and called the Devil?"

"Yes, I did know that." Rune could not help a snort. The irony of the question was not lost on him. "The Saxons call me Devil, you see, on account of the color of my hair."

"Well, doesn't that tell you they don't know what they're talking about? There's nothing more normal than having red hair, I'm thinking. And yet I heard only yesterday morning men talking about having a woman burned for having given birth to a babe with red hair. I mean..." The man laughed. "Her birthing such a babe doesn't mean anything other than she spread her legs for one of us."

The men around them started to laugh but Rune froze. "What do you mean, burned?"

The merchants shouted in their direction, urging them on.

The boat was almost full. Soon it would be their turn to go aboard.

"Can't we continue this conversation once we're on the boat?" the man asked, nodding toward it. "After all, we won't have anything to do for days but talk. I will be happy to tell you all I know then."

"No. Speak now or you won't be in a state to go anywhere." Rune's tone brooked no refusal. He needed to know what the man was talking about now, for he had a suspicion he might not get on the boat after all. He knew only of one woman who had given birth to a red-haired babe. A woman who had disappeared mysteriously.

What if that woman arrested for supposedly consorting with the Devil was Eowyn?

Above the water, the sun parted the clouds and he heard a voice in his head, clear as a bell. Whose, he didn't know, but the words were unmistakable.

Of course, it's her. Who else do you know who had a child with a man the Saxons call a devil? Go after her, you bastard! She didn't leave you, she was only taken away by men intent on hurting her.

"Hey, you, are you coming or not?" one of the merchants called out.

Rune stared at the man, at the boat waiting to take him back home. Of course he was not coming. He could not, he had to get his woman and his son back.

"Damn it all!" he said between his teeth, before turning his back on the boat and running back toward the village.

THE SOUND of the chain being dragged over the wooden door was what woke Eowyn. Against all odds she had fallen asleep on the hard stone floor when Edmund had left her. Perhaps her exhausted body had decided it was the best way to blank out the horror of what was to come.

Too wise to rush to the door, knowing Edmund would not let her pass anyway, she scrambled back to her feet. The last thing she wanted was to be lying flat on her back when he entered. She might well end up there soon anyway.

But the person coming through the door was only a serving maid carrying a platter of food. The girl was young, the same height as her, and curvy as well.

An idea popped into Eowyn's head. Could she...

One woman had entered the room where she was held prisoner. Would anyone notice if the woman exiting it was a different one? She'd seen when the maid had entered that night had fallen and only one torch was lighting the hall. If she acted as if she had every right to come out, she might well be able to slip past the guard who was stationed outside the cell and reach the main door. The man had never seen her face, he might not recognize her. Well, there was no harm in trying. Better to be punished for trying to escape than be raped because she'd not even tried. There was only one problem. The girl might not agree to the deception, for fear of reprisal. No... But if she wasn't given any choice then she would not be able to stop her and would not be accused of complicity.

Eowyn steeled herself. This was for Little Rune. She had to get back to him, now, without delay. The need for him was like a beast gnawing at her insides, and he needed his mother. What would happen to him if she were arrested, hurt, or even simply detained for days, until Edmund had slaked his lust for her?

Before she could think better of the idea, she lifted her hand and struck. A heartbeat later the girl was lying on the floor, still as a corpse.

Horror invaded Eowyn.

What had she done?

It had seemed harmless enough when she had watched Rune do it to Ecberg and the man the other day. A neat blow to the chin to send your opponent to the floor. It did not feel harmless when you felt the person's teeth rattle under your palm and watched them crumple to the floor like an empty sack of grain.

What if she had killed the girl?

No. She forced herself to calm. If a man like Rune, who was strength personified, had not killed his opponents, what chance did she have of inflicting real damage? Except... Except that the poor maid was not a man in his prime like Ecberg and that, unlike Rune, Eowyn had no idea what she was doing. What if she had inadvertently hit a dangerous spot and killed the woman? In any case it was too late to worry about it now, she had to move quickly or she would have hurt the poor girl for naught.

Muttering under her breath to keep panic at bay, she set out to undress her, taking the dress and the piece of cloth covering her hair, but leaving the girl the protection of her shift. A moment later, her distinctive dark hair tucked away from sight and the tray in hand so as to resemble the maid as much as possible, Eowyn stepped out of the door. The hall was as dark as she had hoped. Perhaps if she acted as if she was doing nothing wrong, no one would—

A cry escaped her lips when she found herself swept off her feet and swung over a man's shoulder.

"You took your time!"

All hopes that Rune had unexpectedly come to her rescue vanished when she heard the gruff voice. This was someone she didn't know. Eowyn started to protest, then realized that the man had taken her for the maid and would not realize his mistake as long as he carried her in such a way. He grunted in satisfaction when she grew limp and allowed him to carry her off without another word.

"Come. Alban will be waiting for us at the cottage."

She decided to ignore the fact that not just one but two men were waiting to tumble her into bed, to focus on one single thought.

The providential man was going to whisk her out of here, right under everyone's nose.

If she kept still and carried on pretending she was the maid she had tried to impersonate, she would soon be out of Edmund's reach. Of course, then she would have to face two aroused men who would be none too pleased to find out that she had no intention of talking the girl's place but still, two was better than a dozen and perhaps they would be so horrified by what they had done that they would agree to help her.

No. That was taking it one step too far. But she would take her chances. If she could sneak past the guards undetected and get out of the reeve's house then the hardest part would be done.

A moment later they reached the town gates. She closed her eyes and kept as still as she could.

"Going to the cottage again?" a man's voice asked. Her captor only grunted. "One of these days you will have to invite us as well."

"Not tonight," the man holding her said with a proprietary tap on her buttocks. "Alan will be too shy. It's his first time."

There were more laughs and a moment later they were out into the dark night. Eowyn let out a silent sigh of relief. She was free. Well, almost. She still had to deal with her savior and his friend.

After a short walk in the dark they reached the cottage. The man placed her back on her feet and turned to knock on the door. "Alan, it's us."

While they waited, Eowyn silently crept toward the bushes,

thanking her stars she was wearing a brown gown that would allow her to blend into the vegetation easily.

The door opened on a lanky man she supposed to be Alan. He was grinning widely.

"So? Did she agree?"

The man who had carried her chuckled. "Agree? She fair bit my hand off!"

"That sounds promising."

The voices grew fainter and fainter as Eowyn burrowed into the woods. A moment later she heard the men call out for her. She instantly crouched down and went still.

"Where the devil has she gone to? You said she was willing!" Alan accused.

"She was, I swear!"

Weak with relief, Eowyn watched them hurry in the direction they had just come. When they had disappeared into the night she started to run. Once she cleared the forest she realized she had made it.

She was free.

CHAPTER TWENTY-TWO

"Wolf, I need to borrow your horse again."

"Where are you going?"

Where was he going? That was a good question. Rune had no idea. He yanked at his hair in despair. All he knew was that he had to do something. He would start by going to town and make inquiries. If things were as bad as the man on the boat had said, word was bound to have spread.

He just hoped he was not too late already. The idea of his Angel being burned for sleeping with him was enough to make him retch.

"I'm not sure where I'm going," he told Wolf.

The tall Icelander looked at him. It seemed to Rune he was seeing to the bottom of his heart. What he saw there evidently pleased him, for he nodded his agreement. "Go get her back," was all he said.

Yes. That was the plan. Failure was simply not an option.

Rune was already on Demon, and about to kick him into a gallop when he saw a graceful figure appear at the top of the hill in the distance. It was a woman, unsteady on her feet, her long black hair blowing in the wind. His heart gave a jolt, not hesitating when his eyes might have doubted.

Eowyn.

It was her. He jumped down from the saddle and ran like he had never run before.

"Rune." She fell into his arms, almost knocking him to the ground.

"Angel! Are you all right? Are you hurt, in pain? Are you all right?" He had to stop talking, he wasn't making any sense. Thankfully she didn't seem to mind, or find him ridiculous. She buried herself into his embrace.

"Yes, I'm all right," she said, hiccupping against his chest. "I escaped. I'm fine. I'm free. I escaped."

She wasn't making sense either. There was only one way to put an end to this pointless conversation. He took her mouth in a fierce kiss. It felt as if it was their first real kiss and in a way it was. Before, he had kissed her in a haze of lust, in amusement, or to stop her from talking, but never had he kissed her with the force of his love.

He cupped her cheek with one hand, and wrapped his other arm around her waist to hold her tight against his chest. He never wanted to let her out of his sight again. If he could, he would hold her in his arms all day long and kiss her. Her thoughts must echo his own because she kissed him with equal fierceness. Reveling in the feel, the smell, the heat of her, he wondered how he had not realized before what she meant for him.

Now that he had, he would make the most of it. She pressed herself even closer to him, grinding her hips against his, making him grunt in approval. Ah, so she wanted him.... He wanted her as well and he would take her. But not here, at the mercy of onlookers, not outside.

With great effort, he drew back.

"No!" she protested, bringing him close once more. "I need more."

"Me too," he growled against her lips. "But not here. We'll go to your hut."

Eowyn moaned. Her hair was a wild tangle about her face, her eyes were hazy and unfocused, there were mud stains on her cheek, and she was wearing a dress that was too big for her.

She had never looked more beautiful.

He crushed her into his arms once more. What would he have done if he had lost her before he could win her over, and make her his? It didn't bear thinking about.

Then the reality of what she'd said hit him.

"Wait, did you say you escaped?" Had the man on the boat been right then? Had she really been taken to be burnt? Was that why was she wearing a dress that did not belong to her?

Eowyn shook her head as if she didn't want to even think about it and his hold around her tightened. "The reeve. Albert had gone to him... It's his uncle. He wanted us to get married. But I-I was locked in a room instead, and he—"

"Hush, it's all right. You can tell me later." Evidently, this would be some tale. "You escaped, that is the important thing. You told me once you were not a powerless, meek female, and you've just proven it."

He kissed her again and again, his hands fastened around her waist. He could not stop, he could not get enough of her. He wanted to kiss her, hold her, show her he'd finally realized what she meant to him, make her understand how afraid he'd been when he'd found her and their son gone, tell her how much he loved her.

He drew back, panting hard.

"Oh, Angel, Eowyn, my heart, my love, please. If I haven't done enough to earn your forgiveness, please give me more time and the chance to try again. I cannot live without you."

"You have done enough, what are you talking about?"

Eowyn looked at the man towering over her, so handsome, so masculine, so desperate for her approval. Why did he think he had not done enough?

He closed his eyes like a man in pain. "When I found the hut empty, I thought you..."

He didn't finish his sentence but there was no need. She understood all too well. He'd thought she had fled, taking advantage of his absence.

"You really think I could have abandoned you without a word? Taken your son away from you after what you told me, when I knew the pain you had gone through twice already?" Simply saying the words out loud caused her chest to tighten.

She hadn't meant to sound accusatory but Rune appeared stricken all the same. "Yes. I'll admit that's what I thought. There were no traces of either of you and I... I'm sorry. I should not have doubted you. Again."

"No. I understand. But I had to make it appear as if I had no child, to stall the men coming after me and make them believe they had the wrong woman." She shook her head, realizing how it would have hurt him to see the hut empty. She'd said she would do some thinking. It would have looked as if she had concluded she couldn't give him a chance and had better disappear before he came back and tried his wiles on her. "I'm sorry, there wasn't any way of warning you, I just had to take Little Rune to safety."

He recoiled. "Take Little Rune to safety? I thought this was about Albert wanting to marry you?"

She quickly explained what had happened, what Cwenhild had overheard at the market. By the time she had finished, Rune looked like thunder.

"Where is he? Where is my son?"

My son. Her heart tripped in her chest. There was such

possessiveness, such pride, such love in those two words that she knew their troubles were over. She had forgiven him and he had accepted her past. She loved him and he might well come to love her too one day. They would be all right.

"Rune is with Cwenhild. She took him to her sister's to hide him."

He murmured something in Norse and she knew he was thanking his gods, whoever they were. "I will need to thank her for what she's done. Now, shall we go get him? After so long away from him, you must need to be suckled?"

His eyes flickered to her breasts. It was not a lustful glance, but one of concern for her well-being.

"Yes," she whispered. "But I can wait."

She had expressed some milk before falling asleep the day before, then twice last night in the forest. The need had become slightly less pressing in the last week anyway. Her baby was growing up.

Before they went anywhere there was something she needed to do. She reached into the pocket of her dress and took out the man doll and the five little babies Rune had so skilfully carved. When she had taken her clothes off in the cell she hadn't forgotten to retrieve them. They had become her most precious possession. "I want to thank you for this most thoughtful gift."

Rune's eyes gleamed. Had he been anyone else she might have thought he was about to cry.

"You're welcome. Here." He reached into his purse and withdrew a familiar figurine. "I have the woman, to complete the set."

"How do you...?"

He made a face, as if ashamed of himself. "Forgive me. I took it. When I saw you had left it behind in the hut, I could not resist." He shook his head. "Actually, come to think of it, I should have guessed something wasn't right. You wouldn't have left without her."

"No, I would not." Half crying, Eowyn took the little doll from him and was surprised to see her as damaged as she had been a few days ago, in spite of Rune's promise to restore her to her former glory. "You didn't fix her in the end?"

He brushed her cheek softly. "No, I didn't, because I think she's beautiful the way she is. These traces on her body are the proof of a life well-lived, proof that she was, and still is, well-loved. You shouldn't wish for her to be the way she was before, when she is perfect just the way she is. I know the man doll agrees with me. He wouldn't want those scars erased, considering what they mean. He wants many more babies with her. If that means more lines and more weight on her then so be it. It only means there will be more for him to kiss when he has her in his arms."

His big hands smoothed over her hips, her stomach, her thighs, where pregnancy had left faint silvery lines. Eowyn bit her bottom lip, emotion flooding her heart. "Rune, don't. You'll make me cry."

"So? Cry all you want, Angel, do whatever you need. As long as you do it with me." He paused and his eyes seemed to catch fire. "I love you."

And just like that she burst out into sobs. "Oh. I love you too."

"You do?" He sounded amazed.

"Of course, I do, you silly man!" She laughed through her tears. "How could I not?"

"I'd prefer not to answer that, and not give you any ideas."

For a long while, he cradled her against his chest. Eowyn poured her relief, her love, her hopes, her joy onto him. When she finally calmed down, she lifted her head up to look at him. There was one more issue to resolve. She had done a lot of thinking while she walked to reach her hut in the night and arrived to one conclusion.

She could not stay here.

"Please take me away, take me somewhere where no one will want to bed me because of what they heard about me, call me a whore because of what I did in the past or think my son a spawn of the Devil because of the way he looks."

He growled and drew her back to him, burying his face in her hair, all fierce intent. "Let's go back to Denmark, to my home. There you will be able to start a new life, no one will dare call you anything but my wife and Little Rune will have nothing to fear. He will just be one red-haired boy amongst many. No one will hurt you or him as long as I breathe, I swear. The only man bedding you will be me, and the only one loving you and taking care of you and our son will be me."

Eowyn didn't even hesitate. Going to Denmark was the perfect solution. Rune was offering her a new identity, a new life away from all the pain and mess hers had become, a life with the man she loved and the children he would give her.

"Yes. Take me and Little Rune to meet your parents," she agreed. Then doubt seized her. "Do you think they will accept a Saxon as their daughter-in-law? They probably never imagined they would have—"

"Ah, Angel, don't worry about that. They will love you. Just as I love you."

"But wait... Didn't you send a message to them with Sven and the others, telling them you weren't coming back?"

"I did. So they will be all the more delighted to see me arrive home not only with my child but also with my wife."

The word sent a burst of heat through her chest. "Wife?"

"Well, of course we are going to marry. Do you really think I'm going to let you go now? No chance, you're mine." He tightened his hold around her possessively. "Now, would you prefer to do it here before we leave or in Denmark when we arrive?"

She couldn't help a laugh. "Aren't you supposed to ask whether I want to marry you, rather than where I prefer to do have the ceremony? It is the normal procedure, you know. I doubt it is different in Denmark."

"It's not. But I don't need to ask whether you want to marry me, I already know what the answer is."

"Arrogant devil."

"Yes, that's me." Unconcerned, he placed his forehead against her, the gesture tender. "So what is your answer?"

"Here. Let's get married here, before we leave. I want to take my first step in Denmark as your wife. It might help your parents to accept me better."

"Don't worry about them," he repeated. "It might even be that we reach them before Sven. He only has a couple of days head start and sailing can be unpredictable. Besides, he might not head straight for them upon arrival and it might take him a while to locate their hut, whereas I know exactly where to find them."

"That's perfect. Let's leave as soon as we can find a boat." The more distance she could put between her and the men baying for her son's blood or lusting after her, the better.

The light in Rune's eyes suddenly dimmed. "Are you sure you want to go to Denmark? We cannot stay here if you're in danger, but we don't have to go as far, we could—"

She stopped him with a swift kiss on the mouth. "Rune. You were ready to leave your old life, your country, your family, for Little Rune and me." She placed a hand over his chest and nestled herself in his arms. Her future was with this man, she knew it, in the place where he had grown. "I have no family and my life here has become hell. So, yes, I'm sure. On one condition. You will have to teach me Norse."

He rewarded her answer with a kiss of his own, a far less chaste one. When he drew back, Eowyn was breathless and ready to throw herself into his arms. She took Rune's hand, urging him toward the village and her hut. It was high time they made love properly.

"We will go into town tomorrow," he decided, following her with long, easy strides, "see what is happening. I think not all the boats have left yet."

She nodded. "We'll need to go to the Norsemen village to say goodbye to our friends before we leave." This would be the hardest part, undoubtedly. But she would make new friends in her new home.

"Yes. But first, let's go and find our son. And then, I'm taking you to bed, Angel."

"I'm not tired." Oddly, and despite a night of walking, it was true. Being reunited with Rune, knowing that all this nightmare she had been drowning in would soon be over, that she was about to marry the man of her dreams, had infused her with energy.

"Good," he drawled, leaning to murmur in her ear. "Because I intend to ravish you until you fall asleep with my snake still buried deep inside you."

Eowyn let out a shaky breath. This sounded like a perfect plan. "You really say the most scandalous things."

"To you, my love. Only to you."

"RUNE AND I ARE GETTING MARRIED."

While Frigyth threw herself in her friend's arms and Merewen brought her hand to her chest with a delighted gasp, Rune glared at Sigurd, who looked on with a satisfied smile. A smile he wanted to wipe right off his face.

"If you say *one* word, Beast, I swear I'll cut out your heart and feed it to the dogs!" he growled in Norse.

The wretched man only crossed his arms over his chest. "Oh. I'm not saying anything, Devil. I think there's no need."

Behind him, Wolf smirked. "Indeed. No need at all."

Rune shook his head when he realized he would actually miss the two men's teasing. Who would have thought?

"And then we are leaving for Denmark," he added, knowing there was no point delaying the announcement any further.

This time the women's faces fell.

Eowyn nodded, and explained, her voice trembling. "It's for the best, for Little Rune and for me. We are not welcome here, not after what happened the other day."

Rune wrapped his arms around her. After they had made love last night, she had told him about what had happened with the reeve in that wretched cell. He already knew he would have nightmares about it for years to come. But at least Eowyn would be there, in the bed with him, to soothe him when he woke up in a sweat at the thought of what could have happened to her.

"We will leave with a boat of Danish merchants in two days' time."

This would give them enough time to assemble Eowyn's possessions, say their goodbyes and, more importantly, get married. His chest squeezed when he imagined entering his parents' hut with his wife and son for the first time.

"Come," Frigyth said, wiping her cheek. "You three men look after the babes for once. Eowyn needs us to prepare her wedding dress."

"For once," Sigurd and Wolf grumbled as one. "As if that was not what we did half the time."

Rune only laughed and transferred Little Rune to his other shoulder. Looking after his son was his privilege and pleasure.

"**B**end over, Angel. It's my turn."

With those words, Rune flipped Eowyn over as easily as if she weighed nothing and positioned himself behind her. Without another word, he tore at his braies and lifted one of her legs onto the table, opening her wide for his possession. Yes! Eowyn was so ready she whimpered when she felt him press against her opening, hot and hard. She had already come once but Rune had yet to reach his pleasure. This would be quick, she could tell from the urgency in his voice, and all the more explosive for it. She knew she would come just from feeling him erupt within her.

"Yes!" she rasped. "Now."

A growl, deep and masculine, answered her. "Look at that perfect *rump*. So round, so soft, so golden." As he spoke, he landed a playful slap on her rear. Eowyn moaned. She had long stopped objecting to the word, as Rune had a way of making it sound enticing. "And all mine to play with."

"Ah, Devil, stop playing! Stop teasing me." She always called him Devil when they made love. Nothing seemed more appropriate. He really was wickedness personified when he wanted to be. She loved it. "Take me. Now!"

"Desperate, are you, wife?" he murmured in her ear, bending at the waist to cover her completely. With his heat against her back and his weight flattening her breasts over the table, she felt utterly at his mercy.

"Yes, of course, I'm desperate!" she whimpered. "And I thought I was not the only one." Each opportunity for making love had to be seized with both hands. Little Rune had gone fishing with his grandparents this afternoon, so they had some time to themselves. As soon as the three of them had disappeared though the door, Rune had sat her on the table and proceeded to devour her. She had screamed and probably torn out some of his glorious hair out when a devastating climax had ripped through her.

She couldn't wait for the next one.

Still molded over her bent form, Rune brought his hand between her legs and started to play with her swollen folds. What was the wretched man doing? Only a moment ago he had been poised at her entrance, ready to push in and give her what she needed. Now he was stroking her gently, far too gently, causing her to squirm. She needed more, more friction, more heat, more—

"Feel how wet you are for me? I swear I could come just from pleasuring you and hearing you moan. No one moans like you, my love."

"I can moan all you like, if only you would just… fuck me!" she exploded.

"Mm. Such language! I've never heard the like." There was laughter in his voice but she could tell her brazenness had aroused him. Finally he might break from his iron control. "You want to be fucked then, wife?"

"Yes! *Já*." In what language did he need to be told? Could he not see her desperation? Now was not the time for his scandalous talking.

"How?"

"Hard and fast, and preferably before I expire from need."

With a feral growl he reared up and grabbed her hips in his strong hands, positioning himself at her entrance once again. She closed her eyes. Ah, this was it. One thrust and he would be inside her. Her whole body went liquid at the thought. That first thrust, when he pushed past the muscles guarding her sheath, was always her favorite, and almost as pleasurable as the last one, when Rune reached his own climax. A wail rose in the room. It took Eowyn a moment to realize she hadn't uttered it.

The babe.

Not now! "Ah, Devil, your daughter certainly has a flair for timing," she groaned.

Rune mumbled under his breath as he tucked himself back in his braies. His breathing was coming in short ragged bursts. "I will see to her. Then we will finish what we have just started."

Eowyn was already restoring order to her skirts, knowing the interruption might be longer than they liked. This was why new parents had to seize every opportunity for lovemaking while they could. "She is probably hungry." Why else would a three-month-old baby cry?

"Well, so am I. Ravenous. But I can wait, now that you've had your pleasure."

She melted. Her husband always saw to her and the children's needs first, and this without a word of complaint.

He drew her into his embrace and planted a fiery kiss on her lips. "Let Freya get what she needs. Then it will be your turn. I will fuck you as hard and as fast as you can take it."

Oh, Lord.

He released her before she could push onto the floor and straddle him.

Her heart swelled and almost burst when Rune came back into the room with their newborn daughter cradled against his bare chest. They looked so happy, so perfect together. One tall, one tiny, one male, one female, one strong, one so fragile. How she loved them!

"She *is* hungry, I'm afraid, look at the way she is trying to suckle me!" Rune laughed. "Ah, you won't be getting anything from here, little one!" he chided gently. "Let me take you to your mother. You'll fare better with her."

Eowyn sat down and reddened when she remembered her bodice was already unlaced—and why.

A moment later her daughter was feeding hungrily. As it did every time she watched the babe at her breast, her heart threatened to escape out of her chest. Rune was leaning against one wall, his arms crossed over his naked chest, a smile floating on his lips.

"I will never tire of this view. I'm thinking I might well father a dozen children on you, you know."

"I'm thinking you might well do." Heat invaded her, reminding her that he was waiting to do just that.

He grunted. "Stop teasing me, wife. I can't think of... *this* while my daughter is in the same room as me."

"Mm." Perhaps he had a point. Perhaps it was better to wait until Freya had finished suckling to think about what she and Rune did in bed together.

"Will you sing for us, Angel?"

Eowyn could not help a smile. She knew her husband loved to hear her sing. She also knew it aroused him. It also had the added benefit of sending her children to sleep. It was the perfect idea.

Rune closed his eyes when she started to sing, choosing a Norse song she had learned the other day. She loved it, as much as she loved everything about her new life.

"Do you never miss your country?" he asked when the song had ended, suddenly serious.

"No."

It was the truth. At home, life had become unbearable, and possibly dangerous. Here, as Rune had promised, people only knew her as his wife and, as a consequence, no one dared even look at her the wrong way. Rune's parents had welcomed her and Little Rune with open arms. She had made new friends and a few months ago she had given birth to a beautiful daughter. Soon, other babies would follow.

Eowyn smiled.

Yes. Life with her devil was just... heavenly.

Next Read
Baiting the Bear
Carry on the Norsemen's story with Björn and Dunne's meeting in book 4

ABOUT THE AUTHOR

As far back as I remember, I have been attracted to the Middle Ages, to knights in shining armour and their ladies in spectacular dresses. Now I get to write about them, I feel like the luckiest woman in the world. Being French and married to a Brit makes each book I write extra special, as our countries share a long and sometimes painful past. But in the end, in life as well as in fiction, love conquers all!

I have published several medieval romances under my own name, including series, and also have a pen name, Judith Falcon, for spicier projects, still in historical romance.

Join my newsletter and check out my other books on virginiemarconato.com.

ALSO BY VIRGINIE MARCONATO

The Noble Norsemen

Taming the Wolf

Soothing the Beast

Wooing the Devil

Baiting the Bear